BLOOD MALICE

BRADLEY UPTON

ISBN-13-978-0-578-70001-4

First Printing 2020

For Mom and Dad

ACKNOWLEDGEMENTS

Terry Duquette, there at the start.

Diana Burbano for invaluable suggestions, notes and questions.

Kimberly Davis Basso for being a great sounding board and critique partner. Keep asking tough questions.

Marie, thanks for the proofread and notes.

Eoin Ryan for the assistance with global math.

Cover Art by: Amy Rachlin
Cover photo by: Zerenade Ho
Cover Model: Zerenade Ho
Other Photos by Bradley Upton

PROLOGUE

"I think I'll walk back to the hotel." Fan Sherman said. Her mother tongue, Chinese, was a bit rusty after spending over twenty years in the United States. She spoke it at home with her mother but English was now her primary language for everyday speaking, at work, and for prayer. Now she was in Beijing her language skills were getting a work out.

"What?" Lujiang asked. He glanced out the window at the dark night. It was after ten p.m. "Let me drive you, it's quicker."

Fan frowned for a moment. "It's not far, about thirty to forty minutes."

"You haven't been here in decades. You might get lost." Lujiang said. "Let me drive you. It will only take me a moment to bring the car around."

"I'll be fine." Fan insisted.

"I don't think it's safe."

"Tiananmen Square was last year. Martial Law was rescinded. I can walk two miles without any hassle from the PLA."

"I don't think it's safe," he repeated. Fear grew in the pit of his stomach.

Fan grabbed her heavy coat and wound her scarf around her neck. She pulled on a knitted cap, and secured a mask over her nose and mouth to filter out the pollution. Fan started for the door.

"This isn't the Hutong you remember from when you were six. It's dangerous."

She looked at him. The expression on his face puzzled her. There was genuine fear. "I did it before."

"That was in the afternoon." Lujiang said. "It's dangerous at night. Let me drive you." His voice was anxious.

"I'll see you tomorrow." She turned the knob and opened the door, a wave of cold air billowed in.

"There have been killings in the Hutong."

Fan hesitated. "Really?"

Lujiang nodded. "Yes."

Doubt crossed her mind as she considered his warning. "God will keep me safe." Fan said. "See you tomorrow." She exited the orphanage and closed the door behind her. Lujiang crossed to the window and watched her go down the stairs, across the wide brown lawn, and out the wrought iron gate into the dense Beijing neighborhood.

"I hope so, sister." Lujiang was raised without any religion as was most of the people in China. Only the old might practice some sort of religion and if they did, they did it in secret. The Communist party supplanted God.

Fan walked the narrow streets of Beijing toward her hotel two miles away. Her path led her from the smaller streets without traffic to the larger roads. She walked in a small neighborhood similar to where she grew up in as a child. The low grey brick buildings with old doors hid warm family homes behind the paint peeled entrances. There were bicycles locked outside doorways, leafless trees reached to the sky with bony limbs, there were few people out, all moved quickly, warily.

She walked quickly, the cold night air made her rethink turning down the ride from the orphanage. Up ahead was a small girl, with straight shoulder length black hair, wearing a dirty dress, and swinging a doll as she walked aimlessly. Fan slowed and approached the girl. "Are you alright?"

The girl looked up, noticing the woman for the first time. Her face was oval and a little dirty like she needed a bath. "I'm lost. Can you help me find my mother?"

"Of course." Fan leaned down and engaged the girl as was her generous nature. She sought to help everyone she could, it was her calling. "Do you know where you live?"

"In a grey house," replied the waiflike figure.

Fan glanced around. All the houses were grey brick with small slanted grey roofs. "What color is your door?" asked Fan.

The girl swung the doll as she thought for a moment. "Red," was her reply.

Many doors were red, it was a lucky color. "Do you know your street?" Fan suspected this girl was handicapped and somehow got out of her house where her family looked after her. The waif shook her head. "What's your name, honey?"

"Nühái."

Fan blinked. *Girl?* Was the poor child so neglected that her family didn't give her a name? Had they given up trying to educate someone they thought to be a lost cause? Fan stood up and looked around. Should she take Nühái back to the orphanage to be sorted out tomorrow? It would be a short walk. Fan couldn't leave her out in the cold night air alone. She had to do something.

"Would you like to come with me? I can take you someplace warm and we can find your family in the morning."

Nühái wriggled her nose as she considered the offer. "I think I will go with my sisters."

"What sisters?" asked Fan. The girl pointed behind her. Fan turned, there were two similarly dressed girls quietly watching. "Is she your sister?" asked Fan. The girls didn't answer. Nühái pointed up to the roof. A girl looked down at them, her face a placid mask.

The hairs on the back of Fan's neck rose as fear crept up her spine. The first girl was eerie and to have three others appear spooked her. "Since your sisters are here I will leave you. Good night." Fan turned, another girl stood in front of her. Where did she come from? Fan didn't hear a footfall or the scuff of anyone walking.

"We're hungry," said the girl standing in front of Fan.

She hesitated. Nühái grabbed Fan from behind, her arms circled around Fan's knees and with surprising strength she lifted Fan and pitched her backwards to the bricks of the small street.

"Wait!" cried Fan. The five girls plunged on top of the prostrate woman. Their hands tore at her clothes and mouths clamped to her exposed wrists. A small strong hand covered her mouth, choking off a scream. Sharp teeth bit on either side of her neck tearing the flesh. Mouths suckled at the gushing wounds.

Lord help me! Fan lost consciousness never to awaken again.

CHAPTER 1
ANCIENT TEXTS & HOPPING VAMPIRES

It took Father John Bryant several months to find someone to translate the ancient Buddhist text he got from the Vatican Library. He wasn't able to remove the book, of course, it was far too delicate for that. And the librarian would never allow him to borrow it, taking it six thousand miles away from the Vatican. It was irreplaceable. Xeroxes were allowed under strict supervision.

John now sat across from a Chinese monk, who ticked all the boxes one would expect to have for a Buddhist monk. Orange robe, bald head, old but not ancient, thin, his age was indeterminate. There was a twinkle in his eyes and a calmness; an unflappable air about him. They sat facing one another at a table. A pot of green tea was steeping to the side, two handleless cups waiting for the contents of the pot to be poured.

"You were looking for me to translate a text for you," the monk said.

"Yes. It's very kind of you to look at this, uh, brother uh, I don't know how to address you." John said. He wasn't used to speaking with members of non-Christian religions. The honorifics were beyond his knowledge.

"Call me Shan." The monk said waving his hand dismissively. "I'm not big on titles, Father."

"Great. Call me John."

"The book?" Shan turned gathering the two cups before him and poured the light colored liquid from the teapot. It steamed and a clean, delicate fragrance filled the air.

"Of course." John pulled a large folder out of a backpack and set it on the table before him. He opened it up and started laying out the papers. "This book was at the Vatican Library. It was hand painted on thin wooden slats. I made copies but because of the length I had to do two pieces of paper per page of the book."

The Vatican?" The monk's eyes widened as the pages were laid before him. He'd never seen a sutra so old. Shan set a cup of tea in front of the priest then stood up. He reached into some hidden pocket and pulled out a pair of reading glasses, perched them on his nose and leaned over the jigsaw puzzle of pages. Gazing at them intently he asked, "Is this the whole book?"

"Yes," John replied. "There's more in the file. I'm showing you a few certain pages I'm most interested in. The pages with the paintings or etchings on the wood I would like translated. I don't think it needs to be verbatim, just tell me what it says. I'm also laying out the pages to either side of the paintings in case there's text related to the pictures. If you're able to translate the text for those pages that would be very helpful."

Shan studied the text quietly, he was bent close to the table, almost hovering a few inches over it. As he waited, John picked up the cup, loose tea leaves in the bottom shifted as he moved it. He blew on the tea to cool it and tried a sip. The taste was unlike his normal coffee habit, and very different from the black teas he liked. To his rather crude palate, he didn't taste much flavor at all.

"How's the tea?" Shan inquired without looking up from the copied pages.

"It's good."

"Green tea has healing properties, it has very medicinal qualities."

"Really?" John had heard some stories in passing but didn't feel the need to try it.

"Yes." Shan fell silent again. He picked up a sheet and held it so the light wasn't blocked by his own shadow. He pursed his lips and set the sheet back down. John sat watching him and sipping on the tea. He didn't want to rush the monk. He'd waited months to find someone, what were a few more minutes? "Do you have the cover and the first few pages of this Sutra?" Shan asked. His English was slightly accented. He'd obviously spent a long time in the States, enough time to soften his accent.

"Yes," John pulled out a few pages from the front of the folder and laid them out before the monk. He perused them and sat down to drink some tea.

"This sutra is about three to five hundred years old. It's written in Mandarin. If it was older, a thousand or two thousand years old, it would be written in Sanskrit." Shan said. "What were you looking for in a translation?"

John picked up a couple of the pages, ones with illustrations. Illustrations of beings with fangs. "I'm curious to know what these are. Are they demons? Ghosts? Some kind of blood drinking spirit?"

Shan took the pages and read the accompanying text. He sat thinking for a moment as he worked out how to explain the passages and the creatures. "These are hungry ghosts. In the afterlife of Buddhism you can be reborn as another thing. At one end is human, then there is the Buddha, then there is animal, then there is ghost. Between living and dead are ghosts. This is a drawing of a hungry ghost. Someone who died and their soul was not judged by the king of Hell called Yan or Yama."

"So that would be considered a vampire?" John asked.

"Hungry ghosts can be active in either day or night. They prefer the night."

John nodded.

"There are also jiangshi," Shan said. "The name literally translated means stiff corpse."

"What are those?"

"Those are hopping vampires." The monk said as if that was all the explanation required.

"Hopping vampires? They hop?"

"So the stories say. There are a number of ways to become a jiangshi. I don't think there's a consensus on what brings them back to life. If someone died a long way from home a Taoist priest would reanimate the corpse and the vampire would hop home. Or a person's soul doesn't leave the body after death due to an unnatural demise, suicide, or maybe the soul wants to cause trouble. There are many ways in the folklore." Shan thought for a moment. "They are undead so I guess they could be considered a zombie. But the resurrected person kills people and absorbs their Qi or life force. In the daytime they rest in coffins or hide in caves. That's more the traditional western vampire."

"How would someone defeat a jiangshi?"

Shan made a strange face and thought for a moment. "I'm trying to remember folklore. Tales I heard as a child." Shan paused. "Mirrors. A rooster call. Fire. An axe. Dropping a bag of coins."

"Mirrors?' John asked. "A bag of coins?"

"Jiangshi are terrified of their own reflection."

"Are they that scary?"

Shan shrugged. "I've never seen one. How would I know?"

"How does a bag of coins stop them?"

"They stop to count the coins."

John barked a small disbelieving laugh. "So as the vampire is counting the coins you run away. How strange."

"Running away from a vampire is pretty wise, don't you think?" Shan smiled.

"Yes. It is absolutely the smartest thing to do," said John, reflecting on how often he'd been stupid. He didn't know when to stop meddling with vampires. A sense of justice or honor or something like that made him return to seek out vampires again and again. "Are there other vampires in Chinese folklore?"

"The word for vampire in Mandarin is Xīxuèguǐ." Shan said. "The name covers hopping vampires and Hungry Ghosts."

John raised his eyebrows, he heard the word, but his mind couldn't grasp the sounds and his throat didn't know how to make them. "Could you repeat that name again?" John asked slowly. He knew his ignorance was obvious.

Shan smiled mischievously. "Xīxuèguǐ." He started to sound it out slowly.

"Thank you, but no. Don't even try to teach me. I'm not able to pronounce it." John waved off the idea of ever saying the name. "I'm never going to be able to say that word. I'll stick with jiangshi."

"That's probably best," agreed Shan.

"So the picture on the page here," John shuffled pages and pointed to a figure drawn on one of the Xeroxed pages. "The one with the teeth, the demonic looking one, and the man with the sword. What is it? Is there a story that goes with the drawing?"

Shan looked for a moment at the page. "It's the tale of a warrior who fought demons with a magic sword."

"Is that common for the folklore?"

"There are always magical monsters to fight and magical weapons. There's gods, dragons, ogres, other mystical beings."

"Why is it in this book?"

Shan shrugged. "It seems to be an allegory about bravery and overcoming adversity," Shan read the page again. "Something similar to Jesus in the wilderness being tempted by Satan."

John nodded. He knew the story of course. "Does the monster in the picture have a name? Is it from a specific story?"

"The hero is from Chinese folklore, a holy warrior monk named Huang Gong. He had a magical sword made from a star that fell from the sky. It was a Kangxi Dao called Sui Xing, Shatter Star. He was infamous for hunting Jiangshi," said Shan, he turned the pages and ran his fingers over the text as he read.

"He had a magic sword and hunted hopping vampires?"

"Basically, yes. The vampires weren't the important part. They had no names. The hero did more than hunt jiangshi. He fought injustices by warlords and was unbeaten in single combat. Some thought it was the sword, I think it was the training or merely tales where the hero has to win. The sword was probably forged from a meteor, it makes for a good story when doing show and tell before a fight. I believe his sword is at the museum near Tiananmen Square."

"What do you mean show and tell?" asked John.

"Before a duel you have posturing, 'with this sword I defeated the dragon of Wushei Province.' 'A cloud of arrows blotted out the sky and this armor protected me from harm.' That kind of thing," said Shan.

"That kind of thing happened?"

"If stories of battles are to be believed, yes," Shan replied with shrug.

"How odd."

"Yes."

"That's the way many stories in folklore go. The heroes are bigger than life. You don't have a hero fail, and they are impervious except for some small thing, some weakness. They die a hero's death," said Shan. "That's in any mythology, from anywhere in the world."

"True. Achilles, Gilgamesh," John paused for a second, "Kal-el."

"Superman has never died." The monk said.

"At least not on Earth Prime." John replied. He was quiet for a moment. "Everyone has a Kryptonite."

"What's yours, Father?"

"Hubris," said John without hesitation.

"Yes, that's tripped up many people." Shan smiled in agreement.

"I know," John replied, the thought continued in his head. When I do it there's a body count. "So Huang Gong was a real man and his sword forged from a meteor is in a museum in China."

"I believe it is in Beijing. I don't remember the name of the museum. It's the one for Chinese culture to the side of Tiananmen. It's full of all the artifacts of national pride." Shan paused for a long second. "At least the history the People's Republic wishes to acknowledge. Communism has a selective memory."

"I'm sure it does. History is written by the winners."

"Most certainly." Shan shuffled through the pages again. "May I borrow this Sutra? I'd like to make a copy. I'm not going to get to the Vatican Library anytime soon."

"Of course, take as much time as you need. Feel free to copy whatever you want." John took out a pen and wrote his name and phone number on the file folder. "Here's my number. Let me know when you are done, I'll come get it." The sutra wasn't as useful as he wished. There was no magic bullet for killing vampires. Though there was a magic sword in a Chinese museum. It was more folklore. John's recent education in vampire folklore got most of the facts wrong. The reality was vastly different than the tales and myths.

Chapter 2
An Unpriest-like Education

John finished the service. As he stood outside the church greeting the people exiting he saw someone who didn't come to Mass often. A rangy man, middle aged, friendly in an everyday flannel kind of way. Not necessarily a lapsed Catholic, just a man with a different set of priorities for a Sunday morning.

"Is hunting season over, Mr. Coleman?"

An 'aw shucks' grin crossed the man's face and he nodded his head slightly. "Yeah, Last weekend was the end." He was tall, about forty five, sturdily built wearing flannel shirt and blue jeans with old cowboy boots. "I hope you don't mind me missing sermons."

"I do sermons on other days." John said smiling politely. The collar admonished even if the words didn't. "Like most every day at noon."

"I know, father, but I work during the week. And hunting season isn't that long," Dale replied. He knew the gentle ribbing was light hearted. "I like being outdoors."

"I understand, Dale." John shook the man's big hand. "No harm done."

"Would you like to come hunting sometime?"

The simple question surprised the priest. He'd never known a priest who hunted. Maybe there were some in Montana or Alaska. "I've never hunted before. I don't know if I can kill an animal, actually. In fact, I've never shot a gun before." He had too much empathy. He'd feel bad for the creature and worry about it being in pain. But then John's mind raced through his memories recalling the vampires he killed, and others he watched being shot. Maggie saved him in Las Vegas with her excellent weapons training.

"I can't imagine it'd be taught in seminary."

"Certainly not," John smirked. "Catechism training in the morning and then handguns after lunch? The Church would frown upon that."

"Would you like to learn how to shoot? I can teach you."

John glanced around for a moment considering the offer. It was an interesting thought. He remembered how his life had been saved and how useful weapons were when he was constantly stumbling into danger. He didn't handle them himself and his ignorance was a handicap. "That's a very interesting offer. Can I think about it and get back to you?"

"Of course, Father." Dale said. "Let me know if you want to learn."

"I will, I will," John said earnestly. The wheels in his mind started turning. It could be useful to know weapons and get over the fear of them.

Dale walked down the steps and another person stepped up to chat with the priest. John turned his full attention to them.

Dale Coleman met John at an outdoor shooting range outside of town; it was a short drive into the mountains. The day was clear, the air was brisk, and the sun was sharp. Under a long roof which kept the sun from beating down on them was a concrete table covered with thin gray carpet. It was padded to keep the guns from getting scratched. In front of the table was a flat barren patch of dirt some one hundred yards deep which butted up against a red colored mountain. Small shrubs went up the mountain but the chance for life was limited by the daily fusillade of bullets being shot at metal targets set at thirty, sixty, and one hundred yards. The metal targets were shapes of various sizes and some of the ones going up the side of the mountain were shaped like animals.

On the carpeted bench were two guns, one pistol, a thin rifle, and several boxes of ammunition. Behind them on a bench was another long plastic rifle case secured with a padlock. All around them were people with many types of weapons, the sounds of gunfire and the ring of metal where the bullets struck the targets filled the air. John was a bit unnerved. The sound of the gunfire and smell of the gunpowder brought back frightening memories.

John was standing next to Dale as he talked loud enough to be heard through the ear protection and over the din of gunfire.

"Ok, father, first thing you should know is that guns were invented to kill people. Hunters will tell you that it's for hunting, and the NRA will tell you it's for home protection, but that's not true. They were invented to kill people quickly and efficiently."

John was surprised by his candor.

"Man has always been at war, guns just make it easier and less in your face than hacking someone up with a sword," Dale said.

"I'm sure," John replied. "How long have you been shooting?"

"I grew up in Montana and my dad taught me how to hunt when I was thirteen. When I was eighteen I joined the Army. I was good before I joined the

Army, they made me better. I ended up at Fort Carson in Colorado Springs after being stationed in Germany. When I got out I moved up to Denver."

"I never knew that."

"I guess I'm kinda lapsed. I don't make it to your sermons that often so we don't chat much afterward. And it'd be a weird conversation. Hi, Father, I'm a trained killer," Dale said.

"Quite a few are," John said. "Sorry, lapsed, not trained killers. My church always fills up at the holidays with all the lapsed Catholics. They feel guilty. I don't mind. Everyone has their own path."

Dale nodded and smiled. "You're right."

Turning his attention to the table John pointed to the weapons laying there. "So, what are these?" he asked.

"The pistol is a 9mm Beretta, the rifle is a Marlin 10/22. We'll start you with the small rifle."

"Ok."

Dale set about showing how the guns worked and making sure the priest knew how to handle the weapons safely. After a few minutes John was surprised how easily he could hit the metal targets with the rifle. The ringing of the metal when the bullet hit was satisfying. Dale stood to the side watching and correcting his technique and offering pointers. When John was comfortable with the rifle Dale showed him how to handle the pistol. The pistol was much harder to use competently. Most of his shots went the right direction but there were few satisfying dings of bullet on steel. Mostly he missed the target, dirt kicking up in the background showing where the bullet really landed.

"Don't get frustrated. Pistols are a lot harder than rifles. They are meant for closer combat than one hundred yards." Dale could tell the priest was getting annoyed at his inability to hit the targets. "Pistols are used at about thirty yards or less and to get good you have to have a lot of practice. The military spends a lot of money getting soldiers proficient with firearms. I probably shot tens of thousands of rounds at targets.

John wondered how many rounds his police officer friend Maggie had shot in her training to become a cop. She was good. Good enough to survive a small, privately trained army. After an hour spent sending lead downrange John spoke up. "I think I like the rifle best. I can actually hit targets with it."

"It's a steady weapon with virtually no kick to the recoil." Dale picked up both weapons and moved to the bench behind them. He opened a case and laid them on the grcy foam interior. "Would you like to try something bigger?"

"Sure," John said. He was a little nervous, but he was getting a crash course in firearms. "What else do you have?"

Dale closed and locked the first case and picked up the other long case. "For what's in here we have to go to the other side of the range. It's meant for higher caliber rifles and shotguns. I'll get a card for the clays." Dale handed John both cases and pointed him in the direction of the other range. "Meet me at the end. I'll be there in a minute." The big man grabbed the ammo can and entered the office. John walked with the cases to the end of the other shooting range. It was set up similarly, but instead of a long bench all the way down it had individually molded concrete desks where people set up big rifles on tripods.

These were guns of war, the sounds of gunfire were deeper, the reverberation thumped in his chest when the guns were fired as he passed by. *Shit*, John thought. *That's a hell of a noise.* He wondered what it sounded like without the hearing protection. He looked at the targets of these bigger, more powerful weapons. The distances started at one hundred yards and went back maybe five or six hundred yards. Some of the shooters set out paper targets on the range and some had short telescopes to see if they were hitting the target.

Dale caught up with John and put the ammo can on the bench. He picked up a rifle case from where John set them on the concrete and put it on the bench. He unlocked and opened the case. Two long guns were lying on the foam.

"I recognize that one from Rambo movies. It's an AK-47. The other is a shotgun," John said.

"Very good." Dale lifted the AK from the case and carried it to the concrete desk. "This was designed in Russia to be a foolproof weapon. Mechanically it's simple and doesn't get jammed up like, say, an M-16. This can be dragged through mud and still fire. Russia designed a weapon not for the cream of the crop elite soldier, but for the conscripted lazy grunt who didn't want to be there in the first place and wouldn't take care of his weapon. They didn't think a soldier would rise to the occasion they thought he would react on instinct. And that instinct was to fire blindly at the first sign of battle. Maybe ditch the weapon and run."

"You're kidding."

"Nope. In Vietnam US troops would take these off of the VC because it was more reliable than the weapons they were issued." Dale gestured for John to sit at the concrete desk and showed him how to hold the gun. "Make sure you have the butt of the stock tight against your shoulder, it has a kick that'll surprise you."

John made a concerned face then settled the gun into his shoulder like he was shown. He sighted down the barrel to one of the metal targets much farther away than the pistol range. He took a breath, flicked off the safety, and squeezed the trigger. There was a loud explosion and the rifle slammed into his shoulder. Even prepared, he was still not ready for the impact. "Damn," John said. He looked at Dale who had a wry smile on his face.

"Told ya." Dale said. "Keep going. There's fourteen more rounds."

John settled in again and fired off round after round. He could see where the dirt puffed up from where he missed the target. When he hit the metal shape once a metallic ping reached his ears, he smiled and exclaimed, "I got it!"

"Very good."

After thirty minutes of more misses than hits they put the AK away in the case and Dale pulled out the shotgun. He led John to a machine that had stacks of clay disks on a rotating launcher. A pedal with a button was on the floor near the desk. "This is a Mossberg 500 shotgun. It's very basic but reliable." Dale showed John how to load the shotgun and went first at shooting the flying targets.

He rested the gun with the barrel down, when he said "Pull!" John tapped the button with his foot. The machine whirled and a disk was sent off into the sky. Dale brought up the shotgun from the resting position, tracked the clay as it climbed in the sky and pulled the trigger. Boom! "Pull!" The clays disappeared completely or were fragmented into smaller pieces.

After seven shots and seven hits Dale handed the shotgun to John. He watched as John loaded it and then readied himself for the priest to say 'pull.' John felt a rush of adrenaline right before he said pull.

"Pull." The machine released a clay pigeon; John brought up the shotgun and promptly missed. It broke when it hit the ground. Six more clays landed on the ground breaking on impact. "This sucks. Missing is no fun at all." He sounded and felt like a discouraged teenager.

"Unlike the movies, most things you shoot at you'll probably miss," Dale said. "But let me suggest instead of shooting like I do, already have the gun up and pointed in the path of the clay. That saves you time trying to find it. You can have the clay find your gun rather than your gun trying to find the clay. Does that make sense?"

John nodded and nestled the butt of the gun in his shoulder. He'd seen the path the clays took in the sky as they flew unharmed and pointed the barrel that direction. "Pull," John said. The machine flung a disk directly in the path of his barrel. He made a slight adjustment as he saw the clay and pulled the trigger. The disk powdered. "I got it! I got it!" John cried out.

"Great kid, don't get cocky." Dale said wryly.

John understood the reference and smiled. He continued shooting with the gun in the path of the flying targets. He got a piece of many of them as he continued shooting. They switched off shooting and operating the machine. John was getting tired and hungry. They'd been shooting for over two hours, and the last hour of impacts into his shoulder was taking its toll.

"Dale, I think I'm going to stop now. My shoulder hurts where the stock of the rifle keeps hitting it," John rotated his right arm felt pain where the rifles repeatedly impacted.

"Ok. That's fine." Dale took the shotgun and put it in the gun case and locked it with a padlock. "I'm getting tired too."

"Thank you, Dale. I really appreciate this. It was fun learning experience." John said as they walked to their cars.

"You're welcome, Father." Dale shook John's hand and opened the back of his Ford Bronco. He put the gun cases inside and the now depleted ammo can. "Thanks for coming out. If you want to come shooting again let me know."

"Again, thank you, Dale. I had a good time," John said. "I learned a lot, and I may take you up on that offer." They got in their cars and left. When John was changing to go to bed he noticed a black and blue bruise where the gun stocks were hitting his shoulder. It was the bigger, more powerful weapons which caused it, not the .22 rifle. Maggie would be surprised to hear John was learning how to shoot, though his precision was poor.

Chapter 3
Interlude: Night Terror

A child was following him.

He was sure of it. Down the street, she was there.

He woke in the middle of the night and needed to urinate. To do so he had to leave his house. The communal toilets were outside of his home. Many houses had pans or pails for human waste which are then taken to the crude toilet to dump the contents. Unfortunately for him, he ventured out at night.

The moon was high, a sliver casting a pale light in the dark of the street. He noticed the ghostly figure, a small girl, thin, in dirty clothes, following him silently. He wondered who she belonged to. Since the State instituted it's one child only policy nine years ago, most families wanted male children. Girls were becoming more and more rare as families chose to terminate females in favor of boys who could carry on the family name. Males were more valuable to society.

The child followed him, her steps a ghostly whisper. Maybe she too was headed to the basic facilities. Nervously he kept glancing back. Was she getting closer? In his mind he chided himself for fearing a child. Though he wasn't a big man, he could snap her neck like a twig.

He looked back and she was gone. A sigh of relief escaped his lips accompanied by a slight chuckle. His imagination was getting the better of him. As he continued forward a figure appeared in front of him. Another girl. He stopped and stared at her. It wasn't the same one who had been following him. She stood unmoving ten meters down the street. Where had she come from? The next cross street was further down and the section of wall next to her had no doors.

He stopped walking and made a waving gesture in her direction. "Go home! It's late, you shouldn't be out," he said, his voice subdued because to the time of night. He didn't want to wake the neighborhood. It was February so windows would be shut to retain the heat from small wood burning stoves.

The child didn't move or reply. It stood statue-like. If there was a stone on the ground he would have picked it up and thrown it at her out of anger and fear.

"Leave me alone." He said tersely. "You don't scare me." But she did. There was something about her which made the hairs on the back of his neck rise.

There was a scuffing sound behind him. He spun. Two more girls appeared, entirely too close for his fear level and time of night. His eyes widened. He still needed to pee. He started forward to the toilet, intent on ignoring the girls. A sound came from his right, a stone falling on the pavement. He looked up at the roof. The first girl was standing at the edge looking down on him like a cat would look at a mouse. He choked back a cry and stepped away from the building she stood on. How did she get up there?

He started to run. The toilet was close, the door open, he could turn on the light as soon as he entered. Maybe that would frighten the children away. He got halfway there when a weight fell on him. A small hand covered his mouth with surprising strength, another taloned hand dug into his ribs. Small sharp teeth bit him on the neck. He made a surprised sound and reached over his shoulder with his right hand to drag the attacker from his back.

Small hands grabbed his right arm and pulled down, teeth biting into the crook of the elbow, tearing the flesh. Blood spurted from the wound and a mouth fixed in place over the gash.

He was about to stumble forward to the ground when there was an impact on his leg. His ears caught the sound of tearing fabric and something sharp lanced into the flesh of his inner thigh. Before he could strike out with his left arm more hands grabbed him, creating a new sensation of pain.

The weight of the demon girls brought him to the ground. With their mouths consuming his blood, he quickly weakened. His eyes fluttered before shutting and his anguished voice failed him as he died.

Chapter 4
An Unexpected Journey

"Thank you for coming in," the Bishop said, motioning to a chair for John to take a seat. This wasn't going to be a short conference. Bishop La Paz had replaced his old bishop after the Vatican child abuse scandal forced many clergy to resign or were removed. La Paz had come from El Salvador, and was quickly elevated to Bishop to make up for the sudden vacuum of leaders in the Church. He was a handsome man, thin, with thick black hair. "The Church has a problem and I hope you are willing to help."

"Of course I'll do what I can," replied John. He was leery at the start of the conversation. He expected niceties and a preamble of some kind before the Bishop got down to business. There was an urgency and an intensity coming from the man.

"Do you know a nun named Fan Sherman?"

John recognized the name. He'd met her during his duties for the diocese. She was a nun at the local convent. They helped out at his church during the busy time at Christmas. She was Chinese but spoke English without an accent. In a conversation with her he learned she was born in China but immigrated to the States in a rather desperate and harrowing escape with her mother. They were granted asylum in the country.

"I know her from events at my church," said John.

"She and her mother escaped China when she was four. Her mother married a navy captain named Sherman and he adopted Fan. She was active in the

Church and became a nun. Well, we sent her to Beijing to check on an orphanage we fund through a third party. Since it's a communist country and religion is illegal, she went unofficially, her story was to reconnect with relatives. The government shouldn't have known who she was but somehow she ended up dying. Official word says it was some sort of street accident, at least that's what the family was told. I don't think that's the truth."

"So, what does this have to do with me?"

"You've had experience in other countries. You were in Rome a while back. I want you to go to Beijing to check on the orphanage and see what you can find out about her death. I want to know if she was killed by the government because she was a refugee. Did they find out who she was and kill her?"

"I'm not really qualified for that," protested John, with as much respect as he could muster without sounding obstinate. He didn't want to get on the bad side of his new bishop. "I don't speak Chinese."

"You have a passport with stamps from at least another country. I can't send anyone with a new passport. If it was a clean passport the government might scrutinize it more closely than if someone who has travelled. We also have a contact who can translate for you. "

"It's a communist country. I can't just go like a tourist."

"China is opening up in capitalist ways. They are trying to grow their economy. They have a billion people to feed. Tourism is a growing business. You'll be a business man."

John stared at him in disbelief. He mutely opened and closed his mouth a few times trying to frame a rebuttal.

The Bishop continued. "You'll have to get a visa from the consulate in Denver. It will take about a week."

"You're serious."

"One of our sisters died there. I want to know how and why." Coming from a third world country himself he'd seen atrocities perpetrated by governments and warlords against the people. La Paz personally had known women who were killed or disappeared and it fueled his outrage. "You can't go as a priest. The orphanage is not one of ours but, like I said, we help fund it through third parties."

John sat quietly mulling over the situation. "I don't know if I'm the right person for this job," he said. "This should be looked into by our government, the State Department or something."

"The USA is more concerned about economic treaties with China than the death of one woman, even if she is a nun. It's tragic but not worth upsetting diplomatic ties. And since she was a nun, the Beijing government is a bit miffed having someone who might be converting their citizens in the country."

"I see," said John. Having an anti-religious government involved made everything much more difficult.

"The body arrived last week. A coroner looked at it. There were strange wounds and unusual trauma. It wasn't a car accident. We have a report from the Chinese government but it doesn't make sense. They're covering something up. It looks like she was attacked by animals. There are no animals in Beijing that could do that kind of damage. I need you to go while the incident is still recent."

"Animals? Could it be dogs?"

"Probably not dogs," the bishop shook his head.

"What am I supposed to do?" asked John.

"Talk to people at the orphanage. See what you can find out about her death. The official information is sketchy and doesn't make sense. Ask the police." The bishop leaned forward in his chair. "Do not, I cannot stress this strongly enough, do not preach there. Proselytizing is illegal. You'll be thrown in jail or into a work camp. It might be years before the wheels of bureaucracy might be able to free you. Take civilian clothes and leave the bible behind. If you take a cross leave it under your clothes."

"Really." It was a statement more than a question.

"Really," La Paz said.

Chapter 5
Arrival in Beijing

Around 4 p.m. the plane was descending, the angle of the cabin gently pitched downward. It had been a long flight from Seattle to Beijing in a coach seat. He spent the time reading or napping, only to be interrupted by food service or drink service, or someone in his row needing to get past him to reach the aisle. His mouth was dry from the recycled air. The overnight flight was the best way to travel. Get on a plane in one time zone, go to sleep, wake up in the morning at your destination. Though with this flight he was traveling back through time zones and would be out of sync for a few days.

John craned his head and looked past the people in his row to see out the window. The view was a solid wall of grey. Nothing could be seen as the plane was traveling down through a thick cloudbank. It was winter and rain was common in Beijing. He kept watching hoping to catch his first glimpse of China. He was resigned to the task set before him by the bishop. He was excited to be travelling even if the circumstances were mysterious and sad.

Why the bishop thought he could find out more information about Fan Sherman's death than the police provided was beyond him. John didn't speak Chinese; he didn't have any contacts there. All he had was the name of the man who ran the orphanage Fan went to inspect. Hopefully he'd be able to help him out.

As far as the Church was concerned, one of their nuns was murdered under enigmatic circumstances.

The explanation from the Chinese government was vague. The body had been returned to the States with an official document stating a bogus cause of death. She wasn't in a car accident as Beijing asserted. When the body was examined by a medical examiner before the burial, horrific and unusual wounds covered the body. Fan was buried, closed casket, the strange way she died might be uncovered if John was successful.

The Church couldn't send anyone to Beijing officially. Religion was outlawed and any clergy might end up in prison just for being a priest. The government could accuse someone of preaching and they'd be sent to a labor camp. Someone could travel as a civilian. Tourism was possible and growing in the communist country.

John continued to look out the window. He was nervous and excited. He was determined to find time to do some touristy things as well as work on the Bishop's problem. A priest's schedule and salary didn't give many opportunities for international travel. The plane continued to descend. The view outside the window didn't change; still cloudy. There was a shift in the light and the color outside the window. It switched from grey to murky brown. He turned and looked across the cabin to see what the other windows showed. Fuzzy brown, indistinct shapes. The view worried him. It made him think of a Twilight Zone episode where a flight goes strangely wrong. There were several to choose from, whether traveling in time or arriving without people, something inexplicable always happened.

Unexpectedly buildings appeared as the plane came in for a landing. Where was Beijing? The plane taxied for a long time before reaching the terminal. A rolling stairway was driven to the doorway and the slow process of deplaning started. He shuffled down the aisle and involuntarily ducked his head as he stepped out the open door.

It was nearing 5 p.m. The sun was weak, barely piercing the thick grey clouds. It appeared as an orange disk, indistinct, looking more like a light on the side of a building than a ball of nuclear fission at the center of the solar system. The air outside the plane was thick and chewy. The smell of burnt hydrocarbons, possibly coal or gasoline tinged the air. He noticed the Chinese airport workers were bundled for the cold and wore masks over their nose and mouth. Within a few minutes he understood why. The pollution made the back of his throat itch, and mildly irritated his eyes.

They walked into the building and were taken to immigration. He pulled out his passport and travel information. A hotel name and address in both English and Chinese. He could show the paper to a taxi driver and hope the ride would take him to the appropriate place. Passengers gathered at a luggage carousel to get their luggage then proceeded to passport control.

The line moved quickly, the official looked at his passport, compared the picture to John's face, and looked the visa for entry into China. The serious man asked in accented English what his purpose for his visit. "Tourism," replied John. His passport was stamped and John was sent on his way.

The airport looked like any other airport. It was a medium sized affair with high ceilings, able to handle ten to twelve airplanes at a time. As he stepped into the area outside the immigration arrivals he saw a number of people waiting for passengers. Signs in Chinese were held up, a few were in English. One had his name written on it. "John Bryant" The man holding the sign was tall and thin. He wore a puffy green jacket and grey pants with tennis shoes. He was over thirty with close cropped black hair which was receding at the sides in a scalloped way.

John was surprised anyone was meeting him. He walked over to the open faced, friendly looking man. "Hi. I'm John Bryant."

"Lujiang." He reached out his free hand and John shook it.

"Nice to meet you…" John hesitated at the name.

"Lujiang. But my English name is Jason."

"English name?"

"When dealing with English speakers many of us have an 'English name' to make it easier."

"I see. Which do you prefer?"

"I answer to both. Jason is fine." Lujiang said dismissively.

"Alright. I'll call you Jason if that's okay with you."

"That will be fine." Jason said. "They asked me to pick you up and take you to your hotel." The *they* he referred to was the Catholic Church. John figured that would be the last time it would be mentioned in public. There were too many troops around, even in the airport there were uniformed military patrolling the concourse.

"That would be great. Thank you." John said. Some of his apprehension drained away. One part of the trip was going well. John hefted his small suitcase. "Lead the way."

Jason walked out the glass doors. The chill in the air was sharp, the sky was unusual, dim, and the few stars which peeped through the clouds were veiled by pollution. He led them to a parking lot nearby, and unlocked the trunk of a blue car, the make of which John couldn't identify. It was boxy with dents and chipped paint, there was rust on the fenders and bumper.

"What kind of car is this?" asked John.

"Soviet, from about ten years ago." Jason replied. "We don't make many cars here. No one can afford them. We have bicycles." He unlocked the doors and John got in the passenger side, seat springs squeaked in protest under his weight. He put the key in the ignition and started the car. The engine was loud and rough like it hadn't had a tune up in ages.

"How do you have a car?"

"It belongs to the orphanage. It's not great, but it works. We have some things most people don't." Jason pulled out of the parking lot and got on the road to Beijing. John lapsed into silence and gazed out the window at the dark landscape. The land was ghostly and the buildings they passed were large, six to ten floors, and uniform in shape and size. There was no style, it was large concrete blocks for housing masses of people. It was not what he expected, though it was similar to pictures he'd seen of the Soviet Union.

"So," John started. "You know why I'm here?"

Jason nodded.

"Did you know Fan?"

"Yes. She was very nice, very American compared to Chinese lady."

"How so?"

Jason cocked his head as he thought for a minute. "Not… Chinese mind."

John nodded and understood. She'd been raised in America with a Caucasian step-father. "She must have seemed more like me than like the women you know."

"Yes."

"Do you know how she died?"

Jason pursed his lips. "The government lied to you. What they don't want people to know, because it would be bad after all the recent trouble; there is a killer in Beijing."

"Really?"

"Yes, like the one in England. The Ripper." Jason said.

"Jack the Ripper?"

"Yes, he kills anyone found at night. Man, woman, child, doesn't matter. Police and army die too. No one is safe." Jason looked worried. "Bodies are found in the streets almost every morning. The government hides this from the world."

"How do the victims die?"

"They are horribly cut up."

John sat back in the seat. "Fan was one of his victims?"

"She was walking back to her hotel from the orphanage." Jason paused. The guilt he felt weighed heavily on his heart. "She didn't make it."

"Oh."

"You're staying at the same hotel," added Jason. "So don't walk anywhere at night. Take a cab or a bus or the subway."

The information scared John. He traveled thousands of miles to learn Fan was killed by a serial killer. If the government wasn't so closed and secretive he wouldn't be making the trip. He now had two weeks in China until his return flight. How much would it cost to have his ticket changed and could Jason return him to the airport now? The thought was strong but John dismissed it.

La Paz wouldn't be pleased if he returned within seventy two hours of his departure. John sighed. He would inspect the orphanage and report back. Church money was partially supporting the venture and after the one he saw in Rome, he was leery of them. Rome had been an eye opening experience.

The car continued rumbling forward on the empty road. The headlights illuminated the grey highway. Jason knew where he was headed and didn't say much. The main roads had little traffic. When they reached Beijing it was fully dark but people on bicycles were still out.

"I thought you said it wasn't safe?"

"The people who were killed were alone at night. No one is going to knock someone off of a bicycle and stab them to death." Jason said. "Most of those killed were late at night, in small neighborhoods, small side streets, in poorer areas."

John nodded at the logic. Jack the Ripper also hunted among the poor. "How far away is the airport? We've been driving a long time."

"About thirty kilometers."

"Are we getting close?" John rubbed his eyes and yawned. "I feel like I've been travelling for days. Is there a restaurant near the hotel? I'm hungry."

"We are almost there. Sorry it took so long." Jason said. "There are several restaurants nearby, and one in the hotel." Jason paused for a moment. "Do you want me to go with you?" He silently feared the priest would be murdered too if he was wandering around late at night, lost because he didn't know the area.

"No. I think I'll be fine." John understood what Jason was intimating. Night was dangerous, stay close to the hotel.

The car pulled up to a tall grey building with red paper lanterns hanging from the red cloth awning. South Sea Hotel was written in English underneath Chinese script. The glass front windows showed a lobby with furniture and a front desk, a lone, bored looking man stood behind the desk. John wondered about the name. Beijing was land locked expect for a few canals which crossed the city. The nearest large bodies of water were lakes, some of which were man-made. The ocean was 150 kilometers away.

"Here you are. I believe your reservations have been paid for." *By the Church* was unspoken. Religion wasn't practiced or allowed. Jason wanted to keep the priest safe. The death of the nun shamed him; he hadn't done his job protecting her. "I'll come get you in the morning."

Jason parked at the front and shut of the engine. He and John got out of the car, Jason opened the trunk and handed John his suitcase.

"Can you come by in the afternoon to get me? Around three? I think I'm going to be wrecked by jetlag in the morning." John felt the weight of the time change on his body.

"Of course. I'll call first to make sure you want to get picked up. If you like we can wait a day." Jason said.

"That might be a good idea. Let me sleep on it and I'll let you know when you call." John turned to go up the steps to the lobby. "Thank you for everything. We'll talk tomorrow."

"See you tomorrow." Jason opened the driver's door and got inside the car. He started the noisy engine and drove away.

John opened the glass door and walked into the hotel lobby. The man at the desk looked up. Seeing a Caucasian, he made the switch to English before he spoke.

"Can I help you, sir?"

"John Bryant, checking in."

He looked at his register and found the name. "You are staying with us for two weeks and everything is pre-paid. The restaurant and room service charges are separate. Breakfast starts at six a.m. and the restaurant is still open if you are hungry now."

"You must have read my mind, I'm famished."

The man handed John his key on a diamond shaped plastic fob. "Third floor, up the stairs, down the hall to the left, room 305. The elevator is out of service right now. Sorry. It should be fixed in a day or two."

"Great. Thanks." John took the key and headed up the stairs.

Chapter 6
The Landlocked South Sea Hotel

The room was dark and cold when John awoke. He was confused for a moment then remembered he was in China. He still thought the justification for the trip expressed by the Bishop was dubious. The nun, Fan Sherman, was murdered by a serial killer and the authoritarian government covered it up, which was to be expected from an oppressive regime. He would go to the police to see what progress they had made, but he didn't speak Chinese and wasn't connected to the police in any way. Even if he could communicate, would the police answer the questions he needed to ask?

He glanced at the red LED clock radio on the bedside table. With the blackout curtains pulled it could be 6:33 am or pm. He figured a.m. Hopefully by getting a full night sleep he'd acclimate to the local time zone without being shattered for a week or two.

John swung his legs out from under the covers and put his feet on the hardwood floor. It was cold. He walked to the bathroom and turned on the light. He looked at his face in the mirror. He looked like he had been travelling for twenty hours. Which was true. There were dark circles under his eyes, and his eyeballs felt grainy like they were volleyballs on a sandy beach. He may have slept, but he figured he'd probably need another night before he felt normal.

John hopped in the shower and stood under the hot spray for a few minutes before soaping up and rinsing himself off. The travel grime, recycled air, bad airline food, and bored waiting swirled down the drain restoring some of the humanity lost during travel. He felt more human. He used the small bottle of shampoo supplied by the hotel to wash his hair, and half the small bottle of conditioner followed. He'd ask the maid for more.

He dried off with two towels and put on the bathrobe from the hook on the back of the door. He slipped on terry cloth slippers which were too tight. They were made for smaller feet, but they protected him from the cold wood floor. In the room he turned on the heat and pulled the drapes open to look out on the city. The view was uninspired. The sky was starting to lighten but sunrise was still an hour away. His room overlooked the top of the hotel lobby and across the way was another section of the hotel with windows facing his.

I guess the Bishop is saving money. John thought to himself. He waited for the room to heat up before putting on clothes. He dressed in layers and had long underwear beneath his shirt and pants to fight the cold February weather. John brought cold weather clothes. Beijing was similar to Colorado, maybe a little warmer, and not as skin cracking dry.

He went down to the lobby restaurant after seven. There was a large buffet with a variety of breakfast food, both western and Chinese. Small cards in front of the chafing dishes named the foods he didn't recognize. He picked a selection of food from both styles; bacon, eggs, English muffins, but also cut up chicken in soy sauce, rice, rice porridge, and dim sum, to be washed down with coffee and orange juice.

John ate slowly, his thoughts were distracted. He was in Beijing. Which was both unexpected and fortuitous. The Buddhist monk, Shan, told him the sword of Gong was in the Beijing National History Museum. He had the rare opportunity to go see what a magical vampire killing sword looked like, though any weapon cutting off the head of a mortal or vampire would kill them. No one could live without a head, and John didn't believe in magic. A sword doesn't need to be magical to decapitate a person, it just needs to be relatively sharp.

Up in his room he called the number Jason gave him. The phone rang and what sounded like a female voice answered in Chinese.

"Uh, is this Jason?" asked John. "I'm trying to reach Jason."

There was the sound of the receiver being dropped but not disconnected. John heard a voice call out in Chinese and then there was silence on the other end for a moment before Jason picked up the phone. "This is Jason." He spoke in English, uncertain if the caller spoke English. The girl who answered the phone might have been mistaken.

"Jason, it's John Bryant."

"Good morning, Mr. Bryant." Jason said. "Did you sleep well?"

"Like I was dead," said John. "I think I'm going to take the morning for myself and wander around before I come over to the orphanage. I should be there sometime in the afternoon."

"That will work for my schedule. Should I come pick you up later at the hotel?" asked Jason.

"No. I'm going to do a few things first. I won't be coming from the hotel. I'll take a taxi," replied John.

"Have someone at the hotel write down the name and address of the orphanage for you so you can hand the driver the paper. They might not speak English. In fact, it's very likely they won't speak English," Jason said. "Also take a card from the hotel desk with the address so you can hand that to any driver to get you back to the hotel."

"That's a good idea."

"Be careful with the drivers. Some are not honest; they may drive you around to boost the fare."

John considered the possibility. "I'll be careful," he said, though he wouldn't know if the driver was driving him around since he'd never been to Beijing and didn't know the city.

"See you this afternoon."

"Thank you, Jason."

"You're welcome."

John hung up now concerned he was going to be ripped off, though there was only so much he could do to prevent it. *Forewarned is forearmed,* he thought.

The taxi dropped John off near Tiananmen Square. He paid the driver and got out in the cold air. His jacket was the first of several layers, the bottom was thermal underwear under a t-shirt, then a button up shirt, followed by a sweater, and then the winter jacket he used in Colorado. Living in the Rockies taught him how to stay warm. China wasn't as cold as he was prepared for.

The museum was off to his right. It was a large tan building made of some kind of stone. It wasn't marble. The architecture was blocky and reflected a communist way of thinking. Utilitarian, practical, meant to be heavy as a show of ponderous power.

John paid the entrance fee and walked the soaring large hallways looking at the exhibits. Much of the art and sculptures were post Revolution exaltations of Mao and the Communist party. There were grand depictions of the workers, farmers, soldiers, and average people who created the new China. The China which crushed a student revolution only a year earlier for all the world to see live on television.

John didn't know where he'd find the sword, the guide pamphlet didn't break down listings to individual pieces. He was looking for a section on ancient China, one of folk heroes and emperors. He needed pre-revolution artifacts. When he found a hall full of ancient Buddha statues he knew he was on the right track.

The number of Buddhas was surprising. They were painted or gilded white marble. Some were intact, many were broken, missing hands or arms or legs or heads, but all were undeniably the Buddha. It reminded him of Rome and the artwork there. The statues from Roman times were seldom complete. Parts were missing or broken off. Considering the 5000 years of Chinese history, there was a lot of opportunity for artifacts. It also reminded him of all the depictions of Christ in artwork, and how most of the art from late Roman times until the French Revolution was religious in nature. After that bloody awakening art became more than religious allegory.

John found a room of paintings, tapestry, and artifacts from ancient China. There were items large and small encased in glass and lit with small spotlights. John looked around the room, no magic sword. He passed into the next room, continuing his search. Near one wall was a glass case with a sword, it was curved and from a tapering handle the blade widened to a scalloped end. A plaque on the case was in Chinese and English. ***Shatter Star, Sword of Huang Gong***, along with a description of the man and the weapon.

Swords were not an area of study for him so the weapon didn't strike him as unique. It was obviously not a European weapon. He could recognize rapiers and broadswords. He'd seen representations of them in movies, Shakespeare's Romeo and Juliet, and fantasy movies like Excalibur. The sword in the case was a curved, dark metal blade. It had strange imperfections mottling the length of the blade which made him believe it was made from a meteor. Myths are sometimes true, though he discounted the magic part of the story.

He gazed at it. It looked heavy and sharp, lethal for both man and vampire. Considering how far in the museum it was and the case it was in, he didn't entertain trying to steal it. He might covet a weapon for killing vampires, but it wasn't something he had the training to do. It wasn't in his nature to steal something like that for practical and moral reasons. Thou shalt not covet. Thou shalt not steal.

On the wall behind the weapon was a tapestry that was similar to the illustration in the sutra copied from the Vatican Library. Huang Gong was a national hero from before the revolution that changed the entire nature of China.

John glanced at his watch. He still had time so he continued his tour of the museum until it closed at four thirty. After leaving the building he crossed the street and looked at Tiananmen Square. It was a large flat space, at the end was the Forbidden City, on the wall facing the Square was a huge portrait of Mao. The divine emperor was replaced by a new deity, Mao. The palace was now a tourist attraction. At the other end of the square was a large statue, soldiers and workers united, creating a new China. Everywhere he looked the new religion was the state, the common people wresting the country away from the aristocracy.

That was the myth, but the communist party had its own betters, its own aristocracy. In any system there were those in charge and those under their control. Even John's beloved Catholic Church was the same as a government.

As John walked the air was rough on his throat. People around him had masks to filter out the pollution. He'd heard the pollution was bad and originally thought the grey of the clouds switching to a brown pall in the air as the plane descended was a trick of the waning sun. It wasn't, it was a haze which was everywhere he looked. He was surprised how it affected him; he'd have to find somewhere to buy masks if he was going to stay healthy.

John walked to a street and held his arm up and whistled loudly. Even in Beijing signaling a taxi was a universal thing. A cab pulled up to the curb and he got in the back. Out of a pocket he pulled the name and address of the orphanage written in Chinese. The driver took the paper, looked at it and nodded. The cab quickly pulled into traffic. John was on his way.

CHAPTER 7
THE BEIJING ORPHANAGE

After a fifteen minute drive, the taxi dropped John off in front of a large wrought iron gate, one of two entrances in a tall block wall surrounding the property. Through the gate he could see what had once been a grand mansion, five stories tall, probably dozens of rooms, and none of the architecture was remotely Chinese. This was an artifact left over from the English occupation of China in the 1800s.

The English sailed into the Shanghai harbor wanting access to trade. When the Chinese said no the English frigates bombarded Shanghai for three days until they agreed to trade. Since the waterfront was demolished the English rebuilt it in their own style creating the Bund section of Shanghai. From Shanghai the English traveled to most of the big cities and through a system of commerce and coercion, conquered China. Neighborhoods of Beijing were torn down to build homes for the wealthy like the large mansion before him.

The house beyond the wall was nestled in a Hutong that reclaimed territory after the English were rooted out. Years after the English left the stately home was somewhat rundown and filled with orphans.

John lifted the latch on the gate and entered the grounds, shutting the gate behind him. He wondered if the surrounding neighborhood was safe. The area was grey stone buildings on grey asphalt streets under a grey sky. As he approached he looked at the house. Through the large windows above the door, he could see a wooden stairway. The building was longer down the left side than the right. As he walked up the stairs to the wide porch he saw several young faces peering inquisitively at him through the windows.

By the time John was at the door about to knock it swung open. "Good to see you, Mr. Bryant." Jason said, his friendly face was beaming.

"Nice to see you, Jason. Call me John, remember?"

"Come in. Did you have any trouble finding the house?" Jason motioned for John to enter and shut the door after he passed by.

"No, I gave the address to a cab driver and he dropped me at the front gate." John looked around the interior. There was a wide staircase directly in front of him leading upstairs. Through a set of open double doors he could hear children playing. The buzz of their voices was excited. He figured he was the cause of the commotion. Girls slowly passed by the doorway to look at him. Was the foreigner looking to adopt? John guessed that was the conversation he couldn't understand.

Sadly, no, they would be disappointed. He couldn't save the children, take them all to the United States to loving families. He hoped the orphanage was nothing like the one he'd seen in Rome last year. That was a nightmare. It was closed after it burned down and the children were taken to be adopted outside of the purview of the Catholic Church.

"Come into the kitchen, I'll make some tea and we can talk," Jason led him past the stairway and through a swinging door into a large kitchen. The floor was dingy white and black tiles in a checkerboard pattern. The black and white style continued to the countertops and cabinets. There was a large double sink. The large stove and oven looked old, like it had cooked countless meals over decades. Against one wall sat a small table and four chairs surrounding the yellow Formica top.

Jason motioned for John to sit at the table and picked up a kettle from the stove top and filled it with water from the spout of a large jug on the counter. John watched as Jason put the kettle on the stove and started the burner. He lit a match and placed it in the flow of the gas. There was a quiet 'whoosh' as the flame ignited.

Jason pulled two painted tea cups from a cupboard and scooped loose tea leaves into the bottom of the cups. He brought them to the table, set one in front of John, and sat down as he waited for the water to boil.

"Do you have running water here?" asked John.

"Of course." Jason glance at the jug on the counter and understood the question. "The water in Beijing isn't safe to drink. It's okay to shower and wash dishes but not for drinking."

"Oh," said John. "I'm surprised by that. A big city like Beijing should have safe water."

"We are used to it. We have water delivered for drinking and cooking." Jason shrugged.

"I have some questions about Fan." John said directly.

Jason nodded, his smiling face suddenly serious. "I'm sure."

"Was she here the night she died?"

Jason pursed his lips and nodded again, a small sad motion. "She was."

"Do you know what happened?"

"What I told you last night isn't widely known outside of China." Jason started when the kettle began piping a one note symphony of steam. "Excuse me." He walked over and shut off the stove top. He lifted the kettle, brought it to the table, and set it down on a large ceramic tile on the table. "If the water is too hot it is bad for the tea. I'll let it cool slightly before pouring."

John nodded like he understood, but he didn't. Coffee was his hot drink of choice. "So what isn't known?"

"There have been killings in Beijing. Quite a few."

"You said there is a serial killer," replied John.

"Possibly. It started after Tiananmen; some think it has to do with the protests. Some think it's the PLA killing dissidents after the fact. Retribution, revenge, whatever," said Jason.

"PLA?" asked John.

"People's Liberation Army."

"You think she was killed by whoever is doing that?"

"It seems likely. She didn't look foreign. She didn't dress like an American. I think she was in the wrong place at the wrong time." Jason picked up the kettle and carefully tipped the hot water into the two cups. "Let it steep for a minute."

Whorls of steam rose up and curled in the air, a light fresh scent wafted into John's nostrils. "So what happened with Fan?" asked John.

Jason shifted in his chair, an anxious movement. "She walked," he said. "I told her I would drive her to her hotel. She refused and left. I should have gotten the car out and gone to find her." Jason stared at the cup of tea before him. He played the night over in his mind again. Could he have stopped her? Saved her? He felt guilty that she died. If he'd only done more, convinced her to wait for him she might be alive now.

During the lull in conversation two women entered the kitchen. They started preparing dinner for all of the children. Large pots were put on the stove top; the largest bag of rice John had ever seen was pulled out of a cabinet, multiple scoops, enough for a night at a Chinese restaurant, were placed in boiling water. Meat was cut up and tossed into a large wok with sauce. Vegetables were diced and added.

John watched silently, fascinated by the efficient and practiced way they did the tasks needed to feed a small army. "How many children live here?" asked John quietly as if they might be spies. "Is it safe to talk with them around?" he asked in a hushed voice.

"It's safe to talk here," whispered Jason. Then in a more normal tone, "We currently have forty three children; eight boys, thirty five girls. The ages range from newborns to fourteen," replied Jason.

"Thirty five girls? Why so many compared to the boys?"

Jason glanced at the women preparing dinner and lowered his voice slightly. Maybe it wasn't so safe to talk after all. "About ten years ago the government instituted a one child policy per family to fight overpopulation." Jason paused.

John understood almost immediately. "And boys are valued more by society than girls."

Jason nodded. "Girls are abandoned. There are many abortions so the family can have a son to carry on the name and inherit after the parents die. There's a penalty if a family has more than one child." Jason shrugged. "In the city this might make sense, but for a farm, children are farm hands. One child can't do many chores."

The ramifications of the policy kept unfolding in John's mind like a growing vine of a terrible idea. It was short sighted and most importantly would lead to problems when the millions of boys reach an age where they want to marry and there are too few women to marry. "You're faced with a problem. Your society doesn't want girls and you have a house full of them."

Jason nodded, he sighed. "Yes."

"Why do you have eight boys if they are prized?"

"They are… not…"

"I think I understand." John smelled the food being cooked and watched the women preparing dinner. The stove and the steam heated the kitchen and smells of food made him hungry. The boys at the orphanage were handicapped in some way. Something was wrong with them and they were likewise discarded.

"Is there any hope for the girls to be adopted?"

"Some. We have a few patrons who have adopted the girls," replied Jason, his face lit up. "One in particular, a very rich woman, has adopted a number of girls."

Fear struck at John. He was suddenly worried the girls might be getting trafficked. His time in Rome, experience with the orphanage there, made him less trusting. "Really? That's interesting. I'd like to meet her," said John. "How many?"

"Over twenty. I can probably arrange for you to meet her if you like."

"How are you funded? Is it the government?"

"The PRC does give us money for operating costs and provided us with the building and the land. Your organization provides money as well." Jason was cautious and didn't want to name the Catholic Church. He wasn't sure if the cooks were reporting back to some authority. And though they were speaking English he didn't know if the women understood it as well.

"What about adoptions overseas? I'm sure there are couples in America who would adopt the girls."

"It's possible. It's difficult, time consuming, and expensive. There are a lot of steps for foreign adoptions." Jason replied. "I'd gladly welcome it."

John nodded. "Would it be possible for you to come with me to the police tomorrow? I have some questions about Fan's death and need an interpreter. Do people know there is a killer in Beijing?"

"It's known but the stories are not in the papers. The neighborhoods where the bodies are found know. It's not on television. Also there aren't many televisions," replied Jason. He noticed John was watching the food preparation. "Would you like to stay for dinner?"

John considered it for a moment. "I know you are feeding a lot of children. I wouldn't want to take food out of their mouths. I'll eat at my hotel." He glanced out the window near the kitchen door. Night had descended as they talked. "Since it's dark, could you give me a ride to my hotel or call me a cab?"

"I'll drive you." Both men knew Fan's death was the reason he was there. Neither of them wanted to tempt fate and have him travel alone at night.

CHAPTER 8
INTERLUDE: SOLDIER'S STORY

A pale, wan sliver of a moon was the only light shining on the slate grey streets. The buildings on either side were dark and quiet. It was late, after three in the morning. There was no sound, the city was asleep.

The two People's Liberation Army troops, one of several battalions of pairs spread out in Beijing, Feng Zhào and Yun Dèng, were walking. They'd been walking the quiet neighborhood all night. After nine hours their AK-47s were weighing heavily around their shoulders, the strap biting into the backs of their necks. The rough collar of the uniform wasn't padded in a way to make a twelve hour patrol with weapons and gear comfortable. The packs on their backs contained water and some rations. A radio was in a side pocket, if they ran into any trouble they'd call for help.

They'd be able to go back to their billet in the morning when the sun rose, but in the meantime they were looking for a killer. The assignment was simple. Patrol. Look for the killer who had been stalking Beijing neighborhoods. Stop and question anyone suspicious. Or stop everyone and question them. If they had doubts, detain, and call for backup. The last person they saw was an hour prior, someone going to the toilet. Generally people used a pot and emptied it in the morning. It was more efficient than going out in the cold and the dark.

They weren't the only troops in the city searching for the killer. There were troops all over Beijing.

Dead bodies had appeared in the mornings for months. Only after the protests in Tiananmen did the PRC choose to address it. The news from around the world remained focused on Beijing and it would be embarrassing to the government to have dead bodies appear most mornings.

"My feet hurt." Feng said in a whispered voice.

"Yes. You've told me. Every ten minutes for the last three hours." Yun replied in the same hushed voice. "You've also said it every night this week."

Feng ignored the comment, or it didn't register that he was whining. "We should stop to rest. Have something to eat."

Yun looked at his watch, angled it to find some moonlight so he could see the hands, and grunted his agreement. "Let's find a place to sit. I'm not sitting on the street in this shithole neighborhood." He motioned for them to continue. On another street, a larger one, they'd find a bus bench or someplace to sit.

After five minutes of walking they found five mismatched chairs sitting outside the main entrance of one of the homes. Two of the chairs were child sized, the seats were replaced by boards, possibly a door sawn in pieces and tied to the chair with packing string. One chair was cushioned with a faded red plastic cushion with a gold design. Another chair was black rattan, curved and woven. The last was a wooden seat, the back broken off the chair. Next to the disparate collection of seats was a small pail with sand and numerous cigarette butts.

Feng tapped his partner and pointed to the chairs. Yun shrugged and took off the pack. They both removed the rifles from around their torsos and leaned them against the wall behind the chairs. Feng sat in the cushioned seat and set the pack on one of the small chairs. He untied his boots and loosened the laces to give his tired feet more room to move around, he didn't want to take off his boots but more blood circulating to the extremities would be good. He wiggled his toes vigorously, and sighed.

He dug in the pack and found a container of food and a set of chopsticks. The fish and the rice were cold but he was hungry and didn't care. They ate in silence and drank water from their canteens. "I wish I had a beer," said Feng.

"I wish I was asleep. We've been searching every night this week." Yun gestured at the darkness. "We haven't found anything, and bodies are still lying in the streets every morning."

"I think it has to do with Tiananmen. The dissidents are still killing people." Feng said, his indoctrination by the PLA was still secure. "Look how many troops were hurt. I heard they killed thousands."

Yun munched his dinner quietly. He didn't believe all the scuttlebutt he heard in the barracks. Any truth could be wildly distorted from the time the story entered the door to the time it ended at the last person hearing it. "I heard about twenty were killed."

Feng swung his head to look at Yun in the dark. Even without being certain Yun could sense his questioning countenance. He didn't know Feng well, having just transferred into Feng's unit. He could be reported to command for disloyalty.

"Or it could be thousands," Yun said quickly. Shrugging he added. "I wasn't there. I was in

Shanghai." He marched, he did the job, but he didn't give up his individuality. He was always different growing up and had gotten in trouble for it. In the Army he kept his head down and his mouth shut. Do the job, don't get noticed; it was the easiest way to blend with the crowd.

"I wonder if anyone is having any luck finding the killer."

"Honestly, it's a vague order. Find a killer." Yun said. "We ask the few people we find walking at night what they are doing, where do they live, but unless we catch a murderer in the act of killing someone or find a person with a bloody knife, it's kind of futile."

"I guess," Feng replied. "I doubt anyone is going to admit they are a killer if we just ask them."

"True," Yun nodded in agreement as he scooped some meat and rice into his mouth. He chewed thoughtfully for a moment. "But by having thousands of us on the streets of Beijing, the killer might stop for fear of being caught."

"Well, he'll stop while we're here. Once we aren't patrolling, who knows." Feng took a sip from the canteen. "We can't stay out here forever."

"That would be awful." Yun finished his food and put the container and chopsticks away in the backpack. "The Army might keep us patrolling every night. There hasn't been a murder for days. Our being here is probably the reason. The killer sees all of us patrolling and is too afraid to kill someone. "

Feng thought about it. The PLA was huge, almost two million soldiers over the various military branches. The PRC had enough PLA troops to keep the streets safe at night until they caught the killer.

During the Tiananmen Square siege by college demonstrators, the PLA had anywhere from 150-200,000 personnel to keep the order. Martial Law was only rescinded by the government in January. To have this many troops back on the streets was almost like being back under Martial Law again.

Yun put his watch close to his face and sought out light so he could read the dial. He sighed wearily. "We should continue."

Feng knew what he meant, but wasn't anxious to get moving again. "All right," he said. "Only three more hours of walking before we meet the bus that takes us back to the barracks." He pulled the laces on his boots snug before tying them.

Off to his right a scuffing sound made Feng turn. In the pale moonlight he saw a small figure approaching. A child was walking on the street, something dangled from its hand. When she got closer he could see it was a doll hanging, carelessly held by a sleepy child.

Feng stood and took a few steps toward her. "Child, are you lost?"

She turned to look at him as if noticing him for the first time. "No." Her voice was small and what he was expecting the waif to sound like. She continued to approach them. Both soldiers were standing now, facing the girl.

Is this your neighborhood?" Yun asked. She could be walking to the communal toilet down the street, but at 3 a.m. with a killer on the loose it was a dangerous thing to do.

"No." The little girl replied. She moved closer to them, drawn by their conversation. She stopped in front of them and looked at them quizzically. "What are you doing here?"

"Keeping people safe," Yun replied.

"Safe from what?"

"There is a bad person around somewhere. We are keeping people safe from the bad man." Feng said, automatically talking down to the young girl.

She cocked her head to the side and a small smirk tugged at her lips. "Ok." She said in her sing song voice. She turned away and started walking, the doll swinging in her hand. "Bye." She waved her free hand in the air and spoke without turning back to them.

The two soldiers looked at each other for a moment. "We should…" Feng started to say when something heavy dropped on his shoulders. He gave a short stifled cry as he felt his flesh being lacerated in multiple places. Yun was likewise attacked; he collapsed to the street under the weight of three small figures. They were tearing at his throat, face, wrists and legs. They felt more impacts as more assailants appeared out of the dark.

The girl with the doll dropped the weathered shape and joined in the melee. In less than a minute the two fighting soldiers were subdued by sheer numbers and multiple mouths. They were torn open, their life's blood being drained by the demon girls.

As Yun died his mind careened through the death wave. The adrenaline pumping in his brain made him relive his life in an instant. But also he wondered were these children the killer they were looking for? These hungry ghosts? As he labored to breathe he thought, *I don't want to die.*

The children drained the two men and stood up leaving the bodies behind. Feng and Yun were now trash, not worth another thought. The girls looked around to see if there were witnesses. Had anyone heard them, seen them? If a witness had seen them, they would die too. They were taught to leave no one alive behind. A girl searched each of the corpse's pockets, taking what little cash they had. ID was left behind. Two other girls searched the soldier's backpacks for valuables. Two of the larger girls picked up the rifles and slung them over their shoulders. Magazines and extra ammo were put in one of the packs and a third girl pulled on the pack which was way too large for her.

There was a sharp, single whistle from down the block. All the girls suddenly stopped what they were doing and turned to see a tall figure on a roof several houses down the street. Their Master was calling them back. Another whistle and the girls moved quickly away from the dead bodies.

In the morning six soldiers were found dead, slashed up by some madman. Their uniforms were torn and blood spilled everywhere. The troops were robbed and more frightening to the PLA, their weapons taken. After what happened the previous summer, guns in the hands of dissidents would be disastrous.

The police officer stared impassively at John. His stone face didn't betray his thoughts. He looked at the photo being held out and flicked his gaze to the man translating the words the American said.

"Her name was Fan Sherman. She was a friend of mine. She was killed last month." John said then waited for Jason to translate. "Have you made any progress in finding her killer?"

When the translation was finished the man shook his head and handed the photo back. John put the picture in his coat pocket. The police officer spoke briefly to Jason.

"He said no, it was a car accident, and wants to know why you would fly all the way from America to find out about the death of your friend."

John thought for a moment. The officer was going with the government excuse for her death. "More money than sense," said John. Immediately after he said the common colloquialism he wondered if it would translate since China didn't have the same monetary system to make the phrase a pun. "I'm not with anybody. She was a friend. I want to know why she died. She wasn't in a car accident."

The man spoke and held out his hand. "He asks if he can look at your passport." Jason said after the officer finished.

John felt like his face drained of blood but he couldn't be sure. Was he now being scrutinized for accusing them of lying? He reached into his jacket pocket and pulled out the document and handed it over. The officer looked at the passport and scanned through the pages to see where else John traveled.

"What were you doing in Rome?" The officer asked. The lag time between comment and translation was becoming more and more brief.

"Tourism," replied John. Jason translated, the look on his face was concerned. What foolish thing was the American doing? They could be arrested.

"And you are here for two weeks?"

"Yes."

"Are you going to see the Great Wall while you are here?"

"Yes. I travelled all this way it would make sense to see something like that," said John. "Probably the Forbidden City, too. Do you have anything you would recommend me seeing?"

The officer frowned. He wasn't used to being questioned in such a calm manner. The nature of his job frightened people, put them on the defensive. His office and indiscriminate power to jail someone kept people off balance. "The Temple of Heaven is nice." He handed the passport back. "She died in a car accident." The officer said, his tone steel.

"I see. Thank you. . I'll stop taking up your valuable time," said John slipping the passport into his pocket with Fan's picture. "Thank you for the advice about the Temple of Heaven." John got up out of the chair and turned to leave. He paused and turned back. "If you learn anything else about Fan Sherman could you contact me? I'm at the South Sea Hotel." He hesitated for a moment unsure if he should offer his hand to the officer. John inclined his head, a small bow. "Thank you again for your time." John gestured for Jason to follow him out of the room.

They walked out of the police station silently. Many eyes watched them go. Jason was casting worried looks left and right to see if they were going to be stopped either in the building or outside. John was silent for several blocks as they walked toward the orphanage. When he was comfortable with the distance he spoke. "That went about as well as I thought it would," he said. "They don't have a clue about the killer and it makes them look bad."

"There were some PLA troops killed last night," said Jason.

"Really?" asked John. "Were they armed?"

"They're soldiers, of course they have guns."

"How would someone attack and kill a trained soldier?" asked John.

"I don't know. They patrol in pairs. The killer attacked and killed two trained soldiers," corrected Jason. "That's not easy. Or it shouldn't be easy. Maybe they were taken by surprise."

John made a face and considered the possibilities. The killer might not look like someone dangerous. Then when they get within striking distance they kill their victim or victims quickly. "Wouldn't any attack make noise? They could have yelled or fired a gun," said John. "I wonder if anyone in the neighborhood woke up."

"I don't know. If someone had woken up and went out to see what the commotion was, wouldn't they be dead?" asked Jason.

John nodded. "Probably. Or maybe they'd be too afraid to go see what's happening. They'd lock the doors, wait in the dark, and pray nothing comes after them."

"We don't have guns like you do," said Jason. "We are trained to be… docile, obedient."

John considered the wording for a moment. Trained to be docile and obedient. The government had to indoctrinate the populace at a young age to achieve that kind of compliance. With the proper leadership, one billion angry people could change everything, just like Mao did during the Revolution. They replaced one repressive system for another. The PRC knew they had to keep people docile and obedient or the system they created was in danger from sheer numbers. Tiananmen was a dangerous spark which was snuffed out. The world watched as the government reasserted control.

"We have a lot of guns and a cowboy mentality," said John.

"And a cowboy president," Jason retorted.

"Yes, we do." His political leanings were always for the more humane candidate, and it was never the conservative who was humane to citizens.

They continued walking. John took in the sights of Beijing. There were gas powered carts driven by men, in the back of the carts were crudely crafted brooms made form branches of bushes bundled together. The rustic brooms were a throwback to something in the 1800s. It struck John as odd for a place which manufactured so many products for the world to have such simple brooms for sweeping the roads.

He noticed there were no homeless, there were no dogs roaming and he tried to remember if he'd seen a cat walking on the street. For what he expected of a third world country it was clean and organized.

"Jason, I was wondering." John said.

"About what?"

"You said a rich woman has adopted a number of girls," inquired John.

"Yes. Over twenty."

"Twenty." said John. Why so many? "That's excessive don't you think?"

"I'm trying to give the children the best chance at life I can. She's willing to take on the burden of so many unwanted girls." Jason shrugged. "We don't have many options. Once the children turn eighteen, they have to leave the orphanage."

"That's unfortunate," said John. "Who is she? What does she do with them?"

Jason looked at him quizzically. "What do you mean what does she do with them?" he asked.

"When I was in Rome there was an orphanage which was trafficking children for sex." John said reluctantly. He purposely left out who the children were trafficked to. He was ashamed there were priests perpetrating horrible crimes on the children. The abuse ended but only because of supernatural intervention, worldwide exposure, and dozens of deaths.

Jason inhaled sharply. "Human trafficking is a problem, but I can assure you she is kind and generous. She's adopted over twenty girls. She sends them to be educated, clothes them, feeds them. Madame Xuilan is a great lady." Jason spoke effusively. "She comes from old family money. Her family survived the revolution somehow, and I think they had assets in banks outside of China when Mao took over. She has friends high up in the government so they leave her alone."

John nodded. The rich had protections the poor didn't, even in a communist country. He'd seen it before. Death was the only equalizer for the inequalities of life. "I'd like to meet her. Is that possible?" asked John.

Jason regarded him, his face was calm. "Why do you want to meet her?"

"I'm concerned about the children. Don't you think it's strange she would adopt so many girls?"

"She's generous. She is helping when no one else does or can." Jason was getting agitated. He was defending a patron and friend against an American who knew nothing of his situation.

"I'm sorry if I offended you," said John. "I didn't mean to disparage her. It's just… I don't know. I've never met her. I'm having a hard time believing people are so charitable."

Jason frowned, his disdain showed on his face. "Your job is to be charitable. Your job is to believe."

John stopped walking, suddenly ashamed. "I know. It's not as easy as it was to walk the right path, to live with a humble, charitable heart." John sighed heavily. "I've seen the worst of humanity. It changes you."

Jason watched him. The priest was wounded, by what he couldn't imagine. People on bicycles rode by in the street, a few cars passed, pedestrians walked around them as they stood. "I'll see what I can do. I'll call her estate. If she's in town maybe she will come to talk to you. When do you leave?"

"I fly out in twelve days," said John. "Since I now know Fan was killed by a serial killer, I have a lot of free time."

Jason gestured for them to continue walking. "Let's find some food."

John nodded and caught up to Jason who was walking ahead of him. "Nothing crazy. No fried crickets or scorpions, please." John said.

"In a country of one billion, you eat what you can. Protein is protein" Brain replied. "We will find you some broccoli beef."

John wondered if Jason was mocking him and his limited western ways.

CHAPTER 10
THE SIGHTS OF BEIJING

It took several days for Jason to arrange a meeting with Madame Xiulan. During that time John took in the sights of Beijing and made sure he was back home at his hotel well before 10 pm. He didn't travel alone on the streets after dark, always taking a cab or a bus. The thought of a serial killer made him cautious and paranoid. With his special background he was already wary of dangers in the darkness, though those were not human. When John visited or called the orphanage Jason would tell him if there was a body count the next morning. No information about the murders made the newspapers. Such information was successfully suppressed by the government.

Despite the threat of a serial killer, China had some amazing ancient sights he was unwilling to miss. Breathlessly he hiked up the Great Wall one day, a newly minted UNESCO World Heritage site. The February air was brisk, the sun crisp and sharp. John toiled up the steps from the parking lot, climbing the steep wall. The stone steps were not uniform in height, some were short, some normal, others were a stretch, though the Ming Dynasty section he climbed was more uniform than many parts of the wall. His heart pounded in his chest and he could feel the pulse in his ears from the exertion.

When he needed to rest he turned to look at the distance he climbed and the sprawling vista. The Great Wall snaked and scaled the brown mountainside; countless grey stones stacked creating stairs and ramparts and small fortresses, towers for repelling the enemy. In many places it wasn't as wide as the name suggested, in some areas the stairway up was six to eight feet wide and only ten feet above the mountain and the surrounding grey scrub. He imagined the bushes would be bright green in the summertime, watered by rain, a verdant fringe around the crown of the wall.

At the top of fortress twelve John stood looking out across the valley below. Man could do amazing things when he set his mind to it. The wall was a marvel of engineering, constructed over centuries to keep out invaders, and used to regulate traffic on the Silk Road.

The wind across the gorge picked up, chilling John. He looked at the sky, the sun was moving across the blue expanse, racing to the far side of the mountains. He started down at a leisurely pace. There were buses several times an hour that would take him back to Beijing. Once he was back in the city he would find a place to eat and take a hot bath. His muscles would be sore from the climb up the wall.

On another day John went to the Temple of Heaven as suggested by the taciturn police officer. It was in a vast park in central Beijing. He walked through the park down a long covered walkway. Red painted poles held up the ornately painted roof. On the banister retired Chinese men and women wearing sturdy winter coats and hats played cards and board games and socialized with each other. In another section of the park there were groups doing Tai Chi or playing slow games of soccer. A circle of men were kicking what looked like a shuttlecock with their feet, the feathers of the weighted shape were bright yellow.

A few steps away old men were doing pull ups and bar dips on bars or just hanging to stretch their limbs. Children raced and played, watched by parents or grandparents.

John sat on the banister away from the retirees and watched the people passing by. He wondered what their lives were like having lived under communist rule. Their basic needs were taken care of, but were they happy? Were they content with their lives having known nothing else? The world was denied to them but they didn't know it.

A young girl, maybe eight years old, in pink puffy winter coat, crested the small set of stairs in front of John and spontaneously twirled and spun doing graceful, improvised ballet moves for a few glorious seconds. Then she stopped, turned and waited for her parents to catch up. John smiled, his heart was buoyed by the sight of her unbridled artistry. It was something a child would do, dance for the sheer joy of it. Dance without fear of being judged. He imagined she did it often, maybe she took ballet classes and this exhibition was practice for some future recital. Or it could be done as a lark, improvised for the sake of dancing. John speculated but didn't approach her to ask. It wasn't his culture. He was simply happy to have been there for the ephemeral moment.

John headed to the entrance of the Temple, paid the admission, and stepped over the threshold. He passed by the large, heavy red door which was studded with copper spheres the size of baseballs. The temple was a brightly painted, circular three tiered structure. He found an English tour group and listened to the description of the building, its construction, and marveled something so vast was built before Columbus was born. And all built without the use of any nails.

After the Temple of Heaven he caught a cab and had it take him back to Tiananmen Square to visit the Forbidden City. The walled compound where the Emperor of China lived was magnificent, large ornate buildings in a palace complex which housed the emperor and thousands of attendants and support staff as well as other nobility. John didn't find it odd that such a huge collection of buildings were built to house one man, he'd seen the Vatican. The Chinese emperor was considered divine, having the mandate of heaven, but if there was famine or calamity it was an indication the emperor had lost divine favor. The Pope, once elevated, was the Vicar of Christ on earth and remained in office until death. Both lived in opulence and the Pope was considered infallible.

At all the sites the motif of dragons was everywhere, especially at the Forbidden City. Their long, snake like bodies with four squat legs were represented on all the architecture, along the edges of buildings. He loitered behind an English tour group listening to the guide. The Emperor used the dragon as a symbol of his imperial strength and power. The number of dragons on the eaves of a roof designated the importance of the occupant. Nine dragons denoted the Emperor. Armed with this tidbit of knowledge he looked at the buildings anew.

When the sun was getting low in the sky, John left the Forbidden City and caught a cab to the orphanage. He'd spent the evenings there getting to know the children and tried to teach them English as they tried to teach him Chinese. His attempts at pronouncing words were usually met with polite laughter from the girls.

The cab dropped him at the wrought iron gate. He opened it and walked up the path to the large house. He smiled and waved as a few faces saw him from the windows. Jason answered the front door of the orphanage before John had a chance to knock. The girls had obviously warned him the American was back. "Madam Xiulan will come by tonight after supper," he said before John spoke.

John stepped into the entry way, the large stairway dominated the space in front of them. "Is it safe for her to travel after dark?" The dead were tallied every morning, the serial killer was active and prolific.

"She has a chauffeur driven car," replied Jason. "I think he's really her bodyguard."

"What did you tell her?" asked John.

"I told her an orphan who needed special care had arrived," said Jason. "She occasionally adopts the ones no one wants." He thought for a moment then added sadly, "As much as no one wants the girls anyway." What a terrible situation, raising children a society didn't want.

Chapter 11
The Great Lady

"Why do you adopt so many children?" asked John.

"Because I can," she replied settling into the upholstered chair in the sitting room. Xiulan was beautiful, slim, straight black hair down to the middle of her back. John guessed she was in her early thirties, though he'd had trouble trying to guess the ages of men and women. Only the very old bore the wrinkles of age Caucasians picked up early. She was dressed simply, a dark green embroidered dress, possibly silk, under a long leather coat with a fur collar. Her clothes looked expensive and were different than the woolens and cottons he'd seen most people wearing in Beijing.

John nodded. The answer was as good as any for a selfless act of altruism. He crossed the room and sat in the chair opposite. Jason lurked in the background, waiting to see if she needed anything. He was well aware the advantage having such a rich patron brought to the welfare of the orphanage. She adopted girls but she also supported the institution with generous donations.

"I have money. I can save them from a difficult life." Xiulan replied.

"That's very charitable of you to help poor, orphaned children." John said. "I don't mean to be impolite, but how can you have so much money when the government is communist? Didn't the People's Republic confiscate wealth and possessions from the rich after the Revolution?"

"There are some from before the Revolution who still have wealth and power." She looked at him with devious eyes. "And some within the government now have wealth and power. Communism isn't necessarily equality."

"The Soviet Union has proven that," said John.

Xiulan shrugged and smiled. "Communism works well for those at the top. It doesn't serve the masses well. For example, the government owns all land in China. Someone can own a building but they don't own the land it sits on. My house was built over three hundred years ago. The government can take the land it sits on away at any time. They will pay but I still lose out."

"That's terrible."

"I don't think my house is in danger of being taken away, though. They leave people like me alone," she said. "Most of the time." She smiled like a secret thought amused her.

"Some people are more equal than others. That happens a lot in my country."

"Exactly. Mine too." Xiulan shrugged. "Even with this government, money talks. I have more rights than the workers simply because I have money. My family has been rich for two hundred years. The money is in accounts the government can't reach, so I get a better life and more freedom than most."

"Are you able to leave?"

She smiled slightly, nodding. "Wealth has privileges."

"But you stay," John said, it was a question as well as a statement.

"I have too many charges to care for, I can't abandon them."

"Charges?"

"The girls. I've sent many to boarding school. Some reside at my house. I can't leave them alone. They need my guidance." Xiulan said. "I have house staff but I don't like leaving for very long. It's unfair for them to look after so many children."

"How many do you care for at your home?"

"A few." Her brow furrowed. "Why are you asking so many questions?" she asked.

"In my country it's unusual for the wealthy to care for children in such a hands-on way. They donate to charities or churches, but they don't get their hands dirty with the day to day issues," replied John. Xiulan nodded her understanding.

"What are you doing in Beijing?" she asked.

John looked down at the floor, the shadow of an emotion colored his visage. "Someone I know died here last month."

"You came to get the deceased?"

"No. Her body was returned by your government through normal channels," John replied. "She was murdered. The autopsy in the States showed, I don't know, a wild animal attack. Though I don't know what animals are in Beijing. The PRC covered up the cause of death. They said she died in a car accident. I came to see if I could find out what happened."

Xiulan was quiet for a moment, no emotion crossed her expressionless face. "Did you?" she asked finally.

"No," John shook his head. "Not really. Jason said she was a victim of a serial killer in Beijing."

"Serial killer?" Xiulan looked confused. "I'm not familiar with the term."

"It's a term coined in America to describe a killer with multiple victims. They usually have a pattern, a certain way they kill their victims."

Her eyes widened and the edge of her mouth twitched. "What a strange thing."

"Yes," said John.

"Are you a police officer in America?"

"No." John blinked for an uncertain moment. The Bishop told him not to reveal he was a priest. "I work in public relations."

"Oh."

"I wanted to see where she died. Maybe the police could tell me something more."

"You must have been very close to come all this way for your friend."

"We were," said John softly. He'd met her only once but she was part of the Church. There was an ineffable bond that came with a life of service to the Lord. He understood her motivations and could empathize with her choice. Her death was an unnecessary tragedy.

Jason spoke to her in Chinese, she nodded her head and he left the room. A few minutes later he returned with a delicate porcelain cup, inside was steaming hot green tea. He set it down on the table next to her. She said, "Xièxiè." Thank you. One of the few words John had picked up and retained. Mandarin was a difficult language.

As they talked John was bothered. She was too... something. He couldn't immediately identify it. There was an elusive quality about her, it bothered him. She was… Too practiced. Too human… too ethereal… too something… As he continued talking with her recognition dawned in his brain. He'd seen this before, several times in fact. He suppressed his reaction as soon as it started to show on his face. He stumbled over his words. She noticed the change, the micro expression of realization before it was squelched, a nascent look of shock and fear, and something unspoken passed between them.

She flashed a small knowing, hungry smile, and the blood slowly drained from his face leaving his face a stark white skull stretched with thin skin. Involuntarily John took a look at the cup of tea sitting by her chair. Untouched, it had cooled enough steam was no longer rising from it.

He leaned back in the chair, an unconscious survival instinct to put space between him and the vampire near him. He glanced around the room. Jason and the children were nearby. He obviously knew her but wasn't aware of her dangerous nature. She'd adopted twenty children from the orphanage. Concern flooded him. What had she done with them? Were they food? Disposable victims society wouldn't miss? That was a horrible thought. Malcolm had a Church to lure victims to his larder. Did Madame Xiulan adopt then drain and kill children for sustenance? Surely she needed to feed more frequently than she adopted girls, though there had to be other orphanages in Beijing besides Jason's.

John looked at his watch. It was early. He accomplished what he intended. He met Xiulan. But now he had a dilemma. Should he leave her be, fly home to Colorado and not think about a foreign vampire in a country of a billion? She was six thousand miles away? She couldn't be the only vampire in a country that big. She was another example that vampires were in all big cities. The question was what should he do? He had nine days before his flight.

He wondered if he was finding vampires so easily because they were actually common and he now knew what to look for. Like when owning a different car for the first time you suddenly notice that make and model everywhere on the road. If they were so common, shouldn't he leave well enough alone?

"It's getting late, I think I'll be going," said John, he got up out of his chair and crossed to Xiulan and offered her his hand. "It was lovely to meet you Madame. I'm glad the orphans have such a beneficent advocate."

Xiulan shook his proffered hand. "You are very kind. It was nice to make your acquaintance. I hope to see you again before you leave China."

"Possibly. I leave soon," John replied. He was wary of her and hoped she hadn't noticed. "Jason, can I use your phone? I want to call a cab."

"Sure, you know where it is."

"Perhaps I could give you a ride wherever you are going," Xiulan said.

"No," said John too quickly and with more force than he intended. "I won't put you out. A cab is fine." He exited the room and went to the kitchen. He pulled a card for a cab company from a pocket. He'd used them a couple times in the past few days and one of the dispatchers spoke enough English to make John's request workable.

The dispatcher said a cab would pick him up at the orphanage in ten minutes. After John hung up the phone he was concerned. Should he go back and wait with Jason and the vampire? Had she left while he was making the call? His spike of fear at the realization she was a vampire may not have been noticed by Jason, but he was pretty certain Xiulan noticed. What would she do? Would she harm him?

John killed a few minutes in the kitchen, the women cleaning up after the evening meal noticed him standing looking at the door to the rest of the house, listening to the faint murmur of Jason and Xiulan talking in the other room. He glanced at his watch and stepped out of the kitchen, while zipping up his thick coat.

As he passed by the doorway to the sitting room he waved. "Good night," he called. "See you later." He exited the front door and waited on the porch in the cold, hands jammed into his fleece lined coat pockets. A cab rolled up in front of the gate and flashed its lights. John crossed the barren brown yard and opened the gate. As he closed it he looked back at the large house. He would be driven to find out more about Xiulan. Was she a threat to the children she adopted? He had to find out, but if she was, what then?

Madame Xiulan walked through the compound after returning from the orphanage. The thoughts of the strange American were still in her mind. She was almost certain he recognized her nature. The smell of fear exuded from him after he grew pale. She heard his heartbeat speed up and he started perspiring even in the cold of the room.

How did he know of vampires? It was unusual to see a human who knew of their existence. Was it something common in America or the west? Xiulan had no way to know. Her interaction with other vampires was rare, and it was by choice. She knew no western vampires. Being isolated in China both protected her and limited her information.

She stopped before the entrance to her house and looked around. The large compound was her domain, she was master of all she surveyed. The wife of the caretaker saw her pass and closed the door to their smaller side house out of respect and fear. The compound of buildings was a secure base. The caretaker knew her nature and dealt with all daylight matters. Every night Xiulan woke confident the world worked the way she wanted it to. She spent years manipulating her power and clout. People did what she wanted because she was rich and connected.

Xiulan entered the main house, her house. It was large and elegantly furnished with pieces of furniture she accumulated after being turned during the First Opium War in 1839. She was the mother of two children when she was turned one October night by an English vampire who was smitten with her beauty. After her 'death' her husband raised the two children with the help of family.

Xiulan adapted to life as a vampire quite easily. Her creator was surprised how ruthless she could be. What she was capable of doing scared him; things and horrors he never contemplated. Was it a cultural thing? His nature and morals were proper and English, she was something else. They traveled together for two decades; he tried to temper her boiling passions, but in the end he left her.

Xiulan returned to Shanghai and watched her children and grandchildren and then great grandchildren. She didn't reveal herself but she was a silent protector and shepherded them to a better life. As time passed she distanced herself from the family, too many years and too many descendants. She concentrated on herself until...

Xiulan was being stalked as she sat on the ornate couch, eyes closed, the whisper of soft footsteps ducking in and around the furniture. A small figure in black silk stared at her from over a table, a quiet giggle escaped the figure's mouth. Xiulan heard it and flashed a smirk.

With a growl she rushed forward, fingers and fangs extended, as she leapt toward Xiulan. The master vampire snatched the girl from mid-air and tossed her up toward the high ceiling. The tiny girl, propelled skyward, burst out laughing. As she reached the apex of the practiced arc she shifted and fell into Xiulan's waiting arms.

"Chani, you wicked thing!" Xiulan said with boundless affection as she tickled the squealing child. "How dare you attack me!"

The child in her arms giggled and snuggled into Xiulan's body. "Zēngzǔmǔ, did you bring me any food?"

"You ate earlier, you insatiable thing, you. Maybe your sisters will bring back someone."

"What about Liang? He's in the small house." Her voice was small and dangerously close to becoming a plaintive whine.

"What have I told you about Liang?" asked Xiulan.

"Don't eat relatives."

"Exactly," said Xiulan sternly.

"They aren't very close of a relative."

"No." The tone of Xiulan's voice shut Chani down. The vampire child knew not to push further. "Let's go see what your sisters are up to." She set the girl down and they walked out to the compound. "Look at the sky. When does the sun rise?"

The little girl looked up. "Hour and a half."

Xiulan nodded. She created Chani when the child was too young to really understand the ramifications but she was dying and it was the only way to save her great grandchild. Xiulan felt she needed to protect her more than the others. "Let's find your sisters."

"Yes." Chani chirped. "I heard some of them return."

Hand in hand they went to find the others.

"Jason, could you show me on a map where Madame Xiulan lives?" asked John. He pulled out a map of Beijing that tourists used and spread it out on the table. Boldly placed were sights which tourists wanted to see.

Jason looked at the priest, his eyes narrowed. "Why do you want to know where she lives?" he asked. "She came by, you met her. Wasn't that enough to satisfy your curiosity?"

"She has twenty of your orphans. Have you ever checked on their welfare?" retorted John.

His face clouded over and he flicked his gaze away. "It's hard enough feeding them and keeping a roof over their head, I can't repeatedly check on every child. I thoroughly interview to people adopting and check the homes."

"But twenty children," said John.

Jason slumped in his chair. He knew Xiulan adopting so many girls was unusual, but he was grateful to place the girls in any home. Hers seemed a good option. "I'll get you the address and show it to you on a map since you don't read Chinese."

"Thank you." John said sincerely. "I appreciate it."

Jason studied the map and made a circle with a pen. "This is the orphanage." He bent over and traced a path with his fingers. He circled another section of the map where two streets converged. He pointed to the corner where the streets met with the pen. "This is Madame Xiulan's compound. It is the largest and oldest house on the block. There's an interior courtyard and several houses." He paused. "It's because she had such a large house, with lots of room, that I didn't go back to check on the situation. And with her wealth she could handle the burden of so many girls."

"I understand." John bent over the map and looked at the distance from the orphanage to her house. He couldn't judge whether it was close or not. "Where's my hotel? Can you find it?" He needed a reference point. The cab rides he'd taken to the orphanage gave him some idea of distance.

Jason leaned back over and studied the map. "Here," he circled a spot on the map closer to the orphanage than Xiulan's house. "Here's your hotel."

"My hotel is walkable from here, maybe a bit far. Her house is not walkable from my hotel, though," commented John. He paused for a moment, thinking. "Could I borrow your car tomorrow afternoon? I'll have it back by eleven."

"Can you drive a Russian stick shift?"

"I've driven a manual often."

"You've been in my car. You've seen its condition. It's old. It's Russian. Are you sure you want to borrow it?" asked Jason.

"Yes." John replied confidently.

John picked up the car in the late afternoon. Jason stood watching as he started the engine and made a few lurching attempts at shifting gears before he got the hang of it.

"Sorry!" called John out of the driver's side window with each gear he ground. It had been a while since he'd driven a manual transmission and he had to recall the muscle memory and order of operations. It didn't help that the transmission was rough and the clutch was a bit sticky.

"I can drive you," called Jason, concerned his rattletrap of a car would be trashed by the American.

"No, no, I've got the hang of it now." John rolled up the window and drove out the open gate onto the streets of Beijing. He didn't tell Jason his plan. He intended to go to Xiulan's house at night and park down the street. He wanted to watch to see what comings and goings were happening. She might not be adopting girls and killing them for food. She might be a kind woman. His mind went to the worst case scenario automatically. Although in his dealings with vampires, some were not as bad as the humans. John drove back to his hotel and found a place to park. He locked the car and waited for night to fall over the city. As he ate dinner he studied the map since trying to read the street names wouldn't be possible. He traced the route to her compound with his finger multiple times, trying to memorize the landmarks highlighted on the map.

When he looked out the window it was dark. Time had slipped away from him. He folded the map and fished the keys out of his pocket. The boxy blue car sat on the street looking forlorn. It had seen better days a decade or so in the past. The elements and rough traffic created scars in the paint and dents. He wondered if Jason was a bad driver. Was there insurance to fix the damage or was it not worth the time?

John unlocked the car and got in. The threadbare seats squeaked under his weight. He unfolded the map and put it on the passenger seat. He knew the first part of the trip well enough, after he got further in he'd consult the map as needed.

Traffic was unlike anything he'd driven in. It was not the reckless speedway of Rome he'd witnessed, but traffic laws were more of a suggestion than a rule to be followed. The main streets were wide but there was virtually no car traffic. There were buses and mopeds, scooters and bicycles, but few personal cars. It made the fact Jason had a car for the orphanage, even one as beat up as this, more impressive. The few cars on the road were taxis. There were even rickshaws. Instead of someone running, the rickshaws were attached to the back of a bike and pedaled furiously alongside the right edge of the road.

John drove until he needed to look at the map. He probably had the right path in his head but uncertainty gnawed at him. In the unfamiliar surroundings it would be easy to become lost. Stopped at a light he turned on the interior dome light, a weak yellow glow washed over the map and he glanced down to confirm he was going the right way.

The width of the streets narrowed as he got deeper into a more residential part of Beijing. When he got to her street he drove slowly to look. There was nothing to see of the house or compound save the red front door set into a high wall. Like many homes in Beijing, the exterior walls hid a compound. He circled around the block and looked at the other street. He could see sloped tile roofs where a building abutted the wall.

As he drove the street he looked for a place he could park, a vantage point where he could see if there were any comings and goings from her house. It would be like a stakeout in a movie, where cops are sitting in a car obviously looking at a house. The tactic always seemed illogical to John when watching a movie. Wouldn't the neighbors notice? No one sits in a car all day. At least darkness of night would hide him. Someone would have to walk by the car on the dark street to see him lurking there.

After parking down the street from her front door, John looked at his watch; ten p.m. He didn't realize it was so late and suddenly doubted he'd see anything. If she went anywhere she'd have left already, and it was very dark in the neighborhood. The moon was almost non-existent and the lighting on the streets was poor, an overhead light cast a yellow pall over the grey street every hundred feet or so. He brought water with him and some food, and Jason loaned him a pair of small binoculars. He didn't know if he would stay all night, but he didn't want to be hungry and thirsty. If he started to nod off he'd call it a night and head back to the hotel.

With the engine off the temperature in the car dropped quickly. He had to open up a side window so the moisture from his breath didn't fog up the windows, but that increased the cold in the car. He pulled out the binoculars and looked about. The chill of the night seeped into his bones and he raised his collar and zipped up the ski jacket to retain body heat.

An hour passed. When he noticed someone walking or riding a bike in the area he hastily put the field glasses on the seat next to him. Foot traffic was light and he didn't see any police or military walking around. Had they shown up he would start the car and casually leave. Was it illegal to sit in a car watching a doorway? In China, who knew?

He was watching when some furtive movement caught his attention. He wasn't paying attention but there was a shadow moving on the roof. He lifted the binoculars and saw another shadow flit from darkness to darkness like rats scuttling. They weren't rats, too big. He followed the shapes and two of them dropped to the street after remaining still for several minutes.

Another shadow sprang from the edge of the roof, crossing the street and landing on the roof of the house across the street. The distance was far, even a long jumper wouldn't be able to clear it with a running start.

"What the hell?" John whispered to himself.

The two shadows on the street were joined by two more. He trained the glasses on the figures. They were little girls dressed in simple clothes, shoeless, unconcerned by the winter cold. He looked for the one who jumped from roof to roof. It was down the block with two more. Did he miss their gravity defying leap across the street?

A disturbing thought crossed his mind. What if Xiulan wasn't feeding off of the girls? What if she turned them into vampires? The possibility of such a depraved action appalled him. To be forever a child, the only succor from that fate was death. The killings in Beijing made more sense. There wasn't a serial killer, it was serial killers. Vampire girls were unleashed upon the city and didn't care to hide or didn't know to hide. If that was the case, the girls were dangerous and brazen. It seemed foolish to him for Xiulan to let the girls kill indiscriminately, but maybe after creating them she couldn't control them.

Fear gripped John in its icy hand. If they noticed him sitting in the car he could be their next victim. He slumped down in the seat so he could still watch them but his visibility from the street was lessened. There was a determined quality to their movements, they were on a mission.

He quietly fumbled the keys out of his jacket pocket, inserted them into the ignition on the dash, and waited. If he started the car they would hear the engine. He wanted them to leave the neighborhood before he proceeded back to the orphanage. If they girls knew he was sitting alone in the car would they approach him or leave him alone? If the girls came to the car he'd start it and drive away. Quickly. Caution was needed. He waited, watching, seeing where they were headed.

Seconds ticked by. In the quiet of the street his watch sounded loud, as did his heartbeat. His heart was pounding in his chest like a frightened bird flailing against its cage. Blood was rushing loudly in his ears. He watched the four girls walk away from his car. Good. They were leaving. He could escape.

There was the sound of something dropping lightly on to the roof, the car bounced on worn shocks at the impact. John glanced up. A snarling fanged visage was looking upside down at him through the glass. Black hair cascaded down the slope of the windshield. It was one of the girls from the rooftops. A small clawed hand appeared against the driver's side window, hard fingernails slowly traced down the glass creating a screeching sound. John spun his head, angry dark eyes glared at him, the nails burrowed a line in the tempered pane.

The car bounced again. The girl from the roof was standing on the hood, hands on her hips, scowling, bearing her teeth. John reached for the ignition on the steering column, muscle memory from his own car. There were no keys. He tore his eyes away from the girl for a moment and found the keys dangling from the ignition in the dash. He grabbed it and turned the key.

Nothing happened.

"Fuck!" he exclaimed forgetting the car was manual. He stomped down on the clutch and turned the key again. The engine, cold for hours, coughed and sputtered in protest. He pressed the gas hard pumping the gas pedal. "Come on, come on!" he muttered through gritted teeth. "Start you son of a bitch."

The girl at the driver's door tried the handle, it was unlocked and she pulled the door open with surprising strength. Reflexively, John lashed out with his left hand, back-fisting her in the face. She let out a surprised noise and tumbled away. He grabbed the door and slammed it shut. The engine sparked to life and he shifted clumsily with his right hand, left hand pressing the door lock and grabbing the wheel.

As the car lurched forward into the street the girl on the hood dropped to a crouch, her hands holding on the edge of the hood near the wipers for stability. John shifted from first to second. How to get the girl off the hood? She had a firm grip.

There was a sound from behind him, a call. As he drove forward he saw the four other vampire girls turn to see him speeding toward them on the empty street. He turned on the headlights and clicked on the brights hoping to blind them. Fearless, they crouched in the road like they were ready to spring forward, not the reaction he expected from anyone being bore down on by a speeding car.

He was at the top of the second gear as the nose of the car rushed toward the girls, the motor whined in protest. John stepped on the clutch and stood on the brake pedal. The car screeched to a halt feet before hitting the girls. They didn't flinch, their snarling faces treated the action like it was ordinary and not in the least bit dangerous to them.

The girl on the hood lurched forward, the sudden deceleration making her lose her footing but her fingers held on tenaciously to the hood. She let go of the edge of the hood and hopped up to stand. John slammed the transmission into reverse and hit the gas. The vampire standing on the hood pitched off, landing on the street. John looked in the rearview mirror, guiding the car backwards as best he could in the dark. There was a bone crunching sound as the tires on the left side bumped over something.

As he traveled backwards a small body tumbled into the illumination of the headlights, broken and crushed. It was the vampire girl from the driver's side window. His brain quickly processed the information and wondered if that would kill her or would she be crippled eternally? She must have been advancing as he was reversing, but he was going too fast and she was too small to see in the rapid glimpses of the mirror.

The five girls were running toward the car as he sped backwards. He concentrated on what was behind him and tried to keep an eye on the girls in front. The car bounced as it crossed an intersecting street. He was lucky there was no cross traffic. John stepped on the clutch and hit the brakes hard. He ground to a stop he shifted into first, the car jumped forward and he took a reckless left turn.

The pursuing girls turned onto the street and raced after his car. He was flying down a residential road in third gear, failing to stop at cross streets. One eye was on the mirror, the other looking for impending crashes ahead. In less than a minute he lost sight of the girls chasing him. Apparently they couldn't keep up.

John slowed his frantic pace but kept moving forward with little hesitation at cross streets. It was dangerous to drive like that, but the vampires he left behind him were lethal. When he was miles away he pulled over in a busy brightly lit area, and shut of the engine. He was shaking from fear and adrenaline, his breathing was shallow.

He looked around. None of the buildings were familiar, not that he would know much of Beijing. He needed to find his way back to his hotel. He'd call Jason when he was safely ensconced in his room and tell him he'd return with the car in the morning.

Chapter 14
Shopping

"Jason, is there a hardware store somewhere in the area? I need to get a few things." asked John. He stood in the kitchen of the orphanage after returning the car, weak morning light filtered through the thin curtains. It was cloudy and cold outside, the promise of a winter rain was in the air.

"There's one nearby," replied Jason. "What do you need? I can get what you want since they may not speak English."

John was silent for a few moments. The language difference was something he didn't take into account, again. "Could you come with me in case I have trouble communicating?" He was aware he hadn't answered the question. His purchases might be difficult to explain. *I need a small sledgehammer, a closet clothes rod to carve into wooden stakes, and a machete to kill your patron. Sorry.*

"We can go now if you like. It's not far," said Jason. He reached into his pocket and pulled out the keys John gave him a few minutes earlier.

John's eyes widened momentarily. The car. There had been some damage to the car from the vampire girls. He didn't know how to tell him, and having to explain it would be difficult and was now imminent. "If you a have the time right now, I'm ready," replied John. He followed Jason out the back door to where he parked the car. The forlorn little car sat in front of the garage. When Jason saw it he stopped walking and looked at John. There were new dents added to the existing marks on the car.

"What happened?" he asked. The roof was dented downward, not terrible but noticeable, the hood was dented. The left rear corner showed evidence of an impact of some kind.

John sighed and looked sheepish. He had to lie, he knew he'd have to minutes after the altercation with the vampire girls. He couldn't tell Jason the truth, it would sound insane like every other time he told a person vampires were real. He prepared and practiced for the lie. The best one he could come up with was… "When I parked near the hotel late last night the car was undamaged. I came out and found this. I don't know what happened." It disturbed John that he'd become so proficient at lying. The truth was far more unbelievable.

Jason made a sour face and inspected the car closely. He ran his hands over the dent in the hood. He looked closcly at the disturbed dirt. "Footprints?" he asked.

"That's what it looked like to me too," replied John. "The roof too."

Brain looked closely at the roof. There were two footprints in the depression of the steel. "Very strange," Jason muttered as he ran his fingers over the dents, seeking out contours of the impression. The bends in the metal even showed individual toes. He walked back and looked at the dent on the back of the left rear fender. That kind of damage was common, a crash of a scooter into a car parked on the side of the road would explain that, though there was no paint transfer. Accidents transferred paint.

Jason sighed and figured there was nothing he would do about it. He needed the car and the damage, though annoying, didn't keep the car from working. Most cars in Beijing had some kind of dents. Now his car had three more.

"I'll pay for the cost to get it repaired," said John. He felt bad about the damage. "I'm really sorry. Let me know how much it will cost and I'll cover it."

Jason shrugged. "It's not that important. The car is old and as long as it still works, I can live with it. I just wonder who was jumping up and down on the car." Jason said, he smiled meekly, opened the driver's side door, and got in. He reached over to the passenger door and unlocked the door so John could get in. When he sat down on the protesting springs of the passenger seat he saw Jason tracing the interior contour of the dent on the roof with his fingers, a puzzled look on his face. "Very odd."

He put the keys in the ignition and started the engine. It sputtered to life; he reversed onto the path leading onto the open gate, and drove onto the bustling street. There was morning traffic, mostly bicycles, scooters, and buses. Jason deftly managed the traffic and within ten minutes he pulled over on a bigger street in front of a store. Through the window John could see it was a hardware store without being able to read the sign.

They got out of the car, Jason locked it, his eyes lingering on the dents and his fingers traced over the damage again. John looked at him. "I'll fix it. Tell me how much," he said earnestly. He wondered if car insurance was something China had. The country wasn't car crazy and many people didn't own cars.

Jason didn't answer, he gestured for John to follow and walked to the store entrance without waiting for him. The plate glass door swung in, an electronic chime sounded somewhere at the back of the shop. An older Chinese man behind a long counter looked up from his newspaper. The store was a chaotic mess of shelves and boxes of different sizes. It smelled dusty, a faint industrial odor lingered, a combination of oil, solvents, and fertilizer. It was a hardware store plus much, much more. There was merchandise of all kinds, knick knacks, toys, small pieces to unknown machines in boxes on shelves lining the place.

"Zǎoshang Hǎo," said the man.

"Zǎoshang Hǎo," replied Jason. John recognized the phrase, "Good morning." Jason spoke with the man for a moment and gestured to John. "He doesn't speak English, so I will translate."

"Great."

"What are you looking for?" asked Jason.

John took a breath. He wondered what reaction Jason would have. The items were not anything a tourist or a priest would need. The list defied an easy explanation. "I need a small sledge hammer, three pounds if he has it, or a claw hammer if he doesn't have a sledge. A small hand saw. A machete. A small to medium size knife, like something you whittle with. A couple of dowels about an inch and a half thick. The type you hang clothes on in a closet. Is that a Western thing? Hanging clothes in closets? If they have dowels I can use about ten feet." John stopped for a second to think. When he did so Jason spoke to the man and ticked off the things he asked for. He translated but tried to deduce why John would need such things. He was visiting for two weeks. Why would he need such tools? What was his project?

"I think that's all I need." John said.

The man nodded and disappeared into the eclectic stacks of shelves. Jason turned to John. "What are you doing? Why do you need a machete?" His voice had a hard edge to it. It was incongruous for a priest to need a machete in Beijing. It would be easily obtained but the question of why nagged at him.

"I'm not going to explain," said John. "I'll ask you to trust me."

"That is getting difficult to do."

John nodded. "I understand. I do have a reason for needing these things. I'll explain it when I can." John said. *If I can.* He intended to kill Xiulan and the vampire girls. It was a daunting task and he had no help. In all good conscious he wasn't going to ask Jason for help with the task. The man selflessly cared for children, John didn't want to get him killed if his reckless quest went wrong.

"Is this something for the Church?" asked Jason, he leaned in, his voice barely above a whisper. John quickly considered how to answer. He gave a small, curt nod, Jason inhaled and backed away. It was convenient. The Church had some arcane, unknown reason for a priest to need the odd tools, and that would stop the questions. John breathed easier. He wouldn't have to lie further.

The old man returned, his hands filled with the tools John listed. He placed them on the counter and spoke to Jason before disappearing again. "He'll be back in a minute with the poles." John looked over the tools. The sledgehammer was what he'd used before. The handsaw was a little over a foot long with serrated teeth. The machete was in a worn leather sheath that had a loop for a belt, eighteen inches long and it looked old. John pulled it out, the blade was short for a machete, about twelve inches long, mottled, discolored steel but the edge was keenly sharp. It would work for what he had in mind.

The man returned with three closet dowels five feet long, and a folding knife, the blade for whittling. The old man set the knife on the counter and spoke to Jason. John looked at the knife as they talked. "Three poles are fine. I'll take the extra one." He wasn't sure but he figured he might need more stakes.

John listened to the two men talk. He guessed they were haggling over the price. After a minute or two they stopped and shook hands. A deal had been struck. Jason told John the price. He pulled out his wallet and started counting out the bills.

"I just realized I need a bag to carry the tools in, a backpack, satchel or something to carry this stuff. Would he have something like that? A backpack would work best, I think," said John. Jason engaged the man again. He nodded and disappeared again into the stacks.

He returned with a green, medium sized backpack and set it on the counter. John picked up the machete and made sure it fit inside the pack.

"That's great." John put the rest of his purchases in the pack. "How much for the pack?"

The man replied understanding the nature of the question even if he didn't know the language, Jason translated and John added to the bills he paid the man.

John gathered up the three poles and slung the pack over a shoulder. Jason bowed slightly to the man. "Xièxiè."

John knew the words. *Thank you.* "Xièxiè," he mimicked as best he could. Jason opened the door and they went out to the car. It took a moment to figure out the angle for the poles. In the end they stuck out the open side window of the car.

"Can you take me back to my hotel?" asked John.

"Certainly," replied Jason. After a moment he spoke again. "Will you be able to tell me why you are here? Maybe later, when you have done what the Church wants?"

John nodded. "I'll tell you what I can, when I can," he said. He didn't know if he would, just as he didn't know if he would succeed.

He was about to do something foolish.

Again.

Chapter 15
Through the Front Door

The taxi dropped off John at a corner. In the crisp cold daylight the street was grey, the buildings were grey, there was a strangeness seeing it in the light. The encounter with the demon girls was frightening. John returned to the street where he was attacked the night before. Another dangerous quest in mind. He was inevitably drawn to confront the evil he found though it put him in mortal danger again and again. He stood for a moment looking at the red door to the house. It was daylight so the vampires would be asleep. Somewhere. He'd seen the six girls come over the rooftop so he guessed they slept somewhere at the house. He knew it wouldn't be easy to find.

Over his shoulder was a backpack. The contents he prepared in secret. He had fifteen stakes, the number seemed excessive to him and took long hours to prepare; a small sledgehammer, and a slightly rusty steel machete in a worn leather sheath. They were similar to the tools he'd used before in Las Vegas. Jason stopped asking any more questions when John intimated it was church business. He was instructed to help John however he could, and try to keep him out of prison. It the PRC found out he was a priest he could be jailed even if he wasn't preaching the gospel.

John stood in front of the large door to the house. It was wood, painted red, but weathered so the color was dull. It had two metal bands, one towards the top, the other towards the bottom. A large keyhole was under the knob on the right side. John had a story ready to tell whoever answered the door, he just hoped whoever answered spoke English. If they didn't he would have to find another way in. Being fluent in only one language was a handicap in a multi-lingual world.

There was a button to the right side of the door. It looked new compared to the age of the walls and the door. He pressed the button and waited. No answer. He pressed the button again and waited. Another minute passed. As he was reaching for the button again he heard a lock being turned and a bolt sliding back. The door swung inward and a man stood looking quizzically at John. Whatever he expected to be at the door, a tall westerner wasn't an option he entertained.

"Do you speak English?" asked John.

The man nodded. "I speak small English." His accent was heavy and he spoke slowly as he searched for the words.

"Is Madame Xiulan here?"

The man shook his head vigorously. "She is out," he said. "Try later."

John wondered for a moment. Try later because she's a vampire, or try later because the vampire sleeps somewhere else and would need time to arrive at this house? The man started to shut the door. John put his hand on the door holding it open. "I'm with the orphanage. She recently adopted a young girl and I wanted to check on her to see how she's doing, see if she's adjusting to her new home."

The man stared at him, his eyes narrowed. He looked to his right, to something beyond the door.

"It's important. We need to be sure the child is safe. Not being exploited or harmed," John tried using the authority he learned from being a priest.

"No one has ever checked before," said the man.

"What's your name?" John sensed the man was considering slamming the heavy door in his face. He needed to keep the man engaged. He might have only one chance to enter her house.

Silence for a moment, then. "Liàng."

"Good afternoon, Liàng," said John. "My name is John Bryant. There was a recent incident where an adopted girl was trafficked for sex. We're trying to be sure that hasn't happened with any of the other adoptions so we are making surprise visits to the houses." He suddenly wondered if he should have used a fake name. Too late now.

Liàng considered what John said in a way that made him think the man spoke better English then he was letting on. Again he paused and glanced to his right. Liàng pursed his lips and nodded slightly. He pulled the door open all the way and gestured for John to enter.

Directly in front of the door, about eight feet away, was another high exterior wall topped with a small sloped tile roof. John was surprised. He expected an interior. John stepped over a high threshold and onto a path of paving stones. Liàng closed the door and locked it. A small thin woman about thirty five was standing five feet away looking at John with suspicion. In her hand was a cane made of dark wood. This must be who Liàng was looking to when he turned away at the door. John guessed she was talking to him quietly.

"My wife, Jai," said Liàng. The woman made a small bow but said nothing. John made a slight bow in return. "Follow me, please." He turned and passed John, walking to the right, he whispered to his wife, who nodded. She waited for John to pass then followed, she leaned on the cane for support as she walked.

The thin outer courtyard was painted brightly, the plants were well manicured and thriving. A door was at the opposite end of the wall. This was an outdoor antechamber to the main compound. Someone unwelcome wouldn't be allowed past this area.

Liàng opened the next door and waited for John. Beyond this door was a large courtyard. There were buildings in front of him and on both sides. The house in front was large with a covered porch. The house to the right side was smaller, not as ornate. To his left were some smaller buildings, not houses but something more utilitarian, sheds for supplies. To the side of one of the sheds was a set of angled doors like to a fruit cellar or storm cellar you might find in the Midwest of America. He didn't think tornadoes were a problem in Beijing but he didn't know for certain.

"The child is in school now," Liàng said firmly.

John looked around the courtyard with its well taken care of buildings and foliage. But something struck him as odd. Jason told him Madame Xiulan had adopted around twenty girls though she didn't confirm the number. She might have more than twenty. The buildings didn't look large enough to house twenty growing children, and the grounds themselves were devoid of any indication children lived there at all. Toys of some kind should be visible, even if it was something small left behind, a doll, a ball, or blocks. Maybe a child's drawing on one of the walls but there was nothing obvious. It looked like children didn't live there. It was almost museum-like in its pristine quality.

"She's in school? What time does she get back?" asked John.

"It boarding school. Far away," Jai said defensively. Her voice was brittle with tension.

"What's her name?" snapped John with more anger than he intended. "The girl, what's her name?"

She looked at him silently, her jaw flexed like she was grinding her teeth.

"Is Madame Xiulan available?" John asked.

"Out of town," Jai snapped. Liàng nodded in mute agreement.

"Liàng said she was out and I should try later," John could tell they were getting anxious. The man and woman looked at each other, silently communicating like long married couples do. John had seen it before, an innate understanding, of a hierarchy and order to a pairing. One leads, the other follows.

"My wife is mistaken. I had call from Madam this morning. She will be back by dinner time,"
said Liàng.

Jai shot her husband an angry look. She didn't like being contradicted.

"I'm told that Madame Xiulan has adopted over twenty girls. This house doesn't look big enough to house twenty children," John said. "In fact she's been adopting girls for several years."

Liàng looked at his wife and started to form a sentence. "All in boarding school," barked Jai nervous energy, cutting her husband off.

"Yes. They are in boarding school," he repeated. "Madame Xiulan very generous."

"What boarding school?" John asked.

They looked at one another, something unspoken passed between them. "Come to office. Will get you name," Jai pointed to one of the buildings on the left of the courtyard. Liàng nodded in agreement. He started walking and motioned for John to follow. The small man led John to a building on the left of the compound with tan walls and a porch. There was a closed door with windows on either side. Liàng pulled out a ring of small keys and took a minute as he picked out the correct key for the lock.

Light blazed in John's eyes, a universe exploded. He spun drunkenly but didn't go down. Behind him stood Jai with her cane held like a sword. She swung it again, he turned his body and let the cane land on his side. She was small and petite so the blow hurt, probably caused a bruise, but didn't break any ribs.

While John was focused on the woman, Liàng leapt off the porch and tackled John to the ground. Liàng sat on John's hips. He pulled John's hands behind him trapping the backpack on his back and said something in Mandarin. John saw Jai's feet leave his field of vision as the side of his head was pressed into the rough stone paver. His head swam, her blow wasn't enough to knock him out but he was rattled. He was thankful for her bad aim otherwise he'd be unconscious.

She returned and John's hands were yanked up. He felt rough cord looping around his wrists and being cinched tight. There was the sound of a key in a lock and the creak of a hinge as doors were opened. There was a pair of booming sounds as the wood doors landed heavily against a wall. The man got off John, hands pulled under his arms and he was hauled up, not to his feet, they weren't that strong. So he was half dragged and half drunk walked to the low set of doors.

John was pulled up over the threshold and pushed forward into the darkness below.

Chapter 16
In the Cellar

John pitched forward, his ankles hit the lip of the tiled doorframe and he stared in horror as the angled stairs rushed toward his head. If his hands were free he would be able to catch himself before crashing head first and breaking his neck. Desperately he spun his body and tucked his chin towards his chest, taking the first blow of the stairs on his arms, backpack, and ass. As he tumbled he heard the two doors slam shut and a lock closed sealing him inside. He bounced and his free legs started rotating, folding over his torso. He swung his legs and switched the momentum so he rolled down the stairs on his side, a ball rolling rather than sliding head first to the bottom of the stairs.

He landed after a short unknown distance on his right side at the bottom of the stairs. He lay for a moment listening and breathing hard. He did an inventory to see if he was hurt. He moved his arms and legs checking the mobility, testing for broken bones. Other than a headache, a bruise on his side, some scrapes, and his hands beginning to tingle from the bonds cutting off his circulation, he seemed to be unharmed.

He assessed the surroundings and his predicament as calmly as he could. He was underground in a corridor. The stairs he tumbled down were twenty five to thirty feet tall, though it seemed a much quicker descent. The space was lit with bare yellow bulbs strung near the ceiling on thin electrical cords. The walls were dug out of the earth and buttressed with thick timbers like an old gold mine. The floor he lay on was dry cold red tile, the chill began to seep into him as he lay inert.

He rolled onto his side and worked the ropes tying his wrists together. He needed something sharp to cut the ropes, like the machete in his pack. He knew the top was zippered shut so he wouldn't be able to contort or shake the weapon out of the canvas pack.

John rolled to a seated position and got his feet under him. Carefully he stood up. His head ached and the corridor swam a bit. He wasn't sure but he didn't think he had a concussion. He didn't feel nauseous, his vision wasn't blurred. He would have to get his hands free before he felt his head for a bump. He could be bleeding but didn't see red staining his jacket as he turned his head side to side.

The stairs up were softly worn wood. No sharp edges to work the ropes against. He would look for something else sharp before coming back to them if need be. The timbers holding up the ceiling were promising, after a minute of rubbing the ropes against the edge of the beam he only dug the ropes deeper into his wrists and picked up a few slivers in his forearms from the rough unfinished wood.

John needed something sharper which wouldn't injure him while he cut the cords. Carefully he walked down the corridor. It was about eight feet tall and ten feet wide with supports for the ceiling every ten feet or so. The walls looked like they were dug out of the ground with shovels, tedious work if that was the generation of the tunnel. It wasn't chipped out of rock.

To his right was a closed wooden door. He spun with his back to the door and gently tried the doorknob. It was locked. He didn't make any sound in case there was someone other than him in the underground chamber.

Straight down the corridor was another similar door and then the tunnel curved off to the right. He approached quietly, spun, and tried that door knob. Also locked, and the edges of the door frame and door met smoothly with the wall so there was nothing sharp to cut his ropes. The tunnel to the right showed four more doors and ended about thirty feet down. The light bulbs lit the space with a wan, feeble light.

Down the hall he tried each successive door and each was locked. His mood was sinking and fear dominated his mind. What was the intention of the couple? It didn't make sense to kidnap him. Killing him outright would have made more sense. Now they had a person wandering around their strange cellar. He was determined to escape their trap.

At the last door the knob turned. He pushed when the latch released and spun to look in the room. It was small and cluttered. A yellow bulb was in the center of the ceiling. There were rags of all kinds on the floor. There was clothing, some of it torn and stained with what he deduced was dried blood. Shoes for both genders were strewn about carelessly. Where did the clothing come from and why was it soaked in blood?

More proof Xiulan was a vampire, but were these her kills or could it be the children? Where were the bodies of the victims? Did she kill people and dispose of the naked bodies? That would be an odd choice. It would be best to destroy all evidence of a killing.

"Might as well look," John said as he walked into the room. He gently kicked and felt at the clothes with his feet, moving carefully to see what treasure he might find. The treasure wouldn't be gold, it would be something sharp. He didn't care how big, steel or glass, a knife, a nail, a bottle, he didn't care. In a pair of pants his foot hit something solid. He traced the shape with the toe of his shoe. The shape was small and thin. John knelt down and twisted so his hands could reach the pants.

Carefully he maneuvered the pants so he felt the pocket. It was a shape which sparked hope. He turned over the pants and shook the pocket out on the floor behind him. He heard a dull metallic sound. He turned on his knees and looked. An old pocket knife. He turned again and reached down with his hands. It took a minute to open the knife. It wasn't too sharp but after a few minutes he was able to cut the rope freeing his hands.

John flexed his fingers and rubbed the abraded flesh of his wrists. Blood rushed back into his hands making them feel like he slept on his arms wrong. He closed the knife and put it in his pants pocket. John removed the pack, unzipped it and pulled out the machete. He wanted a weapon and he could use it as a pry bar.

He went to the row of doors and tried the closest one again. They were locked. He pushed the tip of the long blade into the crack next to the latch and used it to slip the locking mechanism open. There was a pop and the door swung inside. Inside the room were shelves floor to ceiling on the three walls. A number of the shelves were empty. The ones which weren't empty had children's toys and trinkets, old dirty dolls and some balls in uncovered boxes. A quick search provided him with nothing he could use.

He pried open the next door; shelves were filled with simple clothes in dark muted colors, small, shirts and pants, but nothing that would fit an adult. The third room was empty shelves. When he got to the next door he paused and looked around. He searched the corridor and rooms unmolested. Why was there no one around?

A terrible thought gripped him. Xiulan was a vampire; she would need a place to hide from the sun. Somewhere safe. A sealed hole in the ground would fit the requirements perfectly. John looked at his watch. It was after four thirty. The sun would be down in less than a half hour, maybe sooner.

"Shit." John ignored the last unopened door in the row, he needed to get out of the cellar before the sun went down. The other rooms provided nothing helpful, it was time to leave. He quickly moved to the steep stairs and looked up. Retrieving the small sledgehammer from the pack, he climbed up the wood stairs. At the top he lay the sledge to one side of him and the machete to the other.

There was no handle or lock on his side. He pushed upward, the door didn't move. He took a few stairs more and pressed his back to the wood and lifted with his legs. Nothing. No movement. He stepped back down and grabbed the machete. He worked the blade into the seam where the two doors met and ran the blade from the top down. At some blockage midway down the door the blade stopped, a latch or lock was in the way. Was it like the other doors in the cellar?

He pulled the blade out and in the darkness tried to release the catch the way he did with the doors below. No luck.

John looked at his watch again, turning his wrist to find the yellowy light from the bulbs below. It was very near sunset. It was winter and the sun went down early. He set the machete down and grabbed the sledgehammer, gripped it in both hands and swung upward with all his strength. The sound was loud, the thick wood flexed but didn't break open. He beat at the door multiple times but it was too sturdy to break.

His ears rang from the sound and he figured the couple outside heard his struggles with the door even if they didn't see the blade from the machete slide down the crack like a shark's fin cutting across the surface of the ocean.

John walked down the stairs. There was a door midway on the right side of the corridor he hadn't tried. That might be another escape route. Or another room with clothes.

Or Xiulan asleep. A dangerous thrill passed through him at the prospect of finding her asleep. He could end another vampire. Glancing at his watch he picked up the pack and slung it over one shoulder. He moved to the door with the hammer in his left hand and the machete in his right. He set the hammer at his feet and tried the door. Locked, of course. He worked the latch like he had the others. It opened with a snick and he picked up the hammer before pushing the door open.

There was a small passage that led to his right. He stepped quietly in and followed the carved corridor. There was pale yellow light ahead. The passageway opened up, the ceiling soared above him and the walls pushed away, far to the sides.

And he saw them.

In the large cavern, on dozens and dozens of small beds, were girls. All were about the same age, all were Chinese, and all were motionless, asleep. For this many children the room was eerily quiet, like it was filled with life size dolls.

These were the orphans Xiulan adopted. How could she have so many? Were they all vampires? No wonder the killings in Beijing increased. She had mouths to feed. He quickly scanned the room. Across the cavern was a banded wood door, sturdy but different than the others in the carved out basement. John looked at the girls again, there were more than twenty girls. He had fifteen stakes. His mind rebelled at the thought. They couldn't all be vampires. They might be human, but asleep. What were they doing in the cavern asleep? Blood drained out of John's face and fear grabbed his heart as his mind crashed into a frightening theory. A terrible thought, *who would do such a thing?*

He stepped carefully to the nearest bed and bent over the girl, her face placid and unlined. He didn't see her breathing. He glanced at the other beds. None of them were breathing. Every girl in the cavern was a vampire. And he was trapped with them. Blood drained out of John's face and fear grabbed his heart. That was why the couple tossed him down there. It would be an efficient way to eliminate him. *Who would do such a thing?* He thought. *What monster would turn young girls into vampires? For what purpose?*

The girl in front of John woke, her eyes flashed open. Instead of seeing the roof of the cavern with its light bulbs, there was a man standing over her. John recoiled in surprise. He thought of hiding in one of the deserted rooms but he missed his opportunity. Around the room, all the girls were awake. It was like a light switch was flicked on and their eyes opened simultaneously. In a few seconds they were all aware of John, all their faces turned, and they stared at him impassively.

"Shit," he whispered.

The door across the cavern opened, Xiulan stepped out looking beautiful and regal and coldly deadly. Her gaze zeroed in on John in a flash. Her eyes narrowed, if she was surprised her face gave nothing away. She recognized him from the orphanage. She didn't know how he found her but he would dealt with swiftly. A child moved ncxt to Xiulan, her hand slipped into her master's hand.

As if from a silent command, a small girl ran to block his exit out the door he used to enter the cavern. It was ridiculous to be afraid of a child, but John was. She was more than a child. She stared at him with a hungry look and slight smirk to her lips like an order of take-out had arrived on the doorstep.

The girls moved slowly, bunching up. John brandished the weapons in his hand and backed up until he could go no further. The wall was behind him. The way he entered was blocked by five girls and a semi-circle had formed around him ten feet away. Like a pack of dogs ready to attack, all their weight and eager potential was on the balls of their feet waiting to be released.

Chapter 17
A Very Bad Day

I'm going to die, he thought.

John was surrounded, his back up against the crudely carved wall. He needed some protection to his blind side since there were too many for him to fight and no obvious way for him to escape. Weak bulbs high in the ceiling lit the moving mass of shadowy vampire children before him.

I'm going to die, the thought slammed through his mind again. *No one will know what happened to me. I'll disappear in China.*

The realization was profound but he was calm and surprisingly resigned to the fact. How he survived his interactions with vampires over the last two years still surprised him. He could have been dead a dozen times. But they were beneficent and they let him live. He didn't prevail over them in any one of his fights. It was a stark realization. One that came too late.

He killed a few vampires in Las Vegas when they were asleep, and he unexpectedly helped others in Rome, but only their tolerance let him get out alive. He was relatively insignificant to their place in eternity and he knew it.

This Chinese Fagin was different. The Fagin in Oliver Twist didn't send his kids to kill. She was going to kill him. There was no way he could prevail over so many of the child vampires with just a machete and a small sledgehammer. He'd need a machine gun and multiple clips. What faced him now was going to be terrible. It wasn't going to be a Bruce Lee cinematic fight where the opponents would wait a turn to have their asses handed to them by the Kung Fu master. This was a swarm of locusts, vampire girls, waiting to be unleashed. It would be unrelenting and chaotic. He might kill a few, maybe ten if he was lucky, but the odds weren't merely stacked against him, he was simply doomed. You can't fight the ocean, you merely exhaust yourself punching the waves.

Even Bruce Lee would fail with these kinds of odds.

John looked to Xiulan. She stood; a shadow in the darkness, a towering over the children, a malignant presence of evil and hatred. The girls under her control were waiting for her signal to attack. Hosea 8:7 came to his mind. "For they have sown the wind, and they shall reap the whirlwind." Meddling in the affairs of vampires for the past two years had been the seeds for this moment thrown into the wind. The pack of demon girls rustling before him was the whirlwind.

"Let me..." he started to call loudly so she could hear him from the far end of the cavern. But the siege began.

A shape darted out of the gloom, he swung the straight blade of the machete. The edge bit into some part of the blurred body, the momentum forced him against the wall. There was an angry growl near him. He wrenched the blade free and pushed back with the hammer in his left hand to give him room to swing the blade. The sharp metal edge came down on the thin neck, cleaving through flesh and bone, the head fell to the floor the body spasmodically moving, blood gushed from the wound.

Immediately he was attacked by two girls before the first body stopped moving. Blindly, without a plan he hacked and pounded at them knowing their necks and heads were the most vulnerable parts. If he removed their heads or crushed their skulls quickly he had a small chance. The surging mass of girls were finite in number, though the number could be as many as fifty. He couldn't tell in the pale light how many he faced. They were moving and he didn't have time to count.

More bodies flew at him, claw like fingers reaching out to rend his flesh. They had no regard for themselves. They were a weapon, cannon fodder, bullets to be thrown at the enemy. He, unfortunately, was the enemy. She had an endless supply of abandoned girls, she would just make more vampires to replace the ones he killed.

He swung the blade and the blunt hammer, striking wherever he could on their flailing bodies to slow them down, Punching and kicking to push them back, create an opening so he could deliver another killing blow.

After a few minutes bodies were piled in a semi-circle around him. He was scratched, bit, and bleeding. The smell of his blood incited them further, infuriated them, inflamed their hunger. The vampires used the fallen as a ramp as they crashed into him like a wave. The sledgehammer was wrenched out of his hand, his arm pinioned and teeth tore at his wrist. He brought his elbow down into the skull of a girl attacking him. The smell of blood filled the air. He cleaved down with the machete and removed her head. A sucking mouth was torn from his wrist. The blow was lucky and didn't severe his hand at the same time.

He pushed the headless girl away from him. More girls attacked. The machete rose and fell, a deadly drumbeat that was less lethal as he was beset. Four hands stopped his descending hand and ripped the blade from his grasp. His ears heard the clatter of metal on the tiled floor some distance away.

Now weaponless John fought desperately, futilely, all knees and crashing elbows in a hopeless attempt to stay alive. There was no real way to stop them and was quickly enveloped by the swarm. The sheer number and weight of the girls dragged him to the ground, teeth and talons tore at him. Blood flowed from multiple wounds.

As his consciousness waned, overcome by pain and fear, the death wave engulfed his mind. Scenes from his life flashed, micro seconds elongated becoming a disjointed collage, a noir movie with a vague plot. The last two years were the most vibrant. Faces strobed in his mind's eye, Sean, Maggie; two of the most important people from his recent past. One set him on this doomed path and the other was a respite from the danger now killing him. Suddenly there was…

Nothing

Chapter 18
A Shock to the System

John's eyes snapped open. The sky was dark but also strangely bright above him. He moved to shield his eyes but there was a clanking of chains and the motion of his wrist was stopped. John looked at his hand, a chain encircled his wrist and was latched with a small sturdy looking lock.

He turned his head to the see his other wrist was likewise bound. Moving his legs he discovered they were also chained. Looking around he could see he was elevated on a rooftop somewhere. From the view he was still in Beijing. By lifting his head he was able to see around him. He was on a flat space about ten feet square. To his left one part of the night sky was growing brighter at the edge of the horizon. He wasn't sure but dawn might be soon.

Then the memories flooded back. He was in a losing battle against the Fagin vampire and her evil demon girls. He'd killed a number of them; their bodies lay at his feet as he swung the machete like a reaper's scythe decapitating them. But he quickly grew tired in the few minutes of deadly exertion and he was faced with what seemed to be a never ending stream of demons trying to kill him. He went down, engulfed by a swarm of gnashing mouths and clawing hands.

The pain from the multitude of small teeth was unique. Once they dragged him down, they drained his blood. He grew weak and succumbed to darkness. Then…

He died?

If he died, how was he alive chained to a roof?

His mind suddenly reeled with two options; He didn't die, he was somehow saved from a no win situation. By whom was the difficult question. No one knew he was there. He had no back up. He foolishly went to find Xiulan by himself. If he had been saved, why was he now chained to a rooftop? There was another option, a terrifying possibility, one he didn't want to contemplate. The horror of the thought was threatening to break him.

He looked at the peculiar sky. It wasn't daytime, not bright enough. It had to be night, though the stars burned too brightly. They weren't pinpricks in the veil of night; they were glowing with an unnatural light. The sky coruscated and moved, like a miasma of slowly shifting vibrant colors. Van Gogh's Starry Night come to life. He looked around, everything was heightened. Details human eyes wouldn't catch were distinct and clearly visible. He could see the fine texture of the concrete where he lay. He could discern the rust of the chains on his wrists.

"Oh God," he whispered fearfully. "That bitch did it."

He was a vampire.

He lay still and listened carefully. It was late or maybe early before people woke for the day. The sounds he heard were that of a city mostly asleep. He was chained to a roof, a sublime death sentence for a vampire. When the sun crested the horizon the rays would strike him. He would burn, a roman candle in the light of dawn.

She wants to burn me, he thought. He was chained for a reason. This was an execution. The sun would inexorably rise and he would be burn the same way he'd seen other vampires burn. He'd disposed of vampire corpses in Las Vegas by exposing them to sunlight. Those were his first real kills as a vampire hunter.

John focused. He could feel his heart beating slowly in his chest despite his rising panic and he felt himself breathing. Vampires were dead. No bodily functions, right? Did he need to breathe or was it merely a muscle memory. That was the myth and like he'd learned quite often the myths were generally wrong. He never asked how their bodies functioned in any conversations he had with them. Another thing he knew as a fact was they were stronger than humans. Tentatively he tried the chain. It clanked as he pulled. One end was wrapped around his wrist. He made his hand as small as he could but was unable to slide the chain off his wrist. He looked at the other end of the chain. It was fastened to a U-bolt mounted to a steel plate bolted to the concrete of the roof.

All the chains were similarly mounted to the flat roof. If ever there was a time for any vampire myth to be true, he needed it to be now. His very life depended upon the legendary strength. He pulled his arms to his sides until the chain stopped the motion, the links straining tight, biting into the bones of his wrist.

He pulled steadily but didn't feel the mount to the roof budge. He relaxed and grasped the chain in his right hand. He took a breath and jerked his arm up and toward himself. Explosively the chain reached its limit, the sound was loud in his ears like a gunshot.

It didn't move. Silence again filled the air. Did she hear his attempt to escape? Did she leave him alone, secure in the strength of her trap? If he tried again would it bring them up to the roof to prevent his escape? He waited for a few minutes to see if anyone came to check on him. He listened. There were no footsteps; the door to the roof remained closed.

"Ok. Let's get noisy," John whispered to himself. With unfamiliar muscles pulled quickly and repeatedly at the chain. The sound and action was surprisingly fast and repetitive, like a machine gun in the quiet night. He felt it giving way and redoubled his efforts. The plate holding U-bolt tore from the concrete roof, the chain swung over him as it broke loose, and he rolled to his left side. Chunks of rock flew over him. The chain with the plate slammed into the flat of the roof, the two inch concrete bolts trapped in the plate adding to the sound.

John kicked upward with his right leg. There was a bit of slack in the chain as it snapped tight. It still held him in place. He tried again and again. The effort was powerful but not as rapid or as strong of a motion as with his arm. The plate tore free from the roof; he moved to dodge the plate as it fell back down. He kicked with his left leg, repeating the process. It came free. He stood up, three limbs were free but his ankles and wrist still bore the encircling chains.

He stood and bent over grasping the last chain holding his left wrist to the roof. He noticed scorch marks where he had lain. This was not the first execution by sunlight Xiulan had done there, though the size of the burn marks from the victims were small. It must have been a punishment for one or more of her vampire demon girls.

As he started to pull the chain with both hands the door to the roof flew open and banged against the wall. He looked down when he heard the noise and saw three of the demon girls staring up at him. They'd heard his escape attempt. Rage suffused their faces as they hissed in Mandarin. John let go of the chain and turned to deal with the immediate threat. With his right hand he gripped the chain with the sharp cornered plate and prepared himself.

The girls jumped from below. The lead vampire child was struck in the head by the metal plate as John swung it through the air. She went down; bits of her skull and brain bursting loose from the impact of the blow, the spray of blood caught by the gentle wind and carried away. Shocked, John could smell her blood. It smelled good. The fact shook him deeply but he couldn't think about it. There were two other killers coming for him. He swung the plate again as the next vampire child alighted on the rooftop. The chain wrapped around her neck, he jerked his hand toward him pulling the chain, the sudden dynamic movement snapping her neck.

The weight of her body falling off the roof dragged his right hand downward as the third vampire demon attacked. Finger claws out, she leapt on him, her teeth biting into his shoulder as she savagely slashed at him. John shook the body of the second girl free from the chain and grabbed the wildcat attacking him by the throat, tossing her away. His new, unnatural strength surprised him. She tumbled away shrieking, falling off the roof, but he didn't hear her land. She must have recovered at the last second to land on her feet. He listened, waiting for her to ascend and attack again. He heard a small growl and the whisper of footsteps going into the building beneath him.

"Shit!" He knew she was going for help. He only had seconds. John grabbed the chain holding his left hand near the metal plate and pulled with all his might. Arms strained and shoulders flexed, he put his legs into the effort and pulled. If he didn't get free now he would be dead. Again. Truly dead. There was the sound of breaking concrete and the metal plate was wrenched free. He was loose but still had chains binding his limbs, impeding his escape.

John turned and gathered the four chain ends in his left hand, the metal plates clanked together dully. He jumped blindly off the raised portion of the roof, landed, took three steps and leapt off of the building. He had no idea how far the ground was but figured he could survive the fall. The buildings in the Hutong were not over three stories tall. He was right; it was a short two story building. He landed softly, but the chains and metal plates jangled like bells as he hit the street below. They would hear him fleeing no matter which direction he went. He was a belled cat and unless he could find a place to hide from the sun quickly. He needed to stop the clarion sound giving away his location to the sharp ears of the girls. If they found him they would run him down and murder him in a more efficient manner than exposing him to the sun.

John studied the street and the building he jumped off of for a moment. To his left was the front entrance to Xiulan's compound. He had been secured to the house next to where he died. He turned to his right and ran. The chains sounded loud in his ears, the noise a telltale sign of his flight. His stride and speed were hindered by the chains but he was still faster than he expected. Running was not something he enjoyed or did often. It was a boring exercise, but he had to be fleet to save his life. He was determined to put some distance between him and the demon girls.

As he ran his mind raced. She had two houses? What time was it? He wanted to look at his watch. There was no way to focus on the watch as his left hand held the plates attached to his chains. He didn't want to lose the vital seconds to stop and look. Where was he exactly? When did the sun come up? He had to get out of the chains and someplace light proof before the sun rose. He'd be dead if he failed to find a dark, sunless space to wait out the day. Terror kept his feet moving, the pounding of his shoes sounded loud to him in the silence of the street. The metallic clinking of the chains worried him. Were they following?

Xiulan had unknown forces, the child vampires, they were her soldiers and thieves, and cruelly, they were expendable. There would always be a supply of callously discarded girls in China for her to save from exposure. How many had she turned?

John slowed, all the buildings looked similar. Low, grey, boxy shapes with weathered doors and small windows, all numbingly similar. The roofs were pitched slightly at an angle and tiled in a uniform grey. Everything in the Hutong was grey. The buildings were uniform, the resident's bleak lives were uniformly grey as well.

An archway was approaching to his left. He turned for the first time to glance behind him. He fully expected there to be a swarm of girls behind him running him down. Like the screaming girls chasing the Beatles in a Hard Day's Night but smaller with sharp gnashing teeth. Surprisingly the street behind him was empty. He looked at the rooftops. Were they pacing him from above? Apparently not. There were no children stalking him from above.

He went under the arch and moved as quietly as he could down the smaller walkway. It was wide enough for bicycles, or mopeds, but too narrow for a car. Not that many owned a car in Beijing. Communism didn't make for gaining wealth and anyone with a car wouldn't live here. The wide boulevards of Beijing were mostly devoid of personal cars. Traffic for people was taxis or buses.

He searched for someplace to hide. He could easily break into a house, but then he'd have to deal with the occupants. He wasn't ready for that. Xiulan intended for him to die a painful death. She left him without the information a fledgling vampire needed to survive. He figured when a vampire created offspring they told them about their new powers and how to survive their new life. Xiulan turned him as an execution.

The street curved gently as he quickly walked holding the chains so they made as little noise as possible. The street had a seemingly organic shape, it curved oddly for a city where uniformity was normal. Possibly a meandering street left over from some ancient path which kept its shape as Beijing was built up around it. To his left was a house with a ruined wall, a ficus tree stuck through the broken masonry and towered over the grey street. John stopped to consider the abandoned building. He might be able to find some dark hole, or build a barrier to keep out the sun. He climbed over the breach, his shoes crunching on the loose stones and detritus on the other side. *It could use a good sweeping*. He thought.

Thankfully his new eyes were able to see in the dark. He walked past the empty door frame, it had exposed red brick slick with green algae where the grey concrete flaked off in large chunks. The roof seemed solid and judging from the undisturbed floor no one had been in the building in ages. A quick search proved it deserted. He found a place deep in the building he could use to hide from the sun. It was a space under concrete stairs, he could pull some ragged sheets of plywood to cover the hole.

With dawn still some time off he settled down in the darkness to wait and watch. He sat with his back to a wall. From his vantage point he could see the entrance to the building. He waited. Were they searching for him? With all the loose stone and whatnot on the floor he would be able to hear any approach. Even a small vampire wouldn't be able to walk completely silently.

He waited. He moved his foot, a restless motion, the chain rustled. Before he settled in for the day he would extricate his limbs from the chains. He looked at his watch. It had been over an hour and the sun would rise soon. The little girls would have to get safely to their rest place so he was probably safe.

John got up and moved deeper into the building. He found a windowless room with a door. He shut it to muffle any sound his efforts to free his hands and feet would make. He rested the old lock holding the chain on his left wrist on a piece of brick. He had an anvil, for a hammer he used the steel plate at the end of a chain. Two sharp strikes where the U of the lock connected to the body broke it. He was stronger than he knew.

He listened. Did any pursuer hear that?

Not that he could tell. Quickly he repeated the process and soon his wrists and ankles were free. The room he was in looked better for a hiding place than under the stairs. It was small with no windows and a sturdy ceiling. The sun wouldn't penetrate the gloomy space. He took a chain and used it to fasten the door shut in case someone stumbled into the ruin during the day.

John looked at his watch. The sun would rise very soon. How did this work? Was it like falling asleep? Was it a sleepy gradual human nodding off? Sean didn't tell him and he never asked any of the other vampires. He rested against the wall across from the door. His mind racing though his body was still. This was a nightmare. How would he survive? He had no way to deal with the day to day…

Oblivion

Chapter 19
First Awakening

John snapped into wakeful lucidity, like a light switch being suddenly flicked on. He could see the ruined room he was in and the weight of his situation hit him. It wasn't a bad dream, it was a real nightmare. Faced with the horrifying truth, John broke down and sobbed in despair. What would he do? Would he expose himself to the sun, a sacrificial suicide? Last night he worked hard to escape that fate. And as much as he was loathe to admit to himself, he didn't want to die.

If he chose to live he would have to figure out how to live. He obviously couldn't remain a priest. There was no way to do the job now. How would he live? Most of his adult life was tied to the church, his residence, his income, his purpose. He would need to do something for a living.

Other vampires he's met had a support system set up over decades or centuries. They had money and help, human help to navigate the business that could only be done in the daytime. They figured out how to live. Money didn't seem to be a problem. John had some money saved but what kind of job could a vampire hold? Night clerk at 7-Eleven? For eternity? That was a depressing thought.

He calmed down, taking a few breaths he pulled himself together. Sullenly he stared at the debris filled room around him. His transformed eyes worked well in the dark as he would expect them to. He was suddenly aware that he hadn't moved from the night before. Did his muscles lock up when he disappeared from consciousness? Shifting around he tested his limbs, flexing his hands, arms and legs. He didn't feel any pain from being in the same position all night. That was a small relief. He stood up and walked to the secured door. Listening carefully, undid the chain and pulled the door open.

There was no one in the deserted building from what he heard. But he did hear the sounds of the neighborhood. People were eating dinner in nearby houses, talking, walking on the street outside the deserted hovel. The problem, as he saw it, was he was a tall white man in Beijing. There weren't many westerners in the Hutong. He would stand out. And if he was awake, that meant Xiulan and her demon children were awake too. They would be searching for him. He needed to get back to his lodgings, but to what end? Should he leave China, figure out how to get home, or should he bring the fight to her?

Xiulan might be able to kill him, a real death, not this new existence. Or he might kill her and save the people of Beijing. She was operating with impunity. The government didn't acknowledge the deaths in a way that hinted to something unusual. The loss of life meant little to the government. The victims were workers. In a country of a billion, there are always more workers.

Carefully he moved to the entrance of the building. His nose caught the scent of cooking food, rich smells of spices and flavors. And he felt no hunger. In the shadows as he waited beyond the ruined doorway, he saw people walking, and smelled them. The reaction of his body surprised him. A sharp pain lanced his guts, a penetrating hunger unlike anything before threatened to overwhelm him.

He needed… blood. There was nothing else which would do. No other nourishment would be compatible to his body now. Would animal blood work? He didn't know but there were no animals available. His mind was filled with questions but the vampire who made him wasn't there to teach him. She'd turned him to punish him, kill him, burn him to death. No vampire would teach him about his new life. He would learn by trial and error.

John could smell people as they walked by. The human smell of sweat, bodies, and blood danced in his nose. It was almost overpowering. Newly born instincts threatened to overwhelm his caution. He needed food. Not food, he corrected himself. Blood. The thought terrified him. If he waited too long he might be driven by the hunger to do something foolish.

How can I do that? He wondered. Once he had killed vampires who were asleep. Last night he killed the demon girls who eventually brought him down. In his mind those situations were different than the people walking by smelling so… appetizing. He tried to force the thought from his brain but the hunger and smell of blood pushed it back in.

I don't have to kill. John thought. *Malcolm's set up at the church showed me that. I can take what I need. From a human being and not kill them. But they will remember. There must be some trick to make a, he hesitated at the word, victim forget.*

If there was a trick, a way to force someone to forget being attacked, he didn't know it. He would have to adapt, figure out a tactic. He stood in the shadows of the courtyard to the house. The darkness of the Hutong neighborhood made him virtually invisible to the people walking outside the ruined house. There wasn't much foot traffic. Most residents were home from their factory jobs or wherever they worked.

John thought about the situation tactically. He needed to be fast, grab someone and pull them into the ruined building. It would be best if he knocked them out so they wouldn't struggle. His heart sank as he realized it would be easiest to snatch a woman. Someone older. A man would put up a fight if he picked someone young enough to fight back. A woman probably wouldn't fight back.

He was horrified by this line of thought. He was thinking like a predator. The same thought process worked for most human predators; serial killers, child molesters. Focus on the weak, the vulnerable. Use overwhelming force to keep their fighting to a minimum. John took a breath and steeled himself. He needed food. This was the only option available to him at the moment.

He waited in the dark, ready to spring out and grab someone. The possibility scared him. How much force would it take to render someone unconscious? Would he be able to stop once he started feeding? He had no fangs as far as he could tell. His tongue felt flat teeth as he pressed the tip against them.

He watched each person and looked at how they moved. Were they predator or prey? Predators walked with self-confidence, an assured look, defiance. Prey moved tentatively even if it was some small tell, a furtive glance around, staring at the ground avoiding eye contact.

A short woman approached his hiding place, from what his heightened eyes could see the rest of the street was deserted in either direction. She passed by his hiding spot. He leapt over the wall to grab her but he wasn't fully in command of his body. The muscles were more powerful than he expected and he launched himself into the air. He flailed drunkenly and smashed silently into the wall of the building across the small street.

The woman turned at the sound and was shocked to see a body fall to the paving stone street as if dropping from the sky. Spooked, she turned from him and fled. He watched her run, within seconds she disappeared around a corner.

"Shit." John whispered. He was unharmed but embarrassed. He got up off the street and brushed off the dirt while glancing around. *An awkward vampire, how embarrassing.* Should he stay and try again? The first attempt was unsuccessful and personally embarrassing. He didn't have the problem when he was fleeing for his life the night before. That was his body replicating running. He was too worried about pursuit to think about how his body was working. Now when he needed to be stealthy and, well, a predator, he fell on his face. Literally.

He moved back toward the deserted house and carefully leapt the wall, this time testing his muscles, using only the amount of energy needed to clear the wall. He landed quietly and settled into the darkness again. The woman who ran away probably wasn't going to get the authorities. The Red Guard didn't patrol the neighborhood and dealing with the local police might lead to a shakedown. Corruption and abuse were always a possibility.

Several people passed by. Two men talking together passed by, three women chatting as they were going somewhere. He didn't understand the language so the conversations meant nothing to him. He needed a solitary person on an empty street. Shortly a small woman came down the street. He waited for her to pass by and crossed over the wall on cat's feet. Silently he came up behind her and with a brisk, sharp motion hit her head. He caught her, lifting her up as her unconscious form started sinking to the street. Lifting her over his shoulder he went back to the ruined building and carried her into the darkness.

He lay her down in the room where he spent the daylight hours. Concerned for her well-being he checked her pulse and could see she was breathing. What an odd thing for a shark to be concerned for the seal he caught as prey. John stared at her face. How did this work? He didn't have fangs. In fact he hadn't determined any changes to the teeth in his head whatsoever. They were the same configuration and flatness they'd been since he was a teenager.

The nearness to her pumping blood made his hunger sharper, more urgent. He could feed off her and leave her to wake up later. He didn't need to kill to survive. But he needed to cut her. There were shards of broken glass in the ruined house. He could carefully slice her wrist, cross ways, not vertically down the arm. After searching the floors for a minute he returned with a sharp piece of glass. He placed the jagged edge against her left wrist and hesitated. He was doing a violent act on a woman. It was what he needed to do to survive.

Unlike a shark or a wolf, the man he once was remained. He was concerned for her, felt empathy for the victim of his need. He wasn't a predator. When he was human he never hunted even though others in Colorado enjoyed the sport. He sympathized with the animal and the fear and pain they'd feel. This wasn't a gunshot from a hundred yards away; this was him cutting a woman to feed. Thankfully she was unconscious, and he needed to get on with it because she might wake soon.

John took the razor sharp edge and carefully sliced her wrist. Blood welled up, the smell of it blood contorted his hunger. He could smell it, the most savory thing to possibly ever grace his nostrils. More appetizing than a rare steak, suddenly more necessary than oxygen, his body knew what needed to be done. His mouth watered as he set down the glass and raised her wrist to his lips. He swallowed dryly before covering the wound with his mouth. The blood hit his tongue there was a pain, sharp teeth flicked out. Fangs. He was now armed like a vampire.

Like a baby sensing mother's milk was nourishing, his body recognized the blood. Primeval instinct manifested, and he sucked at her wound. The blood flowed down his throat to satisfy his greedy thirst. He shut his eyes and moaned in pleasure. Sean told him what it was like. He underplayed the luxurious sensation of it.

He drank wantonly, pulling life from a victim for the first time. After a timeless interval, he opened his eyes and looked in horror. The woman was pale. He tore his mouth away and wiped the blood from his lips ashamed how he lost himself. Blood still seeped from the wound. He couldn't resist and licked the blood away. His action caused the blood to stop and the wound began to knit closed. John looked at her in wonder. How incredible, soon the cut would soon be a faint line across her wrist. Now sated, his fangs retracted into his jaw.

He felt the pulse at the woman's neck. She was still alive. He had to leave her. Staying until she awoke wasn't an option. He had to get back to his hotel and figure out his next move. John imagined demon girls were still hunting for him. Xiulan wouldn't think he died when the sun rose. She was too careful to make such an assumption. She'd want to know he was dead for certain. That would mean her deadly minions would probably be canvassing the streets.

He needed to move quickly to get back to his hotel. He his main problem was obvious, he was lost. His panicked fight into the darkness was directionless. He didn't know where he was. If he could find the subway system he could get back to his hotel. It was near the number 1 line.

Regretfully, he left the woman in the ruined building and set off into the darkness. He hoped she would wake soon and get home safely. The priest in him wished he could do more, the hunted animal now running his mind needed to get moving.

Looking at the signs, baffled, John picked a direction. There were two subway lines in Beijing. His hotel was near one of the lines. His hotel was off of the subway which circled the city. The #1subway line cut across the loop of the #2 line towards the bottom of the loop. He knew what the icon for the subway looked like and kept scanning the signs for an arrow pointing him the right way. He searched his pockets and determined he had enough change for the subway. When he went for Xiulan's he left his passport at the hotel, taking only some cash and his room key. Luckily he still had his cash though the room key was missing. With all that happened, death and reckless escapes, he couldn't guess where it disappeared. Hopefully Xiulan didn't have it.

He needed to find any subway stop to return him to familiar territory. It didn't matter which direction or line, one station would get him started on the way back to his hotel. As he walked he looked at the people around him. He studied the children to see if they were the fearsome children he escaped. None of them were the dirty hungry vampire girls. Most of the children under ten were boys. The prevalence of boys was a symptom of the ten year old "one child only" policy. A bad idea which caused suffering for the girls currently being born and would create unforeseen problems in the future. Nature made a balance in births, generally equal number of males to females. Artificially preferring one sex over the other was selectively breeding difficulties into the country.

None of the signs he was seeing were in English. He wondered if he picked the wrong direction. He wasn't on one of the main city streets, he was in a residential area, but not a street as small as some. It could fit a car, but there weren't many cars. At this time of night there were some old scooters, bicycles, and foot traffic. John kept his eye out for the girls even as he scanned for the subway logo.

If he didn't find it he would go to a bigger street, look for a bus or taxi. Being in a country where the language was a complete mystery to him made the situation harder. He had to make it back to the hotel before dawn. He glanced at his watch. It was after 10 p.m. He needed to rewire his brain to think about time differently. He was exiled to the darkness. Days, or nights rather, were variable like the daytime. Depending on season and location on the earth, nights could be either very long or very short. There probably weren't a lot of Scandinavian vampires. Winters would be great, but Summer nights were maybe two to three hours long and the sun didn't fully set.

His condition, as if being a vampire could be considered a disease, had an off switch, when the sun came up he was out like a light. And if caught in the morning sun, a burning death was the terrible consequence. He needed to adjust fast. A deep sadness was playing around the edges of his mind. The truth of all he lost was slowly dawning on him. Each everyday average thing he could no longer do was a negative revelation. One part of his mind was recognizing the things lost and compiling a list.

The street he was on crossed another boulevard. When he reached the corner he noticed a little girl standing at the corner looking around. John didn't freeze or stop, he turned to the left and trudged on hoping she hadn't seen him. He wasn't sure if she was one of his adversaries, but she was the right age range and wore a simple dress like the others he'd seen. Like the others he'd killed before they killed him. He noticed she was shoeless. As had been all the child vampires so far. Was the waif a demon girl or some poor child out in the cold night?

John walked head down trying to diminish his height. He stood out, at least half a head taller than the native Chinese men. He listened, hoping his ears would discern if he was being followed. A barefoot child on a stone street would be silent as a panther in the jungle. The Hutong neighborhoods were the demon girl's jungle. The street he was on was wider, there were more lights and more people. He needed to know if he was being followed. Was the girl merely a child or was she one of the vampires he imagined were scouring Beijing to find him? He took a risk and turned to the left to look behind him as he walked. There was no one there. He turned to the right and about one hundred feet away on the other side of the street was the barefoot girl. She was looking at him and keeping pace with him.

A completely rational fear gripped him, he wanted to run, but without knowing where he was fleeing would be the wrong choice. He required a safe destination. He had his hotel, but that was it. He couldn't pound on a random door and beg for help.

The language was a barrier to him as was the fact the occupants of every house was now food.

Regardless of these new problems, he'd been found, but was it only one demon girl? She had no way to get help, there weren't many payphones around. John picked up his pace a little bit. Panic teased around the edges of his mind. His fear was justified. They had killed him once. Even if he were a vampire it was possible to die again at their hands. He glanced back. She was still there. A second child was ten feet behind her, the same serious, hungry look on their faces.

They were the cat. He was now catlike too, but in this situation, unarmed and lost, he was the mouse. A large mouse hunted by kittens.

"Shit." John muttered to himself. He still searched for the subway icon which would lead him to safety. He knew where the children were behind him and kept track of them as he walked. He'd been found and trying to be nonchalant was a stupid waste of time. The demon girls knew he'd seen them, and they didn't care. They could pace him and wait until there was a secluded place to attack. Somewhere unseen by humans would be best.

As John was looking for sign posts for the subway he noticed a small figure on the roof about one hundred feet ahead. He shook his head and exhaled a curse. "Fuck. Can I get a break, Lord?" The Almighty didn't answer and John didn't really expect Him to. He allowed John to be turned into a vampire. If that wasn't a big belly laugh and a big "Fuck you!" he didn't know what was. The street was mostly empty. It was a good time to attack.

The girl in front of him didn't move. With his enhanced eyes he could see she was like the others behind him. He could see her eyes following his progress toward her. Two were behind him and one on the roof in front. He would have to do something unexpected or actually expected. His options were few except for running. There was no safe convenient place to hide, he had no weapons, and turning into a bat and flying away seemed unlikely, or if it were possible, no one had taught him how. As a vampire once said to him in Las Vegas, *"What's the physics of that?"*

As he approached, the girl on the rooftop moved to the edge and looked like she was preparing to jump. John didn't give her the chance to leap down onto him, he bolted. He broke into a sprint and was past her before she could land in front of him or on him. He ran faster than he'd ever run, it was not really graceful, he was still hampered by unfamiliar muscles, but they were strong. His legs pumped and the sound of his shoes reverberated off the stone walls as he passed. Running like a panicked deer was a momentary save, he still needed to escape the demon girls behind him. They were as tireless as he was. They knew the city well and he was blindly running in a direction. He needed transportation. He needed something to hinder the girls. A hand grenade would be good, pull the pin, roll it behind him. A shot gun would suffice as well. He could pivot and shoot from the hip as they rushed him. Sadly, he had neither.

Ahead the streets were getting brighter, more and more busy. He didn't slack off. If he did, they'd catch him. He kept pounding forward trying to avoid crashing into the humans in front of him. His eyes saw the subway sign well before he passed it. An arrow pointed to a street to the right. He glanced over his shoulder as he crossed the street. The three demon girls were now four. Where he picked up another one he didn't know. They were a ragged group behind him about forty yards away, but still chasing him. He needed to prepare.

John stuck his right hand in his pocket and fished out change as he ran being careful to keep his fist clenched once his hand left his pocket. If he lost the change he'd have to jump the turnstile. If there were security or police or PLA that would get him stopped and questioned. He might even be arrested and get thrown in jail. His curse would be discovered as his body lay inert on the ground or, depending on the cell, sunlight might creep in through a window and burn him as he lay insensate. The three demon girls kept easy pace with him. His longer strides helped keep them at bay.

People stepped aside as the five figures wove in and out of the sidewalks at breakneck speed, stepping onto the street to avoid a particularly congested spots on the sidewalk. The speed they travelled was quick, faster than most runners, even Olympic sprinters. People wondered at why the Englishman was being chased by children. The fear on his face and the hunter-like visages of the children made observers know this was serious. It wasn't some child's game, it wasn't Tag. Something was very wrong and before anything might be done to help the man, they were gone.

The subway was about a quarter mile from where he'd seen the sign. The girls were gaining on him when he saw the sign and the brightly lit subway entrance. John doubled his effort, wind ruffled his hair and he marveled at what his new body was capable of doing. When he got to the stairs he didn't slow, he launched himself into the space recklessly. Luckily there was no one on the landing below as his feet touched the ground. He took another jump and cleared the next set of stairs.

John landed at the bottom with two leaps, the tiled entrance to the subway station gaped before him. There were some surprised Chinese looking at him. They were shocked to see a white man come flying down the stairs in two leaps. John nodded to them and glanced up the way he came. The four demon girls were at the top of the stairs in a small cluster. They were talking and pointing at him. It was encouraging that they didn't immediately rush down the stairs after him. It made him think they were told to stay away from crowded well lit places. He turned and entered the station.

John opened his fist when he got to the turnstile and put in coins until the light switched from red to green. He passed through the turnstile and moved into the station, picking a place on the platform where he could see the entrance. Two of the girls cautiously walked down the stairs, hugging the walls. They were determined, John had to give them that. He looked around the platform. Hopefully the train arrived soon. He quickly studied the subway map learning where he was and discovering where he needed to go. About this time he noticed the other entry to the subway from the opposite side of the street. The other two girls were at the other set of turnstiles on the far side of the platform.

The people on the platform waited. Thankfully they didn't pay much attention to John, and the demon girls seemed to be invisible to the city dwellers. Beggar children were ignored in China as easily as they could be ignored in America.

I guess people are the same everywhere. John thought.

The hot breath of the approaching train tugged at John's clothes. The smell of the diesel grew more pronounced. The demon girls smelled it too and moved. They ducked under the barrier and walked toward John. His eyes grew wide. They were going to move on him in front of people! He stood several feet from the edge and put his back to the oncoming train. He would make a break for an open door when the train stopped.

A sudden fear hit him. What if they didn't intend to catch him, what if they pushed him in front of the train as it was pulling to a stop? He'd probably be just as dead. John could tell the direction of the train from the wind. It grew stronger as the train exited the underground tunnel. John walked sideways, parallel to the track, weaving through the people on the platform as he moved. If the demon girls had planned to push him onto the tracks, his movement using people as a shield thwarted them.

The brakes shrieked loudly and the train rumbled to a stop. He was ten feet from an entrance as it opened. A number of people exited and as people moved to board, he joined them slipping in. He stood at the entrance of the car, just inside the door. An announcement was made in Chinese and the door started to close. As the doors in front of him slid shut, one of the three demons tried to slip in at the last moment. John expected this and lashed out with his foot. He caught her square in the chest and she flew backwards a surprising distance. She landed on her back and slid. His foot barely made it back inside before the door pinched shut.

He watched as two of the vampires stared at him as the train pulled away; the third got up off the floor and was looking at the subway map. Would they be able to run to the next station? John turned around. Several people were scowling at him. They saw him kick the child as the door closed. No one said anything to him, even if they did he wouldn't understand. But the car was suddenly filled with anger and animosity toward him.

He found an empty seat and sat down. John craned his head to look at the train map on the curve of the ceiling, trying to figure out where he was and where he needed to go. Something suddenly bothered him.

Three.

Three.

Three vampires were on the platform when the doors closed.

"Shit," John muttered. He sat up and scanned the hostile looking crowd in the subway car. Many of them glared at him with baleful eyes. Kicking a child made him a monster. They didn't know he was kicking a monster. And he, himself, was a monster. He could smell the people in the car, the stink of the unwashed and the scent of blood underneath that sang to him, a dark, hungry song.

John scanned the map and confirmed his destination. He would be getting off in four stops and transferring to the #1 line. His panicked flight had brought him to the #2 subway line which looped around the central part of Beijing. His lodging was off of the other subway line.

He looked around the car carefully as it rumbled and lurched on the tracks. He figured the fourth demon girl had to be on the car with him. While he was concerned with the danger in front of him she probably flanked him and entered the car through another door, or she entered another car and would be looking to see where he exited.

When the train stopped at a station John watched carefully for the demon girl. People were exiting and entering. In the confusion the little vampire might try to get closer to him. He didn't doubt she knew where he was sitting. He saw something out of the corner of his eye. Wait! There she was. At the end of the car, in the second to last row he saw a child's head rise up over the back of a seat like a crowning moon. Luminous eyes watched him passively. There was no hate in her eyes, just patience. Infinite patience.

At the second stop she was still watching to see if John was making any move to exit. He remained seated and watched her as well. She didn't approach him in the crowded car, seemingly content to wait him out. Neither wanted violence in the car with human witnesses.

John looked at the map again when the train stopped the third time. In his head he counted how many seconds it took at the stop. The time the doors remained open depended on the passengers getting on or off. He needed to work out his exit at the next stop. Would he stand up, be prepared to leave as soon as the door opened? Doing so would give the demon a hint of his intention. She would easily be able to follow him.

John didn't notice the PLA soldier get on the train at the station, his attention was fixed on the girl. A woman approached the soldier and spoke with him, pointing at John. The man's brows furrowed. He nodded his head and fixed his gaze on John. He worked his way through the passengers and stood to the right of John, his chest puffed up with authority.

The harsh tones of the military man broke his attention, John shook his head and looked up at the man uncomprehendingly. The soldier gestured as he spoke, pointed to the woman. John glanced over and recognized her as one of the people on the train when he first entered the car, and kicked a little girl across the platform.

Shit, John thought. He noticed the train starting to slow; it was reaching the transfer station. His mind raced. He had to exit the car, ditch both the demon girl and the soldier. Shit.

The soldier stopped talking and stood expecting an answer. He either didn't speak English or figured John could speak Chinese. John guessed he was being asked for his passport or some form of papers, maybe the man was asking why he punted a child in the train station.

The door opened. Several people got off, a number of people were getting on. Timing would be everything. He still was unsure of his muscles but John sprang out of his seat as the doors were half way closed. The distance to the door was less than ten feet. John pushed past a few people and resembled superman flying as he leapt through the closing doors. The soldier was surprised to see the Englishman move with blinding speed. The doors slammed shut a second after his feet passed the threshold of the car. John rolled on the platform, regained his feet and moved away quickly. The subway car lurched forward and disappeared into the dark tunnel. Several surprised people watched him as he recovered from his exit from the train. What an odd thing to see, a man flying out of the subway car and rolling to a stop.

From behind a pillar John watched the train exit the platform. He ignored the people who regarded him fantastically. Would the soldier stop the train? Did he contact the driver in the front car by some intercom system? John waited for a moment to see if it stopped its forward progress and returned to the station so the PLA soldier could pursue him. The rumbling of the train swiftly diminished as it continued on to the next stop. John let out a breath he didn't know he was holding.

The more important question, did his abrupt exit from the train leave the demon girl behind? Was she taken by surprise? John stepped out from his hiding place.

No. The she was standing twenty yards away. John figured there were too many people in the subway station for her to act. She would wait.

John followed the signs for the #1 platform. The girl shadowed him, lagging behind him and to the side of wherever he stood. He found the correct direction and stood on the platform eagerly awaiting the next train. The demon girl was nearby, silently waiting. She was going to be hard to shake.

John realized he wasn't going to shake her. She knew which stop he would get off at. She'd follow him to his hotel. Then she'd return with others. He had to kill her. The priest in him hated the idea, but the vampire he now was knew it had to happen. Also there was the fact that so far all the demon girls had been little psychopaths fixated on killing him. She wouldn't let the opportunity escape. She would probably try to kill him this evening.

John was a killer too and he needed to kill her to survive. The realization was difficult for a man of the cloth. He was against taking life, but there was no choice. He couldn't run from her, he had to lure her into a place where there were no witnesses, and try to kill her. What a cruel hand he'd been dealt.

The hot breath of the approaching train started as a sigh and strengthened. The subway rumbled, slowed down the length of the platform, brakes screeched loudly and the cars lurched to a stop. The doors opened. John looked at the girl to his right. She waited to see what he did. There was no reason to be stealthy so John walked on the car and took a seat. The little vampire entered the car from the next set of doors and settled into a seat where she could watch him.

John sussed out how many stops until he needed to exit and kept a count ticking off in his head. His focus was on the girl. He wondered if he could talk to her. Did she speak English? If she did, would she listen to reason? What could he say to a deathless eight-year old to persuade her to let him live? What were the effects of being turned so young? He'd never heard of a child vampire. Such an idea was an abomination. What twisted mind turns a child into a killer? The Fagin vampire was a monster for making children into vampire slaves. That's what they were. They'd never be able to function without her. They didn't have enough life experience to understand the world. The girls were wholly dependent upon her. She turned them into thieves and killers. Without a strong leader, what would they do? Could they be stopped?

If he survived the trip back to his hotel he would go after the leader. She needed to be stopped; stopped from making orphaned children into vampires. She needed to be stopped from using them as thieves and assassins. The children deserved to grow up even if they were orphans unwanted because of their gender. The cruelty of the government filled the orphanages with the cast off girls.

The train slowed to a stop and the doors opened. John kept his eye on the demon and she likewise was watching him. She would exit when he did. He knew it. He glanced at the map at the top of the curved car wall. She noticed and looked at the map as well, her eyes narrowed in concentration. The second station away was his destination. He considered his options of escape.

Should he run out of the subway car? His longer stride and knowledge of his destination might help him lose her. She didn't know where he was going and he might be able to outrun her. He doubted she knew the neighborhood. Though he didn't know it very well, and certainly not well at night.

Should he try to kill her? She would return to Xiulan. She was going to know he was alive, the three girls he ditched at the first train station would tell her. This demon girl might be able to tell her where he was staying. He couldn't disappear in one night, find a new place to sleep the day or make it to another city. He didn't have time. Daylight would come before he would be able to make arrangements and move.

The train stopped again. The next station on the line was his. He had mere minutes to decide what action to take. He was still uncertain what to do when the train slowed and shuddered at his station. John stood up, the girl mirrored his action, her eyes watching him intently. He gestured to her to follow him and calmly walked out the open doors onto the platform. The move was a bluff. He didn't feel secure at all.

It was later and fewer people were travelling. John walked to the exit and the demon girl paced him. She didn't rush him nor make any indication she was going to let him escape.

John stood by the stairs leading to the street, maybe twenty vertical steps and he would be on the street. People passed him going up and down to the street. Still too crowded to move the way he wanted to move. The demon girl stood twenty feet away watching. He needed to get in front of her far enough he could do something to ambush her. There was going to be a confrontation, John was certain of that, he wanted to do it on his terms.

They stood staring at each other, lifelike statues subtly vibrating with explosive potential. The girl, with the patience of a predator, was waiting for his action. They both knew it. But he was predator too, a brand new animal, inexperienced, but dangerous nonetheless.

Out of his peripheral vision John saw the station, it was mostly empty. No one was paying him any attention. With surprising swiftness he bounded up the stairs, leaping three to four steps with each motion. He crested the top step and started running. The direction he chose was not the way to his lodging. He was moving off the main streets and looking for a quieter street so he could deal with the demon girl.

John's path zigged and zagged, taking a left or right street as they appeared, looking for a deserted place in the city. With his extraordinary hearing he could hear her soft footsteps fleetly running behind him. The plan, such as it was, worked. She was pursuing him.

John turned a corner and skidded to a stop. He pressed his back against the wall eight feet from the corner and waited the few seconds for her to enter the street. She didn't burst around the edge of the building. Her footsteps stopped. As he could hear her, she could hear him clumsily pounding down the street. She heard him skid to a stop after he went around the corner.

He was waiting for her and she knew it. The little monster was not as dumb as he thought. John listened. There was no sound of movement. She could be waiting around the corner just like he intended to do with her. He cursed himself for underestimating his adversary. Instead of going to the corner John stealthily walked across the street, his attention on where she should be, with a few steps to the cross street he'd be able to see around the corner.

John moved carefully, his eyes focused on the edge of the building looking for his pursuer. He was able to see down the street. It was empty. Where is she? She didn't give up. John thought. The one I was trying to ambush is looking to ambush me.

A weight hit his back and he crashed forward to the ground. Pain bloomed in his neck. This is how he died the first time. But this demon was alone. John reached back and grabbed a thin arm and her neck with his hands. He quickly pulled up and forward throwing the biting devil off him. She tumbled to a stop a few feet in front of him. John sprung to his feet and rushed the girl. She leapt forward to meet him.

With his longer reach he grabbed her by the head; he twisted his body and with all his might smashed the child's head into the pavement. Her skull was crushed with a sickening sound. Disgusted, John shook loose the skull fragments and brains from his hand. It was an effective execution, quiet, efficient, brutal. If he'd had anything in his stomach he probably would've thrown up. He mused at the thought. Never again would he feel a full stomach. Thanksgiving with the myriad of delicious foods was now a memory. Hunger for blood was his companion now. Things like dark chocolate and a smooth, smoky whiskey were lost to him.

Despite having killed again, he stood mourning another in a growing list of the simple human things now denied to him. He then remembered there was a small dead body at his feet. He would have to get rid of her. He could leave her, she would be added to the secret PRC statistics of the people she and her kind killed. He took her thin coat and swept up the pieces of brain and skull, grabbed the body, and leapt to the low roof of a nearby building. He placed her body where the first rays of dawn would find it, burn it. Her body needed to be destroyed. If it was a fitting way to execute him on his first night as a vampire, it would be good enough to dispose of a demon girl's corpse. *I'm becoming better at this than I want to be*, he thought. *I'm being coldly logical about killing to protect myself.*

John jumped down from the roof and retraced his steps back to the subway station. He walked quickly. He was nervous about being seen, how many white westerners in Beijing kicked a girl at a subway station? What if the PLA was looking for him? Did the soldier on the train notify his superiors about a white man kicking a child? There were witnesses and his escape from the train made him look guilty.

Chapter 22
At the South Sea

John glanced at his watch as he approached the hotel. It was late but there were still a few hours before sunrise. If it was like the previous night he needed to find a secure place in his room to prepare, make light proof. The transition from awake to asleep was uncommonly fast. He was awake then he was not. During the day he would be insensate, and that was unnerving. Normal sleep crept up gradually, this was a light switch. On. Off. Awake. Oblivion.

To insure his safety he would need to take precautions. When he got inside the hotel he walked to the front desk. A diffident Chinese man was the unlucky person to pull the graveyard shift, the nametag on his suit read "Ron." Upon seeing John approach with a determined look he spoke first.

"Can I help you, sir?" Ron's English was good but heavily accented. His real name wasn't Ron, John was certain of that.

"Yes." John looked the man in the eye. He was aware his clothes were dirty and he was disheveled. Had any hotel employee notice he didn't come back the prior day or night? Would it matter to them if someone did notice? "I'm in room 305, I want to leave strict instructions that I'm not to be disturbed at all today. I don't want any maid to clean the room, I don't want new towels, nothing. No one is to come in. Do you understand?"

"Yes, sir," Ron said. "I will make a note for the day staff that you are not to be disturbed."

"And no one is to enter."

"Of course." It was an odd request, but the hotel meant to serve the guest's needs.

"Thanks. And do you happen to have a spare key? I seem to have lost mine." In his mind he quickly played over the events of his death but still couldn't recall where he lost the key. For all he knew it was on the floor where the child vampires overwhelmed him.

"If you don't find the key there will be a charge for the loss."

"I understand. I may have left it in the room."

Ron opened a cabinet door behind the desk, there was the jingle of keys as it swung open. He pulled a key for 305 off of a hook and handed it to John. "Here you are."

John searched his pocket for a gratuity. He pulled out a fifty yuan bill, did a quick mental calculation, and slid it to Ron across the desk. It was more than he wanted to give, but he didn't have anything elsc in his pockct. Dying had tapped him out.

"You're welcome sir." Ron slipped the cash into his jacket pocket. Westerners over tipped, but he didn't mind. The man walked to the stairs and Ron wrote a note that the man in 305 was not to be disturbed.

John walked up the three flights of stairs to the dimly lit corridor. He stopped in front of his door and listened for a minute. Had Xiulan taken his hotel key with the plastic tag stating the name of his hotel? Was there an ambush inside his room? He didn't hear any noise but vampires didn't make much noise if they wanted, so he put the key in the lock and unlocked the door. He turned the knob and pushed the door open. It was black inside the room but his new eyes could see surprisingly well.

He flicked on the light and waited outside in the hallway. No one attacked. There was no rush of demon girls to kill him again. The room looked the same way he left it two days before. He walked in, pulled the 'Do Not Disturb' placard, written in both English and Chinese, from the inside of the door, and placed it on the exterior doorknob before shutting and locking the door.

John searched the room for demon girls. Finding he was alone he glanced at his watch. There was two hours before the sun rose and he went to sleep. He had time to shower and change clothes before figuring out where he would spend the daylight hours.

He stripped off his dirty clothes, leaving them on the floor, and walked into the bathroom. He turned on the shower and waited for the water temperature to heat up. As he waited he looked in the mirror, another myth shattered. His face was the same face he grew into and looked at as an adult for fifteen years. John Bryant, dead at thirty five, alive for who knows how much longer.

He washed his face at a bathroom while finding his way back to the hotel, but he needed a shower. There seemed to be a layer of dirt on him and his clothes. The thick, dirty air permeated everything. It was hard on the lungs and contributed a griminess to the city.

He stepped into the shower and grabbed the soap. He cleaned his body but also took inventory, checking to see what was different, if anything was different. Did the attack which killed him leave visible scars or had his transformation smoothed out the injuries? He examined his limbs and was pleased to see he wasn't disfigured or mutilated. He looked human, which was a relief.

John shut off the shower and dried off with a rough towel, one that was once upon a time soft, but had been washed too many times to stay that way. He went to his bag and put on fresh clothes. He wasn't sure what to do with the clothes he died in. Doing laundry wasn't high on his priorities. Figuring out how to survive was. He had to live through the day while helpless. To do that meant finding a sunlight tight space in a room that never had a reason to be light proof.

The closet was the obvious choice. It had a sliding door and was at a ninety degree angle to the window. When John checked in he didn't notice if the window had a view of the sun. Such a thing wasn't a priority. He didn't spend much time in the room. There were sheer curtains along the window and heavier black out curtains which covered those. He pulled both tight, overlapping the edge of the heavy curtain. He walked to the light switch and turned it off. With his extended abilities he didn't see much light bleed from the sparse lights outside. He stepped into the closet and slid the door shut. There was no visible light, even to his eyes.

Convinced he had solved the issue he pulled the blanket off the bed and checked the door was bolted and the chain restricting someone from outside opening it. The chain was a poor security measure, a swift kick would breach it, but it made him feel better.

He knew roughly what time he was blindsided by sleep the previous night so he waited. When he had what he figured was ten minutes he sat down in the closet, his back against the wall, and covered his body with the heavy blanket. He didn't want to know how often it was washed, but he guessed not very. Washing or changing sheets was common, the blanket above the sheets, not so much.

He covered his head and waited for whatever happens when the sun rose. As a human, sleep was an opiate. Sleep was restful, there were dreams and nightmares, but what he experienced the previous night was an unconsciousness of the soul. Nothing was remembered. No dreams, no leisurely waking up, just a jolt to wakefulness. It was disconcerting.

Minutes crept slowly. John suddenly realized he needed to make a call before sunrise immobilized him. He scrambled out of the closet and went to the phone. He retrieved the number and dialed. Because of the time of night, he expected and got the answering machine.

"Jason, it's John. I need you to get me something by tonight. I know it's a strange request, but I'll need two machetes with sheaths," John said like it was an everyday ask. He treated it like it was nothing more strange than asking for a pen to write something down. "Thanks, I'll call you tonight." He hung up the phone and went back to sit back down on the closet floor. Door slid shut and blanket over his head, a last barrier from any unexpected situation where sunlight was in the room.

He remembered an old phrase, Hobson's Choice. He didn't know the origin of it, but it meant taking what was available or nothing at all. Life as a vampire or nothing. Drinking blood or death. It was a scary thought; one he would…

Blackness

After getting the two machetes from Jason at first dark, John arrived in the neighborhood where Xiulan's compound was the exterior wall for two streets. The houses in the area butted against each other. Hers was the largest on a street of bigger than normal residences. Beyond the walls were private compounds similar to homes he'd glimpsed in Rome, a plain outer building hiding a beautiful inner courtyard. Oddly, or maybe not so oddly, the PRC let her be. Whether she was paying someone off, or she had influential friends, John couldn't guess. Sometimes vampires had powerful connections to insulate them from everyday problems. Wealth was power for human and undead alike.

It was after ten p.m. The streets in front of her compound wall were somewhat busy but he saw enough openings in the flow of people and bicycles to do what he intended. John figured all the demon girls would be gone by now, out hunting for victims to rob and feed. Xiulan, he suspected, was a spider placed in the middle of a web. She was pulling at tendrils and feeling the vibrations of the city. She didn't need to venture out if she didn't want to, food would be brought to her. Dirty work was for her girls, why risk exposure? The city was recently released from martial law and she was expanding the number of girls under her control. She would need to replace the ones he killed. How many little girls did he butcher? He didn't know. He was trying to survive.

John shook his head. *No. They were monsters.* He thought. *They weren't girls, they'd never grow up to become women.* In a sense, they were trapped in amber, never growing older, never developing as people, never learning anything more than killing and stealing.

When there was a lull in traffic on the smaller street and no one could be seen for over a hundred yards in either direction, John leapt straight up and landed on the slanted tile roof. He moved over the apex to the side not visible from the street. Traversing the roof he crept to the building the human caretakers occupied. He needed to subdue them before going down to the underground spaces Xiulan occupied.

John landed in the second ring of the courtyard. To the north was a large building, pale light shone in the windows. He had prepared; held in place by a belt high around his ribcage were two machetes in leather sheaths. He left his puffy winter jacket behind for a dark colored, closed jacket. It concealed the weapons when he was travelling but the tight belt made his torso movements stiff. Walking around with long knives, even if they were farm implements, would make him stand out more than a tall white man in Beijing naturally stood out, so he concealed them under the coat. He needed weapons and guns were impossible to get, not that he'd be very proficient since he learned how to shoot only a few months back.

He unzipped his jacket, undid the belt buckle, and dropped the machetes down around his hips to a spot low, like a gunfighter's rig and buckled the belt around his waist again. He tied the leather cords at the bottom of the sheaths around his legs to keep them from bouncing as he walked, or worse, lifting up when he tried to draw the blade.

John walked to the caretaker's house on the right side of the courtyard and ascended the steps without a sound. There were openings for windows which had sturdy wooden shutters protecting the occupants from little vampires who might not follow orders all the time. From under the door a yellow light shone, they were awake.

John knocked. After a moment he heard quiet footsteps approach the door from the other side. The door opened a cautious crack and a pair of eyes focused on him. He pushed open the door and stepped into the house. John grabbed Liàng by the shirt and punched him on the side of his head. The unconscious man was laid on the floor. John needed to be violent, but it still repelled him. He heard a gasp from another room and saw a door as it slammed shut.

With quick silent strides he approached the door and without slowing, forced it open. The doorjamb cracked and the door swung open, he entered before the swinging door had a chance to bounce back and hit him. He ran to the woman and hit her one the head as she was trying to conceal herself under the under the low bed.

When he had been captured earlier and tossed into the corridor beneath the compound, he'd only seen those two people, the man and the woman. A quick search proved they were the lone occupants of the building. Thankfully they had no children. He didn't know what he'd do if there were kids to deal with. He found some cord and tied their hands and feet, and found fabric to gag their mouths. He didn't want to kill them, but since they were here and he needed to feed…

John concentrated, unsure how it worked. His teeth flicked out, small and sharp, something he would have to get used to. He punctured the neck of the man and fed. He needed to eat if he was going into battle. Everything so sharply contrasted to his mortal life. His new senses were astounding, almost intoxicating. He knew he could easily become enraptured by something simple he ignored as a human. Textures were interesting, smells more differentiated and delicate, hearing was difficult since there was so much information coming in all at once. It was a cacophony he hadn't learned to mute yet. And taste. So far all he'd consumed was blood. He didn't feel the urge for any other food, though he hadn't tried anything else. He didn't know if his body would accept something other than blood. It would be an experiment for the future if he survived the night. If he lived.

John sealed the wound on the man's neck, carried him to the bed. Next he pulled the woman from where she lay, half under the bed and set her next to the man. For an extra measure he tied them both to the bed. He needed to make sure they couldn't escape if they woke up before he was done. He'd set them free later, or if he didn't survive a vampire would help them.

When he was satisfied they were immobilized he left the building and walked into the courtyard headed to the entrance of the underground spaces. The door on the large opulent north building slid to the side when he was in the middle of the stone path. Light spilled out illuminating the area directly in front of him. Xiulan stepped out on the covered porch followed by eight demon girls. They moved, four to one side, three to the other, and one clung possessively to her like a privileged child clinging to her mother's leg. A favorite.

"You survived. I'm surprised," she spoke softly knowing his hearing would pick up the sound.

He said nothing.

"I can make you rich," she said.

"You can't make me human again," John said softly.

"No, I can't." she replied. Xiulan looked confused. "Why would you want to be human? They're frail. They die."

"That's part of the deal. Finite time; Live, love, learn, die."

The seven girls were shifting, spreading out on the wide porch. John's eyes flicked quickly down the line. Xiulan cocked her head to the side, a sly smile on her lips.

"Would you like one of them to play with?" she asked. "They don't just kill and steal."

"What?" John's anger flashed hotly.

She smiled wickedly. Offering the girls for sex infuriated the American. Their morals were so limited and simple.

Swiftly he pulled both machetes out of the sheaths and rushed forward. The line of girls jumped from the porch to intercept him. Xiulan stepped back to the doorway, watching.

Inside John's mind a primordial thing unwound and raged. He'd experienced the instinct of fight or flight in his other dealings with vampires. He was one of them now and didn't fear them like he did when he was alive. Anger rose as he faced the oncoming demon girls, the desire to fight was forefront. They'd killed him, and he wanted revenge.

John wondered for a millisecond about the ethics of killing feral eight year old vampires. They were an abomination more than being a vampire was an abomination. Little kids, true, but lethal, amoral, remorseless killers. They'd killed others, including himself, and robbed them of their money, leaving the drained corpses to be found slashed and torn on the streets.

A small figure reached John first, he brought the raised blade down swiftly, it cleaved into her shoulder cutting deeply. The blade came to a halt midway through her body. She crumpled into a heap. He didn't have time to check if she was alive, she was out of the fight. He wrenched the blade free and swung at the next girl as she reached him. He caught her in the throat as he side stepped, her head fell away and the momentum carried her body forward to fall, crashing on the stone pavers.

Five more rushed him with dangerous recklessness, their positioning to him staggered. He met them as they came. The demon girls had no tactics, just rage and numbers. The machetes in his hands rose and fell, flashing in the wan light, and the thin veneer of civilization sloughed off leaving an untrained barbarian with a binary choice; fight and survive, or fail and perish. He hacked wildly at the limbs and necks of the unarmed children, the sharp weapons cleaving cleanly, killing the creatures. Out of the corner of his eye he saw Xiulan speak to the girl at her side. The master stroked her hair and spoke in a whisper. The girl nodded and leapt off the porch at John, her small face was rage and hatred personified. Xiulan disappeared inside the building. There were no reinforcements available, all her girls were out hunting.

When the last girl fell to the ground dead John pursued Xiulan, entering through the open door. A pair of fashionable shoes lay on the floor. She ditched them for speed. He could hear her footsteps as she fled. He paused briefly trying to figure out which way she had gone. The room was large and gorgeous; high vaulted ceiling, dark polished wood floors and furnishings, antiques hidden from the communist regime, or allowed to remain due to her power or connections. There were large ancient embroidered tapestries on the walls. To either side of the room were doorways. John heard the footsteps to his left and moved that direction. The sound drove him deeper into the building. He followed Xiulan before she could escape somehow. There had to be a contingency for her to survive. She was too old not to make plans within plans within plans.

Chapter 24
Or Flight

When the third girl fell, Xiulan's sly, smug smile faltered. Fear started growing.

When the fourth girl perished, she edged back toward the open sliding door. Panic rose inside her.

When the fifth girl died, she slipped off her elegant shoes and stood on the hardwood porch waiting.

When the sixth girl failed, decapitated, she scowled, cursing herself for choosing weak children.

When the seventh girl fell, she slit the side of her tight silk dress up to the hip in preparation. She would need freedom of motion.

Xiulan looked at the precious child clinging to her, the small face impassive as she watched her fellows die. Xiulan reflexively stroked the child's hair, a simple gesture. One she had done over the decades, it comforted them both. "Chani, my love, protect me." The small child nodded and left Xiulan's side. She jumped off the porch, talon's raised, slashing. She reached John and she died, body cleaved with swift, cruel blows from the machetes.

Xiulan saw her shadow die, and she bolted.

Of the two options open to her, she chose to run into the mansion. She passed by the office and fled to a safe room which held a secret. Her acute hearing could hear the clumsy feet of the man chasing her. She was angry with herself for not killing him outright. She was cruel and wanted him to burn, dying terribly at first light. He woke too soon and was able to escape. Now he harried her and her very settled, comfortable existence.

At the end of a corridor she entered a small room, shut the door and slammed a large bolt home, locking it. Without any hesitation she moved to a panel and pressed a hidden button, a knot in the wood pattern near the floor. A latch released and the panel opened. She crouched, stepped inside and shut the panel tight behind her. In the dark she knew where the next release was, the door on the other side of the space opened and she entered into a small deserted room. Even in a country of a billion there were empty houses.

She grabbed a key ring from a nail inside the small passage and shut the hidden door. Xiulan exited the abandoned home and went several streets away to another small house. She inserted the key into the old but oiled lock, and turned it unlocking the plain exterior door. She glanced around and entered unnoticed. The courtyard outside the house was a riot of weeds. She hadn't used the safe house in a long time. She crossed the short stone path to the front door of the house and unlocked the door with the other key on the ring.

The entry hall was empty, devoid of furniture. She moved deeper into the house looking to see if anything was disturbed since she'd last been there. Had any thieves broken in? Had squatters taken up residence? No, all was as she left it.

She turned on an interior light revealing a simply furnished and light proof room. This part of the building had no windows. It was a furnished tomb. She sat down on a chair and contemplated her next move. On the walk over she hadn't found any of her children. She couldn't attack the man by herself. She needed help, her children were expendable help.

Her girls were far away, miles away, for they could travel swiftly and silently. If there were too many deaths in her own neighborhood, unwanted attention would focus on the area. She instructed them to cover all of Beijing so they moved out in ever widening circles.

The American had killed many of her girls in a few days. She would always make more but there was time and effort spent training them to serve her purposes. Replacing them would be time consuming. She would need to find other orphanages to supply her with children the right age. The orphanage where the American found her was ruined. She needed new sources for young girls. Too young and they weren't easily controlled. When she first started turning children she didn't have any self-imposed age restrictions. Quickly she learned and she had to kill the youngest ones. They were uncontrollable and too young to understand the necessity of her rules.

Xiulan wondered what the man was doing at her compound. She might be able to go back and spy from a nearby rooftop, but if he saw her she would be in danger again. Having fed before the attack, it was safest to stay where she was and wait until the next night to discover the damage being wrought upon her life.

She didn't live the past hundred years being overtly foolish with her own life.

John followed the sound, machete in his hand, arms pumping as he moved. He didn't try to move quietly, he sacrificed stealth for speed. He could tell he was close on her heels, not quite seeing her but hearing the uncharacteristic pounding of her feet as she ran through the maze-like building. He exited an office, ahead was a lone door at the end of a short hallway. By now his sense of direction was screwed up, he was so focused on catching her he hadn't paid attention to his path.

The door clicked shut and he heard a slide lock slam home. John stepped to the side of the door, unsure of his next move. It didn't make sense for her to lock herself in a room unless it was a fortified bunker or she had weapons. The thought worried him. With the connections and wealth she had she'd be able to get some kind of weapons. John knew he could be hurt and even killed by guns with enough rounds. Would she shoot through the door? John stepped to the side in case she did.

Should he wait her out? Try to talk to her? He pressed his ear to the door and heard nothing. He looked at his watch. It was twelve minutes since he went over the wall. He'd subdued the humans, killed eight demon girls, and given chase to the master vampire all in twelve minutes. Now he was thwarted by a thick, darkly stained door.

He listened again. There was the sound of a click, something within the room, like a door. Maybe it wasn't the dead end he thought. With precious time ticking away, he moved and kicked at the door. It shook inside the frame but didn't break. If she had a gun she could shoot through the door and with a reasonable amount of certainty, hit him. He stepped again and slammed his foot near the door handle. Again it held, but the wall seemed to vibrate and shake.

One more kick by the handle did the trick, it broke and the door swung in. He stepped into the room, machete up, ready to fight. The room was empty. It was a small plain room, dark wood panels on the walls, little furniture, and there were no doors or windows. *There's a secret door*, he thought. He tapped around the walls listening for a change in tone. When he found a hollow sound he examined the wood closely. There was a tight seam which lined up with the panel.

He pushed the sharp edge of the blood spattered machete in the crack chipping and marring the old wood. He tried to pry it open. After a few minutes he released the latch and carefully pulled opened the hidden door in case she was waiting on the other side. It was an empty space three feet deep and another door. John listened and ran his fingertips around the edge of the door until he found a release. It made a soft click and he carefully pushed the door. She could be lying in wait, armed. She could have more human helpers stationed ready to kill him.

On the other side was another house. The room the door opened to was empty and was in a state of disrepair. Xiulan was gone. It had taken him ten minutes to get this far and she slipped away while he struggled. He backed out of the small tunnel and closed the door.

The big question, was she gone for the night? Was she gone forever? No, that would be too hopeful. John figured she was gone for the night. She had to have someplace safe to stay other than the grand compound and the underground caverns hidden below. Was she gathering her girls and returning, or hiding out, waiting to return when it was safe?

Then there were still the demon girls to contend with. They wouldn't have a safe house like Xiulan. She was ready in case of an emergency. They had only one home, one safe place to return to; the compound and cavern below. It was cruel but wise of Xiulan to keep them subservient. Their education halted, their view of the world would never change. Their safety and welfare were totally taken care of by the master vampire. They lived or died at her whim. She had expendable tools. If they rose up against her she would be overwhelmed, but the thought would never enter their minds. It was a societal thing as well as an instinct drummed into their heads from birth. In a world of masters and servants, they were servants. They would always be servants.

John looked at his watch as he retraced his steps to the exterior. It was a half an hour after he surmounted the walls. He figured he had hours before the demon girls would return, and started searching the house.

There were many rooms to the house, all marvelously furnished, the wealth of the occupant was on display for no one to see. He doubted she had visitors, all the opulence was a memory of a bygone era, before the PRC, and solely for her.

John found an office. Curiosity got the better of him and he started searching without a clear objective. Offices held secrets. She might not hide those secrets because the whole compound was a vault.

There was a large mahogany desk, obviously an antique, one would expect to find such a desk in an English manor house. The English had occupied in the late 1900s and when they were replaced their influence and furniture remained. There were book cases on the walls filled with books. John scanned the titles and saw only a few English volumes. Almost every book was in Chinese; that was to be expected. There were a few volumes in English but the titles didn't make him stop to consider why she read them.

One wall had a large cabinet, dark wood, reaching almost to the ceiling. He tried the doors, it was unlocked. Inside were guns, lots of rifles, AK-47s, and pistols. "Jesus," John whispered to himself, "Where did she get these?" He learned how to shoot with Dale back in Colorado. It was a powerful feeling, the buck of the rifle against his shoulder, the ring of metal when he hit the target. The sound wasn't as frequent as he would have liked. He picked one up and checked it like Dale had shown him. It was loaded; the banana clip was at capacity, there was a round in the chamber. He could smell the gun oil and steel of the weapon. On the shelf were more clips of ammunition. He didn't find boxes of ammo when he searched the cabinet. The bullets were either loaded into magazines or loose. John suddenly felt lucky she didn't run into the office and grab a gun. She had enough of a lead she could have killed him, though it would take some effort.

He set the rifle back inside and left the cabinet open. He moved to the desk and sat in the western style leather chair. He opened the drawers and went through the papers. As he worked, he didn't bother trying to make it appear he hadn't searched, she knew he was there, might as well be obvious. He piled the undecipherable papers on the desk and kept digging for more. In a large bottom drawer he pulled out business check books, the kind in elongated leather embossed binders. There were three of the books from three different financial institutions.

John set one on the desk and opened it. He studied it carefully. He was unable to read the Chinese, but the numbers were self-evident. The balance was large. He looked at the next bank book; it had an even larger balance. He looked at the third. It was similar to the second book. He did rough calculations in his head. It was tens of millions of dollars, not Yuan. John leaned back in the leather chair and exhaled.

Xiulan had enough wealth to escape China and set up a life anywhere. He could burn the place to the ground and fill the caverns with concrete, but with the resources in the bank books she was immune to anything he could do short of killing her. A plan formed in his mind. She needed an imperative reason, something dire, to draw her out. Abject poverty would probably do it.

He closed the three bank books and put them in a pile on the desk. He moved to the cabinet and pulled out three rifles and placed them near the door. He took another AK and slung it around his body, checked the clip and pulled the slide to see if a round was chambered. It was.

He continued searching the house but the other rooms didn't reveal anything as interesting as the office. He looked at his watch. Midnight. Dawn was hours away. The demon girls would be returning at some point. They had no idea what happened so they would go down to the caverns to sleep for the day. Unless, that is, they saw the bodies and blood on the stones in the courtyard. He needed to get rid of them and clean up the blood as best he could.

John walked around the large courtyard checking buildings. He needed to stash the bodies. He needed to hide them and mask the smell of blood from the girls as they returned. They couldn't know anything was amiss. He found a gardener's shed with tools and implements for taking care of such a large property. He thought for a moment and turned to look at the condition of the flowers and trees. They were truly beautiful. There was a delicate symmetry to the garden which blended perfectly with the mansion. How did he not notice?

He admired it for a few minutes, walked around smelling the flowers, the lilacs and night jasmine, before turning to the unpleasant task before him. The bodies of the vampires lay on the stones, their blood staining the granite. He got a wheel barrow from the shed and started with the bodies which were more intact. He carefully piled them in the shallow wheel barrow and when he had four bodies, he rolled them to the shed.

As John picked up and moved the bodies into the shed, a task which earlier would have horrified him or caused him to puke from the smell and the gore, a small change happened he didn't seem to notice. The progression of 'do whatever it takes' was becoming more extreme. From the ability to pound a stake through a heart, to acquiescing to a massacre, to perpetrating a massacre himself, a change was happening and not for the better.

As he cleaned up the carnage he was working toward a goal. He sought the annihilation of Xiulan and her vampire girls and in doing so his humanity was slipping further and further away.

He found a garden hose and turned it on. Restricting the end of the nozzle changed the lazy flow into a spray which he turned against the discolored stones. The water powered away the pools of fresh blood. It hadn't dried so it diluted and flowed into the cracks between the stones and washed into the grass. He continued until his nostrils were not smelling the blood he spilled. Hopefully the girls wouldn't notice.

He turned the hose off and returned it to where he found it. John looked at his watch. Never before had he been a slave to time; now his life literally depended on it. Two thirty. He swung the AK from around his torso and moved to the doors leading to the carved out underground. He pulled one of the doors open and looked down the dirty wood stairs. His eyes were able to pierce the semi darkness. He could see the yellow light from the sparsely spaced bare bulbs hanging against the roof and walls. They seemed bright.

He needed to assure himself there was no one down below.

Chapter 26
Descent

John opened the doors to the basement and looked down the stairs. It was similar to the last time he'd been down there, when he was tossed down there a few afternoons back to be eaten by vampires when they awoke. Three AKs were slung around his torso, his pockets bulged with extra clips, and a fourth rifle was ready in his hands. If he was right, the caverns would be deserted. If he was lucky, all the demon girls were out hunting and stealing for their master.

He walked down the stairs quietly and waited at the bottom, listening for any sound. He moved forward when he was satisfied he was in no immediate danger. The corridor was deserted. John checked room to room, alcoves and odd hewn spaces in chambers until he reached the main chamber where the children slept and he died. It was empty, there were cots in rows and the dirt floor was stained from where he killed some of the girls a few days before. Thankfully the bodies were gone, and the chamber unoccupied.

Xiulan's crypt was across the chamber, the only room in the underground complex to have a solid sturdy door. It was the fortress where she stayed when she was the most vulnerable. The door was unlocked and John went in. Compared to the roughly dug and coarsely hewn beams supporting the chambers and corridors outside the door, the room was appointed like a classic hotel. Bed, furniture, small elegant pieces of art, all placed according to feng shui.

John looked at his watch, three thirty a.m. He had only a couple hours to wait. He also needed to worry about getting back to his hotel in a timely manner. He checked the weapons and placed three of the rifles next to the door. He practiced reaching down for a fresh one. He didn't know how many demon girls were left, but he wasn't fast enough to change magazines under pressure. It was easier to drop the weapon and pick up a fresh one. If he needed more than eighty four shots, then he'd worry about reloading the rifle. He could slam the door and lock it while he reloaded the clips into the guns.

He shut the door. To kill time he searched the crypt. He found old personal items, pictures of people, some with Xiulan looking as young as she was now with people long dead. Under the bed he found a PLA military pack stuffed with cash. Loose Yuan in small bills, John deduced this was stolen from the girl's victims. He set the pack aside and waited.

Sounds penetrated the door, chirping voices. The girls were returning. He had put off thinking about his next move, but with the growing sound and advancing time, he had to act.

Five fifteen a.m.

He needed to begin a terrible deed and then get back to his hotel. John stared at the floor for a second, stood up, and crossed to the door. He pushed the door open a crack and looked out. He could see a slice of the large chamber, there were a number of the girls sitting on the cots chatting with each other in Mandarin. They'd just killed and stolen from people all over Beijing, but they were talking like nothing happened. Or maybe they were telling tales of their conquests, John couldn't tell.

He opened the door slowly, the rifle in his right hand was hidden by his turned body.

"Were you kids looking for me?" John asked in a booming voice, one he learned from speaking to crowds when not supported by a sound system. He wanted all of them to know he was there. He needed them to focus on him.

The demon girls looked up, their eyes widened and their faces contorted in anger. This man killed their comrades, their friends. They all got up and began advancing on him. It was exactly the reaction he wanted. Not wanted, really, needed. He didn't want to slaughter innocent children. But they weren't innocent. They were vampires, killers.

John waited until they were closer then pushed the door fully open and stepped back into the room. The other rifles were to his right, safeties off, a half second away from his hands. He raised the rifle and started firing. He discarded one rifle and picked up another. And then another.

It took less than two minutes. The chamber filled with smoke from the weapons making his eyes water, the sound of gunfire echoed off the walls and rang in his sensitive ears leaving a hiss of hearing damage. He lowered the smoking gun. Nothing moved in the room.

"Oh god," said John. The gun slipped from his hands and clattered to the floor. The room was suddenly silent. No. His sensitive ears picked up something subtle. There was a liquid sound, blood leaking from ruined bodies. All the girls were dead, their voices silenced. He stared at the glistening horror of shattered bodies and torn limbs. His mind reeled as the reality of his actions sank in. He killed children.

No. They were feral vampires. Killers. Thieves. And eight years old. Tragic victims of a cruel master. John's heart broke in a way that might never recover. He killed children. Their poor souls were corrupted, the potential of their lives stolen. In Rome he saved orphans from a terrible fate. These children were lost, irredeemable. Their humanity was cruelly snatched from them.

He walked around the room checking for any signs of life, the smell of spilled blood and gunpowder thick in his nostrils. There were no demons, little girls, left alive. They were homicide victims twice. Once by Xiulan and now by John.

John's memory flashed to the massacre at the LVPD. It was the same smells and sounds. Only this time he was the executioner. He was the killer. He blocked the memory out. This new horror by his own hands would supersede that older memory.

John moved back to Xiulan's crypt and grabbed the pack and the full AK. He swiftly left the basement, climbed the stairs, and standing outside the doors he listened. Had the neighborhood heard the roaring of the guns underground? There didn't seem to be an audible stir in the area. The cavern must have been deep enough to muffle the sound.

John walked across the courtyard and entered the north house. In the office he put the three bank books in the military pack. At the cabinet he took two pistols and a spare clip for each and put those in the pack as well. He left the rifle in the cabinet where he found it. There'd be no way to get from her house to his hotel with a full sized rifle.

Before John left the office he took a sheet of paper flipped it over to the blank side and wrote quickly with a pen, a short message for an audience of one. He carefully set that in the center of the desk. It would be the first thing anyone would see when they sat down.

He slung the pack over his shoulder and left the building and the compound. He had an errand to do before he got back to his hotel. Time was short. And he would need to hurry.

CHAPTER 27
A LITTLE BIT OF LARCENY

It was almost six in the morning when there was a knocking at Lujiang's door inside the orphanage. "Yes, yes, I'm coming." He called out in Chinese. Was it one of the girls? Was there a nightmare which needed to be chased away? It wasn't unheard of but most of the older girls didn't need to have monsters scared away. It was the young kids who needed protection from the dark. He opened the door and was surprised to see John.

"What are you doing here? How did you get in?" Lujiang asked. He was concerned that a door had been left open.

"I don't have time right now, Jason, and I can't explain. But I need someone to help me with an important project," John said. "I need you to help me drain these bank accounts almost completely, whether by forgery or just writing checks for cash." John pushed into the room, he was wearing sleek black clothes and had a Chinese military backpack slung over one shoulder. Under the other arm were three large notebooks, he walked into the room and set them on Jason's desk. "Since her signature is in Chinese characters I need someone to duplicate it." John paused. "And I need it done first thing in the morning. This morning. I can't do it. I'm unavailable today when the banks are open unless you know of someone who banks at night. My biggest problem is I don't speak Chinese. I need your help, and time is of the essence."

Jason listened politely, his face registered confusion and alarm. What the priest proposed was a crime. Where had he gotten another person's bank books? From the insistence, Jason assumed this was not a trivial sum of money. No one is going to risk Chinese prison for a pittance.

"I need the funds in two or three accounts. I want one of these accounts to have five million dollars in funds to be given to your orphanage. You need it." John said. For what she did to the girls, she deserved to pay. "I'll dispose of the other accounts with charities stateside."

The man's concerned look softened. "The orphanage? Who's money is this? Who's bank accounts are these?" Jason asked. He'd done extralegal things before, but small crimes, and for the good of the children. Acquiring food or needed medicine. He hadn't broken laws because he wanted to; he'd broken laws because he needed to.

"A mobster, for lack of a better word." John said, glancing at his watch. He needed to get back to his hotel.

"A Chinese mobster!" Jason's voice was urgent but hushed as if the syndicate could hear him. "That's going to get you killed. That could get me killed!"

"I don't think so." John shook his head. "They'll come after me not you if they come after the money."

"What are you doing? This is insane," Jason said. "First you have me get you machetes and now this? You didn't kill anyone, did you?"

"No," John said solemnly. "I didn't kill anyone." *They were already dead, like me.* "The checks are just bank accounts. It will look like a normal transaction."

Jason stared at him silently. The priest had gone mad.

"I need this done. It's important," John pleaded. "It's a matter of life or death."

"Your death. Maybe mine!" Jason protested.

"I need this done. I need it done today. You won't be in danger. This is white collar stuff. Shuffling of money around," said John. He looked at his watch, sunrise was soon. "I need your answer now," he implored. "Will you do it?"

"Is it the mob?"

"It's not the mob. I can promise you it's not the mob," said John, his voice was urgent. He needed the task done, and it had to be today. It was all about leverage.

Jason reluctantly nodded. "I'll do it. I have a cousin in the banking world. He should be able to help." John suspected it wasn't a cousin, probably none of Jason's cousins were cousins, but it didn't matter if he was able to drain her accounts.

"If new accounts can't be opened, put the money into bank drafts, cashier checks, whatever. The money needs to be liquid and easily portable. It's imperative." John pushed the ledgers forward.

Jason gave a curt nod. "Alright, I'll help." Money was going to go to the orphanage, he was always underfunded.

"Excellent," John glanced again at his watch. *I have enough time to get back to the hotel. I think.* "I'll call you tonight to see how it went." He moved to the door and closed it. He snaked his free arm through the other strap of the backpack and in a moment he was running, out the orphanage and onto the street. It was six a.m. The sun would be up within the hour. He had several miles to go before he was back at his hotel. He was literally chasing the sun, or rather the sun was chasing him.

The cold night sky was warming in the east, the horizon was hidden by buildings but the dark night sky was greying, lightening, and the clouds were being painted orange at the eastern edges. The air was moist with the threat of possible rain in the late morning. The pack bounced on his back as his legs pumped quickly. There were some people out on the streets. Some traffic, buses, bicycles, pedestrians, John ignored them all and ran like the devil was after him. If the devil promised an eternity of fire, the sun promised the same for him. His fiery death would be the last moments of his time on Earth.

John knew where the hotel was in relation to the orphanage. He'd made the trip on foot a number of times, but not at this speed. His fleet passing was noted by many but they questioned if they really saw what they saw. No one can run so quickly. Were he human his heart would have burst or cramps would have stabbed him in the side, slowing his pace or stopping him completely. His new abilities were astonishing.

When he was a hundred yards from his hotel he slowed to a regular human run, before he got to the doors he slowed to a brisk walk. He opened the glass door and waved to the night clerk at the desk. The man waved back. John crossed to the stairs, as soon as he was out of sight, he sprinted up the stairs taking them two at a time. On the third floor he pulled the key out of his pocket and unlocked the door.

"Made it." He said to himself as he put the Do Not Disturb sign on the handle and locked the door securely. Hopefully his instructions for the daytime would still be heeded. He checked his watch. He had ten minutes. He opened the closet and stowed the military pack with cash on the top shelf. John checked the curtains covering the window, they were still safe and secure. No light would penetrate the coarse fabric. He sat on the floor of the closet and slid the door shut plunging him into darkness.

What the hell am I doing? His mind replayed the events of the night and his actions. All of them. *I've killed little girls.* He saw their bodies flying apart as the bullets sprayed the oncoming crowd. *They were monsters. Demons. They were going to kill me.* The justification was pale in comparison to the images in his head. *I'm stealing*, he thought. "I need to draw her out. It's the only way." He said to himself. His voice seemed loud in the closet.

Guilt for his actions was …

Oblivion

Jason studied the ledgers John brought him. The amounts were extremely large, astronomical in Yuan, and still a large fortune in American dollars. The distressing part of the favor was the name, the owner of the fortune, Madame Xiulan. She was a powerful benefactor for the orphanage and she had adopted many girls over the years. To steal from her was unforgivable. If he was religious he might have called it a sin, but since the State didn't allow religion it was an unethical and illegal ask. He'd done questionable transactions before but nothing on this scale. This was government corruption numbers.

Jason did know someone in the banking world, though not technically a cousin. He called anyone he asked favors from, or did favors for, a cousin. He thought it a funny joke, though when he said it many people believed he was telling the truth about having a cousin in such and such industry. China used to have large families, how else does a country get a population of over a billion?

He ventured out of the orphanage, the check books in a large satchel. He didn't want to walk down the street with large binders emblazoned with bank logos in gold leaf. It wouldn't be prudent. The 'cousin' Jason was going to see worked at a large bank nearby. The building itself wasn't large but was a branch of a bank that had a footprint in China, Hong Kong, South Korea, and Japan. As China embraced capitalism, the bank grew larger and more powerful.

Jason opened the glass door and walked across the marble lobby floor bypassing the tellers behind their windows. He approached a man in his thirties, about Jason's age. He was thin or maybe that was a wiry kind of fitness under a grey suit. He had black hair cut short and glasses. The nameplate on his desk said 'Peng Shào, Assistant Manager - New Accounts' in both English and Chinese. Peng looked up when he sensed someone approaching his desk.

"Cousin Shào," said Jason.

"Good morning, Lujiang, what are you doing here?" Peng knew Lujiang didn't have any accounts with the bank.

"Is there somewhere we can talk in private?" Jason asked calmly though his insides were flip flopping about what he was going to ask Peng to do.

"Of course," said Peng. "Follow me." He rose from his chair and lead from the main bank floor to a stairway. They climbed up while talking about the weather. Peng led them to a small office, he opened the door and gestured for Jason to sit at a small table. A window looked out onto the busy street outside. Peng sat down across from Jason, he was wary. "What is it you need? Why are you asking for privacy?"

Jason opened the satchel and pulled out the ledgers. He slid them across the table for Peng to inspect. "I need to withdraw the money from these accounts. Almost all of the money." Jason's tone was serious but a degree of nervousness in his voice belied the calm façade.

Peng opened the first binder and quickly took in all the salient details. He repeated the process with the second and third binders. "These don't appear to be your accounts," said Peng diplomatically. He recognized the name on the account. Most anyone above a peasant knew of her by reputation alone.

"Yes." Jason said. "I need the money withdrawn from the accounts, nonetheless."

Peng scrutinized Lujiang for a long minute. His bank was not unknown to this type of under the table activity. "To move this kind of cash is a somewhat specialized transaction. The amounts are too large to withdraw in one lump sum, it's better to make it a number of withdrawals and checks. Say one thousand or more." The bank had a few questionable 'businesses' which needed clandestine movement of money.

Jason's eyebrows rose in surprise. "One thousand? I need this done by end of business today if possible."

Peng leaned back and steepled his fingers in front of his mouth, pursing his lips. Should he ask what was going on or simply do it? "That's very difficult to do." Now was the time to offer his pitch. The service he could provide was special. Few would be able to accomplish the task. He would make a reasonable request since he was doing all the work and taking all of the risk. "I can do this by the end of today. It will take a lot of effort, and for my effort I will be recompensed." Peng remembered the numbers from the books in his head. "I want three percent of the gross amount. I will have the rest moved to a numbered Swiss account." He did the mental calculation of the time difference between Beijing and Zurich in his head. Beijing was seven hours ahead or seventeen behind depending on how you looked at the day. It was after nine a.m. which meant it was after two a.m. Zurich time. But international banking never sleeps. He would be able to take care of these transactions. It was simpler than he told Lujiang, most of the process was electronic. He just needed Lujiang to think it was difficult to earn his three percent.

Jason was amazed his 'cousin' was going along with this scheme. "Can it be more than one account? Make one of the accounts about five million US." That was the money for him and the orphanage. "The rest put in two or three accounts, whatever is easiest."

Peng nodded. "Leave the books here. I need the tracking numbers to the accounts and the balances."

"Whatever you require."

"Excellent. I'll call you tonight after it's done. Meet me after the bank closes and I'll give you the account numbers and passcodes. And I'll give you back the books. I suggest you burn them."

"Of course. Thank you, cousin." Jason and Peng got up from the table and shook hands. He left the bank wondering if this was so easy because the bank laundered money for the Chinese mafia. An honest bank wouldn't be willing to do something illegal. At least not an honest banker.

****

Awake.

John sat against the wall of the hotel closet. Still alive. He was a little surprised a maid hadn't stumbled onto him dead in the closet. Nothing happened during the daylight hours to change that. Would he always be surprised when he wakes up? As a human when he went to sleep he took for granted the fact he would wake in the morning and he'd always been right in his assumption. No one goes to bed thinking they are going to die. The past three nights John became insensate not knowing if he would wake. So many things could happen to him if someone found him. They could try to help him. People trying to help by taking his catatonic body to an ambulance would cause combustion. His world was becoming oddly dangerous.

John exited the closet and looked around the room. Everything seemed the way he'd left it. No maid had come into clean the room per his instructions. His made bed was tight and immaculately made.

He walked to the phone and called Jason. After three rings the phone was picked up. Jason said hello in Mandarin.

"Jason, it's John."

"John!" After the initial surprise Jason lowered his voice to a conspiratorial tone. "Do you know what these ledgers are?"

"Yes."

"She's a patron of the orphanage!" Jason protested. She was a good woman who adopted the older children when no one else would.

"I know, but she's responsible for the nightly killings in the streets Beijing." John didn't say how she was responsible. That information would veer wildly into surreal territory.

"What? How is that possible? There have been multiple murders in a single night," commented Jason.

"She has help, lots of help." John's tone was serious.

"Do you know what you're saying?"

"I do," John said. "Did you do what I asked? Did you get the money from the accounts?"

There was a pause on the phone. "Yes. The money has been removed from her accounts. It's now in several Swiss bank accounts."

John was surprised his request had been accomplished so easily. He didn't know how but assumed Jason's 'cousin' was involved in darker banking than is normal in business. "Good. Thanks. Did you take money for the orphanage?"

"Yes."

Did John hear a note of guilt or shame in Jason's voice? He couldn't be sure but he instinctively knew the man had done questionably legal actions to help the orphanage survive and take care of the kids. "What was your cut?"

"Five million dollars like you said," said Jason, his tone was flat. He wondered if John would object to the large amount.

"You can use it. But don't do anything foolish. Don't buy the kids a yacht or anything."

"How did you do this? Why did you do this?" Jason asked.

John didn't answer immediately. He needed to draw her out so he could kill her. She had no reason to seek him out and after killing all her girls she would disappear unless she had a good reason to surface.

Her money. If she remained in Beijing she'd be wary of him. She needed a reason to find him.

"I'll be over in an hour to get the account information from you," said John, ignoring the questions. He hung up the phone. He showered and changed clothes.

John was hungry.

Chapter 29
Xiulan Returns

The next night Xiulan approached her house with a sense of apprehension but her haughty face didn't betray the emotions underneath. What would she find upon returning home? The American was surprisingly lethal as a vampire. He'd killed her girls, but they were unarmed and uneducated. She would have to train the next ones she turned, they needed to fight better. Ambush would work when overwhelming unsuspecting pedestrians, facing an armed opponent it lead to their slaughter.

She took out a key to the large door and unlocked the stout lock. She pushed open the heavy door easily and paused to look before stepping inside the walls. In front of her was another wall, to the left was another door, one leading to the inner courtyard and communal living space. The inner door wasn't normally locked. She moved into the small courtyard shutting and locking the exterior door behind her.

She opened the next door and scanned the courtyard. There was a familiar scent in the air, and flies were in the air around the gardener's shed. She walked over and opened the door. There was a buzz as the resting flies took flight. A swarm lifted off the bodies and cascaded randomly in the darkness. Her lip snarled at the smell and the sight. Inside were the eight bodies of her girls. He hid them for some reason. She would have burned them. Burning rubbish was allowed and within the walls no one would see bodies being consumed by fire.

She shut the shed door and walked across the courtyard noticing the stones were cleaned of blood. Xiulan moved to the doors to the underground caverns and pulled them open. They fell to the sides with a resounding bang. From her right she heard a human noise in the caretaker house. She'd deal with them later. She wanted to see her children first.

Stepping into the cellar she smelled it again; death, blood. She moved silently and quickly down the stairs. The bare bulbs were still blazing toward the ceiling. The smell of blood got stronger as she got closer to the roughly hewn cavern. She opened the door and saw the carnage.

Her remaining girls were dead near the door to her crypt. She couldn't be sure if this pile of gore, limbs, heads, torn up torsos, and parts were all of the children. The bodies were so mutilated it would be hard to do a correct body count. She crossed through the chamber to her crypt. She could tell they were killed by bullets. The expended brass was littered all around the entrance to her crypt. On the floor were three AK-47s.

She stared impassively at the bodies of the girls. She was sad, it would take a long time to replace them. The inside of her crypt was turned upside down. The murderer had searched it. She noticed the large military pack with cash was missing. He was gone but the fire she felt for revenge still raged in her. She would find him and kill him.

When she emerged from below she went to the caretaker's house. Technically all the buildings were hers, the caretaker and his wife resided in the smaller one. The man was a relative, one of her great, great, great, something grandchildren, over one hundred years later made her uncertain how many generations that was. It wasn't important.

Xiulan found the two caretakers tied up and secured to their bed. Having been restrained for over a day made the bed soiled and them thirsty and hungry. There were signs they struggled against their bonds, but failed to release themselves. Wrists were raw and dried blood stained the ropes.

The man's eyes widened when she strode in the room. He tried to talk thru the gag. She came directly over to him and tore off the gag.

"How could you let this happen?" she screamed.

The man's voice was hoarse and dry in his throat. "Ancestor! He took us by surprise. He was like you. I couldn't do anything to stop him."

"Fool!" Xiulan raged. "All my girls are dead. My house has been defiled, you are useless!" She yelled down at him, but made no move to untie him.

"Ancestor, I'm sorry. I have served you faithfully for twenty years. Please untie me so I may fix everything that is wrong," he pleaded. He'd seen her angry but her rage was never directed at him. The fury suffusing her face scared him more than anything he'd ever seen before. She looked demonic.

"You have failed me." Xiulan swooped down and bit his jugular. Blood started pumping into her mouth. She was hungry and she needed to feed and the useless man needed to die.

He cried out for a moment in pain and fear but her hand covered his mouth to muffle the sound. She drank deeply, there was no reason to be dainty or careful, he was guilty of crimes and the punishment was death. His wife bound and gagged next to him was frozen in wide-eyed fear. Was she going to die next?

She sensed he was close to death and stopped feeding. She looked at the woman next to the dying man. Her need for blood was sated but her anger remained. The woman should have done something. Xiulan reached over the body of her progeny, many generations removed, and snapped the woman's neck. She wasn't being merciful; the woman wasn't worth any more effort than a broken neck.

Leaving the caretaker's house she made a mental note to replace the mattress on the bed. It was ruined now if it hadn't been from the ordeal of their captivity.

Xiulan inspected her north house, the one she fled through twenty four hours before. If she had gone to the office and pulled a rifle from the cabinet to confront him the girls would still be alive and her house wouldn't be defiled. Her decision to flee cost her dearly. The rooms looked mostly intact, all except for the office. The desk was searched and the cabinet with the rifles was wide open. Obviously he pulled the guns out of the cabinet and used them on her children.

She sat in the leather chair and rolled it close to the desk. A clean white sheet of paper was on top of the piles of documents and files, carefully placed so she would notice it first. On the paper four words were written in English.

I HAVE YOUR MONEY

Xiulan's eyes flashed, she tore open the lower desk drawer. The large bank registers, check books, were missing. The American had stolen her records and her check books. They were gone, but he'd need to get to the money in the accounts. She wasn't sure if he had the help to do business in the daytime. Such a thing took time to create. He'd been a vampire for two days, he was new in Beijing, and didn't have the support structure necessary to access her money. He needed human minions and he didn't have any.

Or did he? He hadn't time to cultivate human help. If he knew anyone in Beijing, would he trust them with the information? Revealing his new nature would be difficult. He said he'd only been in China a week. If he knew anyone they'd probably be at the orphanage. Someone there might know how to reach him, know where he is staying, know something.

If the note was true and he was successful taking her money, Xiulan needed to retrieve her fortune. She'd worked carefully to accumulate such a vast sum. Starting over from scratch was possible, but it would be simpler to get the money back then kill the man. She pushed back from the desk and looked at the open cabinet, her mind taking a mental inventory. She walked over and carefully counted. All the rifles were accounted for, including the three down in the cavern. The handguns were another story. Two were missing and she wasn't sure but extra clips and bullets for the 9mm guns.

He was armed. She would need to be careful. He didn't need to leave her a note. He was trying to draw her out. Stealing all of her money was certain to make her expose herself. He intended to kill her like he killed all of her kids. Was he successful, had he drained her accounts?

Xiulan dug into the desk drawers and found her address book for business matters. She dialed the phone and reached the first bank she used in Hong Kong, an institution away from the reach of China, at least until 1997 when the United Kingdom returned the territory to China. Because Hong Kong was a financial hub for the Far East the bank had bankers available at hours conducive to businesses in the UK and the USA.

The phone rang and was swiftly answered, "Feng Wa Bank, how may I direct your call?"

"Account services," replied Xiulan.

"Please hold." Music played on the line for a minute while the call was transferred.

"Accounts."

"I need to check on balances for my account," said Xiulan, nervous of the possibility the American was successful.

"What are the account numbers and passwords?"

Xiulan read off the account numbers and the corresponding numbers which allowed her to transact business over the phone.

"One minute please." The man said in Mandarin. She could hear the sound of swift keystrokes on a computer key board. He read off the last four digits of the account and the remaining balances in each account. She had less than one thousand Yuan remaining in the account. Xiulan was silent for a long moment. The man sensed something was amiss. "Is the amount incorrect?" he asked.

Xiulan took a calming breath. "I've been robbed. My account has been fraudulently accessed and drained."

"I see." The man could be heard typing on the keyboard. "Are you sure? This wasn't one or two transactions. There are several hundred transactions of smaller amounts which is what kept it under the radar, for lack of a better term. If it had been millions there would be a holding period for the funds."

"Hundreds? How is that possible?" She asked through clenched teeth.

"It seems to have been spread out over a half a dozen banks and the destinations were several accounts."

"What can you tell me about the accounts?"

"Not much," he paused briefly. "The accounts are Swiss and have no names, only numbers."

"This is fraud. I've been robbed, can't you do something?" Xiulan was practically screaming into the phone. The man on the other end was more and more frightened. He imagined her reaching through the phone and tearing out his heart.

"Let me transfer you to the fraud department. Please hold."

The music came back on the line. After an eternity of fifteen seconds the phone was answered. "Fraud Department, Mr. Hangzou speaking."

Xiulan talked with the fraud department for half an hour. The situation was unusual as the amounts were ultimately substantial but removed in small amounts.

Beyond substantial, it was a fortune. She was instructed to contact the Beijing police. Once that step had been done she should contact the bank again. Since the money had been transferred electronically it would be very hard to recover. It wasn't just reversing the electronic steps which drained the accounts. This was harder; especially since it involved the Swiss who were known for their secrecy. Nations, clandestine organizations, criminals, religions and billionaires used the Swiss to hide or move money.

"Follow the steps I've laid out and get back to us. We will see what we can do to get the money back in your account." Mr. Hangzou said, his voice was soothing but did nothing to quell her growing rage. In his humble opinion the woman on the phone was thoroughly fucked, but his professional obligations to the bank didn't allow him to elaborate on his opinions.

"Thank you. I'll call you tomorrow night." Her voice was calm, calm and murderous. She called her two other banks and learned quickly that those accounts had been liquidated in a similar way. After repeating the same conversation with the other banks and bankers she hung up the phone then flipped the large, heavy desk over as if it weighed nothing. Her rage was expended on the walls and contents of the office.

She would find the priest and end him. She looked at a clock on the wall. It was after nine. She had most of the night to track him down and she knew just the place to start.

CHAPTER 31
JOHN'S DILEMMA

John stood for a minute considering feeding. He never thought much about eating before. It was a simple process, especially in the States. If you had money you bought food at a store or a restaurant. The animals you were eating were dispatched in some way and delivered to the kitchen or table processed and clean of any moral judgments. That luxury was over. His meals were walking around. They felt pain and fear and he would be the cause of their distress.

He needed to figure out how other vampires did it. How do they feed without losing their humanity? Or do they all lose their humanity? The vampires in Rome were brutal but only to the guilty. Malcolm in Las Vegas figured out how to feed without killing. Madame Xiulan was another story. There seemed to be no last vestige of humanity left in her, the fact she turned little girls into vampires and trained them to kill and steal illustrated the point. .

John walked down the stairs to the lobby. The night desk clerk recognized him and nodded to him. "Same instructions as before, sir?" he asked before John got too far away.

"Yes, please," John replied. "Everything has been great so far, thank you."

"Very good, sir." The man said, it was a reflexive phrase, one he'd said thousands of times. It was an acknowledgement and polite dismissal. The night clerk looked down and continued working as John exited the lobby to the cold, damp night. The moon hung low in the sky a sly sideways smile that seemed to mock John's predicament.

It was after six p.m. He looked around at the sparse traffic and the abundant bikes and pedestrians. Finding a meal was easy, having it in private, discreetly, was another thing. He would wait until he could find a … victim . . . safely. The word bothered him. Victim. For him to eat, someone had to hurt, and he would see it, feel the panic, smell the fear.

He pushed the thought away and started walking to the orphanage. Jason was waiting for him with the accounts which held Xiulan's money. He knew she would come looking for him where she first met him. It was a dangerous calculation. Last night he didn't have time to think of a place for her to meet him and write it on the paper. He was looking to enrage her, make her leave the safety of her compound. When he wrote it he wasn't sure he would be able to take her money. He wanted her to come to him and her money was leverage.

As John walked the streets he noticed soldiers in pairs or groups of four patrolling the streets. He noticed their guns. They held rifles in their hands and in holsters on their belts were pistols like the two he had back at his hotel room. It could be a coincidence, or Xiulan had her demon girls kill soldiers and take their weapons. If that were the case the Chinese government and military would be in a panic. They'd be worried the guns would fall into the hands of people sympathetic to the demonstrators from Tiananmen Square the previous year. The trouble back then was bad, it could be worse if any new demonstrators were armed.

John arrived at the orphanage and rang the bell by the front gate. He waited for someone to leave the main building and come to open the ornate red door. After a minute he heard the bolts slide open and the locks unlock. When he came by in the morning he climbed over the high wall and entered the building easily to wake Jason. He was being discreet now.

The large door opened and Jason stepped out over the low ceremonial threshold. "You rang the bell like a civilized person. Why didn't you break in like this morning?" Jason said, he was still shocked and a little angry John had disturbed him in such a scary way.

"I'm sorry for that. I didn't have time to rouse you from sleep normally." John said as they walked to the large converted house.

They climbed the wood steps to the porch surrounding the building. Jason opened the front door and motioned for John to enter. He led them to the kitchen. "Please sit, I'll be a moment." Jason entered his office and returned with a piece of paper in his hands. "I did what you asked." He held out the folded sheet of paper, John took it and opened it up. There were three numbered accounts in three different banks, the amounts in the accounts, the sixteen digit passcodes, and phone numbers to access the accounts.

"Thank you. I'm surprised you did it in a day," said John.

"Quite frankly, so am I." Jason admitted. "I'm now wondering how honest my 'cousin' is."

John frowned. Were the numbers real? He would have to call to verify the information on the paper was true. "Is this the only copy? Did you take some as well?"

"Yes to both questions, and my cousin took a small percentage for his trouble and risk." Jason made a motion with his hands and held them up in front of them, a dismissive gesture to say his hands are clean. "How do you say? I'm washing my hands of this whole thing." He stepped passed the doorway again and came back with a canvas bag which he handed to John. "These are the bank books you left me. I suggest you destroy them."

"Great. I'll take care of these." John took the canvas bag. "I'm headed back to my hotel, call if you need me." John said making certain the last comment registered with the man. The comment seemed off handed, like it was no importance, but it was crucial he remember. "Thanks for doing this. I really appreciate it."

"You're going to have to tell me how you know what you know about Madame Xiulan."

"I just know," said John.

"We need to go to the police or the army. They are patrolling the streets at night now. We can stop the killing," implored Jason.

"I think it will stop. Taking her money will stop her," said John. "I'm going to go. I'm starving."

"Come eat with us. We have plenty for dinner. One more mouth won't make a difference."

John stared at Jason. The man couldn't figure out the expression on the priest's face. Was it wistful? Was it desperate?

"Thanks. I've got to figure out my own supper," John said, a small wry smile on his lips, the tone of his voice was gentle. "See you later. You have the number of my hotel if you need me." John knew he'd probably see him sooner rather than later. He was making a dangerous calculation and knowingly putting people at risk. Not people, children. Orphans. And Jason. Xiulan would come looking for John. Unfortunately she'd only ever met him at the orphanage before he invaded her house. She'd want her money returned, and he had it. He prayed she would take a course of action which didn't harm anyone. She could make a simple phone call to resolve the issue.

John walked back towards the hotel in the cold night air, and despite having heightened senses, the cold didn't bother him much. He acknowledged it but wasn't uncomfortable. It was another surprising change to his body, one which was welcome and would be handy when he got back to Colorado. Would he find the same reaction to heat?

His pace was brisk and his route meandered. He was hungry and needed to feed, but how and where? The night was still early and people were still out on the streets. Alongside the street was the royal canal the Emperor used to sail to the Summer Palace. The water way was shallow but deep enough for the royal barges that went from the Forbidden City to the Summer Palace, a journey of some twenty miles. The lake at the other end was three meters deep and man-made. The dirt excavated was piled up creating a mountain near the lake.

John glanced at the water shimmering lazily in the darkness, catching the light from the distant moon. A lone figure was at the side of the canal in the darkness, a fishing pole in his hands. John stopped and looked at the solitary man. His hunger moved him forward, off the road and into the darkness, stalking the oblivious man.

As he approached his teeth flicked out, unexpected and sharp. It was instinctual reaction from his body. His tongue involuntarily moved up and caressed the unfamiliar shapes, testing the deadly points. John paused behind the man, a dark shadow in the inky night, and silently set down the canvas bag. Fishing at night was foolish when there are vampires around. John scanned the area one last time to be sure he wasn't being watched, then he struck.

His hands closed on the man's throat from behind. He squeezed hard enough to constrict the blood flow to his brain, the man passed out in seconds. John released him and laid him down on the side of the canal. He checked his breath, the man's respiration created swirls of steam that corkscrewed in the cold air. Good, he hadn't killed him by accident. John lifted the man's wrist and cut him with a fingernail. Blood welled up. He fastened his mouth over the wound and drank. He watched as he did so. He didn't want to be seen even in the secluded area by the canal.

John fed his hunger and sealed the wound so the man wouldn't bleed out. He looked at his watch and picked up the bag. Eight o'clock. He wanted to get back to his hotel. He would get a call soon, he was almost certain of that.

The prone man would be alright. That was what John told himself. It was what he needed to tell himself. He was going to have to figure out how to feed. His conscious and uncertainty about the human body might lead him to starvation. He needed to learn what he could do with a … human so they don't die and aren't damaged in the process. There it was; he was beginning to think like a predator and humans were his food source. The realization frightened him.

John's victim woke an hour later cold and confused. His neck hurt and his right wrist itched strangely. The fishing pole was by his side, and the string of fish was still in the water of the canal where he left them. He must have fallen asleep. Despite his heavy coat the man was chilled deeply but fine. When he stood up he was light headed for a moment. Strange, he felt very tired even after his nap.

Chapter 32
Xiulan Calls

Back at the hotel John nodded to the night clerk and said good evening in English since his Mandarin was embarrassing to non-existent. The clerk replied in English and thought nothing of it. It was not uncommon for the guests, especially the Americans, to forgo trying to speak Chinese, it was a difficult language.

John climbed the stairs to his room and opened the door with the key on the plastic fob. He stood in the doorway and flicked on the light. He inspected the room from the doorway to be sure nothing had been moved, no one had been in it. He listened carefully. He heard other people on his floor, the sound of televisions, his room was silent and unoccupied. He shut the door, flicked the dead bolt as well slid the chain in the slot. He was playing a very dangerous game with a lethal opponent; one that wouldn't hesitate to kill him.

John was putting Jason and the children at the orphanage in danger. He was heartsick at the possibility of what she could do. He had to get her out in the open. How he was going to kill her was the big question.

After eleven o'clock the phone by the bed rang disturbing the silence. John didn't answer immediately. He didn't want to seem like he was waiting for the phone to ring. He picked up after the third ring.

"Come to the orphanage now with my money, or everyone here dies." Xiulan was practically yelling.

Her voice was loud on the phone and John imagined the volume in the house. He hoped none of the girls were awake to hear her. Some of them had to understand English.

John recognized her voice. It would be foolish to agree. "No. I'll meet you in Tiananmen Square. By the Soldiers, Workers, Farmers, Students statue at three a.m."

"I may kill everyone here and meet you in Tiananmen square, then kill you, and take my money back." Her voice was a malevolent hiss on the phone, a sound filled with poison and anger.

John considered his options for a quick second before speaking. He tried to make his voice match the lethality of hers. "Before we meet I'm going to call Lujiang. If anyone at the orphanage is harmed or killed, any man, woman, or child has a hair out of place, I'm gone with your money, like smoke in the wind." John was as serious as he'd ever been. He believed her threat, she needed to believe his.

She would indeed kill everyone if he didn't do something to stop her. He wasn't there to be an immediate threat, but he had her money. The only thing keeping them safe was her millions in his hands. She was a special kind of evil, something he never imagined before. An adversary like no one he'd opposed before. She was a powerful being without remorse and completely unlike any of the other vampires he met before.

Xiulan was quiet for a moment as if she was planning.

He took her hesitation as a chance to continue. "If you harm them I'm gone. I'll live a very nice, comfortable life for a very long time and when you've forgotten me I'm going to come back and kill you. I'll burn down everything you love," John said though he doubted she loved anything. "Hell, I may burn your compound tonight if you piss me off."

"I don't trust you," she said.

"You shouldn't because I don't trust you either," he replied. "You kill soldiers and steal their guns. The PRC wouldn't like that." He needed her to fear what he knew and what governmental danger he could expose her to. Even she feared the government on some level. Wealth and power wouldn't save her if the PRC descended on her life. If he knew that, what else might he know as he searched her house?

She said nothing.

"Fine. I'll meet you. 3a.m." She turned her body to block the human's view of the phone and pressed the disconnect button. The human was watching but couldn't see her motion. "How do I know I can trust you?" she asked though she disconnected the call. She surreptitiously pressed the redial button. The phone rang once and was answered.

"South Seas Hotel," The night clerk answered. "How can I direct your call?"

"Fine. 3 a.m." She loudly hung up the phone. The night clerk heard the dial tone and hung up, confused.

She knew where he was, she heard the human ask for the priest's room. She faced Jason and thought for a second. She wouldn't kill him tonight. Just in case. There was time to exact her revenge on him later. Maybe tomorrow night.

Xiulan swept from the room and left the orphanage. Jason let out a slow breath. Hearing one side of the conversation scared him to death, possibly his and all the children's deaths. He quickly went around the entire building to lock all the doors and secure all the windows, even the windows on the upper floors.

The door exploded inward, the door frame splintered from the tremendous, instantaneous force exerted on the wood. A blur entered, John was lying on the bed unprepared for the attack. He was milliseconds too slow, taken completely by surprise. Xiulan was on top of him her hands on his throat, sharp talon-like fingers digging into his neck. When they pulled out she would shred his neck. "Where's my money?" she asked, waiting for an answer then she would slay him.

Desperately John lashed out with his right hand, fingers separated in a V, and he struck Xiulan in the eyes. His aim was hurried but he felt one of his fingers hit her in the eye, the other struck above the left eye near the supraorbital ridge. She shrieked in pain and released his throat without rending his flesh. She covered her eyes with her hands. John took the moment to land a vicious right cross to the side of her face. She fell off him to the left, rolled and came up eight feet away. Her right eye was ruined, blood streamed down her face, a look of fear in her remaining eye.

John rolled to his right and put the bed was between them, blood seeped out of the wounds on his neck. Behind him was the ruined door. He could turn and bolt into the hallway, he might be able to make it down the stairs and out the front doors.

The information she demanded was in the pocket of the jacket he was wearing. A gun he stole from her was in the drawer of the nightstand next to where she crouched malevolently. The other gun was on the floor of the closet. He needed her to move, and he was aware the noise they were making would bring other people. In this moment, curiosity would get onlookers killed.

"Give me my money!" she snarled again, this time her voice was colored by rage and pain.

"Okay." John held up his hands in a placating way, showing her he was unarmed and trying to keep her from attacking again. How did she find him? Did she kill Jason? Threaten his girls? His imagination was racing on the question when he needed to focus on the raging beast standing in front of him.

He needed to get to his gun. They were in two different spots in the room and unfortunately not on his person. The one in the closet seemed a dead end. If he fumbled for the gun on the floor he'd be trapped. The one in the nightstand seemed the prudent option, it left him with escape routes, either out the door or out the window.

At the gun range he was a bad shot with the pistol, but that was at one hundred feet. She was less than two strides away. There was no way he could miss. Not true. He knew she had supernatural speed, but now so did he. She had an injured eye. A speck of dust on the eyeball was painful, having an eye gouged out must be excruciating. "I'll get you the paper with the new accounts." He started to move.

"No," she said. John stopped moving. "Point to where it is," she hissed.

John nodded. He had one chance to bluff and calculated how fast he could get to the weapon in the nightstand. He should've rested the gun on top of the small cabinet. He would have to get across the bed and open the drawer before she could hurt him.

John pointed to the dresser across the room from the gun. "Top drawer, under the clothing."

There were sounds in the hallway. Inquisitive people had left their rooms to see what the disturbance was. Xiulan would kill them all or take a hostage if it gave her an advantage. She moved to the dresser. When she noticed a face in the doorway she said something in Chinese. The man fled.

While she was distracted for the moment, John vaulted over the bed, tore open the drawer with his left hand and scooped out the loaded gun with his right. He pointed it at her. Nothing. The trigger didn't move. The safety was engaged. Xiulan lunged at him, he flicked the safety off with his thumb and fired point blank into her torso. The noise was deafening in the small room. The bullet torc into her, missing her heart but ripping into the upper left side of her torso, and out her back. Before John could fire again she slashed him across the chest with her nails, his jacket and shirt tore. So did flesh. Blood flowed out of the ragged wounds. Xiulan bolted right, curled into a ball and hit the blackout drapes over the window.

Glass broke, the drapes bulged out the window but didn't pull free from the rod. She rolled out of the drapes and plunged to the roof below. The fabric kept her safe from lacerations but as she spun she couldn't correct her fall so she hit the roof curled into a ball. Groaning Xiulan uncoiled and staggered upright. She'd broken bones, possibly crushed her shoulder where she hit. She would need blood to repair her injuries, and she knew just where to go.

Pain ignited as he touched the cuts on his torso to see how deep the wounds were. Blood welled out of the furrows in his flesh, they were bad for a human, but John was no longer human. The dark jacket and shirt hid the blood staining them. He heard the window break and turned to see her fall, spinning like a ball. He couldn't let her escape. He rushed to the window, pulled the drapes aside, and saw her land. The way she got up he knew she was injured more than the bullet wound. She ran as best she could and dropped off the roof of the hotel, landing in front of the glass lobby doors.

The night clerk saw a flash of movement and was shocked by the sight outside the doors, a woman, bloody and bent was hobbling down the stairs and out to the street with a surprisingly fast gait.

John ran to the closet, retrieved the gun on the floor and ran to the window. He didn't stop or slow; he'd seen the terrain of the roof two stories below and was prepared. He jumped out the broken window with a gun in each hand and as he fell hoped his new body could survive the landing. He'd jumped over walls without a problem and prayed he wouldn't shatter both ankles.

He hit the roof and stumbled a little not expecting the intensity of the impact, but otherwise he survived unscathed. Maybe being a vampire wasn't so bad. He turned the way Xiulan fled and ran after her.

The night clerk was opening the glass door to the hotel to see about the woman when another figure landed in front of him and sprinted into the cold, damp night. He was about to step out further when the front desk phone rang. He hurried back to answer and noticed all the lines of the phone were lit up, blinking. "Front desk," he said.

"There was a gunshot!"

"One of the room doors was kicked open!"

"I heard glass break and I think I heard a gun!"

The night clerk grabbed his keys and locked the front doors. He climbed the stairs to the third floor. There were a number of guest in the hallway clustered around an open door. He recognized the room. It was the strange American's room. "Please step back. I need you to return to your rooms, I'll take care of this! Now!" he said authoritatively. Several people moved away, a couple people went back to their rooms but watched from the doorway.

The night clerk's mouth dropped open when he arrived at the American's door. It wasn't open, it was off the hinges, the doorjamb was shattered, wood was splintered on the floor. "Everyone, please step back!" he demanded. He cautiously entered the room, all was quiet. The room was cold from the jagged maw of the broken window letting in the night air. There was a drawer pulled out laying on the floor like it had exploded forth in an arc. A red dripping stain was on the right wall, blood spatter from a gunshot? There was a hole was high up in the wall.

He took in the whole scene. The bedspread was disturbed, askew from where it should have been, like there was a struggle atop it. The sparse room didn't look like it was occupied. The man's luggage looked mostly packed, he hadn't put clothes in the dresser like a long term visitor would. On the floor of the closet was a blanket from the bed, wadded up. On the top shelf of the closet was a plump PLA military backpack.

He needed to call the police. He couldn't shut the door so he shooed all the onlookers away then pulled out a handkerchief and picked up the room phone carefully. He dialed out and called the police. Then he placed a call to the banquet manager, there had been an event earlier and the staff was still tending to the ballroom, clearing tables and whatnot. He needed someone to wait in the room for the police to arrive, and he needed to be downstairs when they did.

Chapter 34
The Search for Evil

John landed on the stairs of the hotel. Xiulan was nowhere in sight. He looked down and saw drops of blood leading down the steps and to the right. Where would she go? A terrible thought crashed into his brain. She threatened to kill everyone at the orphanage. She had two options that he could see. She could go back home tonight to recover, or she could exact revenge for all she lost. Knowing what little he did of her, he guessed she would choose the latter. Now she was injured and enraged, she had more of a reason to keep her promise. She was hurt and needed blood. Beyond that she needed revenge.

And there was another reason to go. In the same way he used her money to draw her out into the open, by going to the orphanage, she was drawing him out. He wouldn't let her slaughter innocent children. She knew that and so did he. A more frightening thought came to him; she wasn't going to the orphanage because she slaughtered them before she attacked his hotel. Could she be so evil? Were all of them already dead because of his hubris?

In her injured condition he would be able to make it to the orphanage on foot first. If she took a cab, he'd be too late. But what cab would pick up a woman covered in blood? John stowed the guns in the pockets of the ruined jacket and closed it up as best he could. He only had the rounds in the guns. He didn't think to grab the extra magazines. He didn't think he'd follow her out of a third story window either. There were sixteen bullets in one gun and fifteen in the other, and one canny, hard to kill vampire running from him.

John started running. He followed her out the window abruptly, without money, so he couldn't hail a taxi. But he figured Xiulan couldn't get a taxi either being grievously injured. If a cab wouldn't stop for her, they wouldn't stop for him. The blood was dark on the shirt and jacket. If they hadn't been torn he might appear normal.

So he ran, the weight of the guns bounced in the side pockets of the jacket. His hands kept them from bouncing out as he raced through the darkness. He was desperate. He had to be faster than the injured vampire. Many people could die if he failed. Children. Children could die.

By now John knew the way. He ran quickly but not at his top speed. There were still people out on the streets and there were police and soldiers around. To people he passed he hoped he looked like some crazy fitness fanatic westerner and not some panicked person trying to prevent a massacre.

He wondered why his actions led to people dying in massacres. His intentions were honorable. He wanted to fight evil and save humanity. That desire always seemed to come with a body count. And now he was a vampire, the situation became even more muddled. He was the menace he originally wanted to fight. The universe was a chaotic and ironic place.

As he ran without growing tired or sweaty he marveled at the body his mind now inhabited. It wasn't a nefarious thing to become a vampire. It's how one used the power and abilities. Like Stan Lee said from the mouth of Spider-man, "with great power comes great responsibility." John felt responsible for the kids at the orphanage. His meddling put them in danger. He needed to atone for his actions. He needed to stop her if he could.

The orphanage loomed ahead of him. Its uncharacteristic building silhouette was dark against the miasma of the night sky. It was a large four story building which was left over from the English influence.

John slowed to a walking pace when the house was before him, and looked around. He listened carefully. Up ahead at his destination he heard faint cries of distress. Muffled screams and plaintive sobbing reached his sensitive ears. Had Xiulan somehow reached the place before him? It was unthinkable as hurt as she was that she would be able to beat him to the orphanage.

He quickly jogged the perimeter, aware of the people on the street, anxious, afraid of what was happening on the interior of the building. When he had a clear moment at the back of the building he vaulted over the iron fence and landed quietly. On cat's feet he quickly crossed to the back door and found it ajar, the wood of the door jamb splintered, the heavy door split in half.

She forced her way in like she broke into his hotel. He listened for a moment, the sounds were coming from upstairs. He followed the sound in the dark building. As he moved swiftly the floor creaked and gave way under his careful passage, the grumble of the building sounded loud to his ears. If she was paying attention she'd know someone was coming.

At a stairwell off of the kitchen the sound of crying descended from upstairs. John pulled a gun out of his pocket and walked up the stairs, hugging the wall hoping the old wood was sturdier at the edge and would make less noise. The sounds were coming from children, girls. He could tell by the timber and pitch of the voices even if he couldn't understand the language. Pain is a universal tongue.

At the second level the sound was still coming from above him. Carefully he moved up the stairs to the third floor. There were no lights on but he could see well enough. An old wood door was open at the end of a corridor. John padded hastily to the end, the sounds of crying children covering his treading feet.

He pushed open the door, the gun leading the way into the room. Xiulan was standing in the middle of a large room that had ten beds. The only light was what moonlight filtered through the thin curtains. Her mouth was latched to the neck of a small girl who was limp in her powerful arms. In a second he took in the scene before she noticed him.

There were six girls huddled in a corner, fearfully sobbing, tears streaking their faces as they watched the monster feeding on their friends. She'd fed on three already, the limp bodies discarded carelessly, like bloody rag dolls tossed on a bed. Xiulan's luminous eyes flicked up and saw him enter, gun raised. As he pulled the trigger she spun, the gun flashed in the darkness and the sound made the cowering girls scream. Xiulan used the child as a shield, with blinding speed, her body went one way and she moved the child into the path of the bullet. The round hit the small body, it shook soundlessly with the impact. Horrified John paused for a flash of a moment. Xiulan dropped the body and rushed him. She was moving forward before the body crumpled on the ground.

From her motion and speed it seemed consuming the blood from three or four girls had helped heal her. She didn't move with any impairment from the fall from his window and the bullet hole in her shoulder didn't seem to be a problem either. Her arms were forward, taloned hands reaching out to strike at him.

John backed up out the door and ran down the hall. Retreating seemed the wisest thing to do. He felt her hands dig into his shoulders and her weight was forcing him forward. Their momentum crashed their bodies into the railing of the stairs. The old wood broke and they tumbled forward to the stairs below. The impact shook her hands free from his back but they clawed and slashed at each other as they tumbled down the remaining stairs to the second floor.

The gun disappeared from John's hand in the fall. He didn't see or hear where it fell. At the bottom of the stairs he kicked her torso with his right leg and rolled away in an effort to gain his feet under him. She was moved several yards by the force of his kick and skidded to a halt. John reached down with his right hand, picked up a spindle from the broken railing and held it before him like a club. Maybe he could use it as a stake and plunge it through her heart.

She got to her feet and growled like a dangerous animal. Words weren't necessary. There was no accord to be reached, no negotiation to end the fight. There was only one way for it to cease. One of them was going to die, and the contest to decide which had just begun.

Xiulan ran at him. Before she reached him she jumped over him and landed on the stairs behind him, spinning she kicked him in the back. His back arched from the blow as he was propelled forward. Using the momentum rather than fighting it he bent forward, tucked and rolled. He rolled down the stairs and came up in front of a large window which looked out to the street. As he turned she barreled into him. They crashed out the window, their force started a rotation in the air. She would be on the bottom when they hit the ground.

She let out an explosive grunt as all the air in her lungs exited upon impact. Her arms flexed, pushing forward against his back. John rose up unexpectedly and flailed in the air coming down on his knees ten feet in front of her. The spindle had been lost somewhere in the fall and he remembered the second gun. He fumbled for a second in the left coat pocket and his hand came around the starred grip of the weapon. Since it had a shorter barrel than a Berretta 9mm it came out of the pocket quickly.

With his right hand he was a lousy shot, with his left he had no idea if he could hit a barn in an emergency, and this was an emergency. John spun from his knees and sat down on the ground, legs before him. He brought his right hand up to the bottom of the gun to help with the aim.

She was gone.

Chapter 35
Aftermath

John stared into the darkness, his head swiveling from side to side expecting an attack from virtually any direction. He even looked straight up. She might have jumped up and was coming down on top of him. Nothing. She was nowhere to be seen. She'd escaped him again.

"Dammit!" hissed John.

He stood up and spun in a circle looking for her. He switched the gun to his right hand, it was pointed at chest high and he was ready to fire. The front door of the orphanage burst open. Jason came out cautiously with John's missing gun in his right hand. His left hand held a flashlight. He stood on the porch swinging the light side to side, looking for the woman. His face had a haunted look.

"John!" he spoke in a low voice, afraid if he was loud she would attack out of the darkness. "Where is she?"

"Gone," his voice was bitter. "I think." He wasn't sure if she was gone. He only knew she disappeared. He groaned as he stood up. He failed, again. He didn't kill her here, so he would have to find her again. There was only one option in his mind, her mansion compound. John looked at his watch, it was after midnight. He needed to continue his hunt; he couldn't go back to his hotel. The police would be there by now and his room was wrecked. The police would find his backpack full of stolen cash and digging down inside the pack they'd find the spare clips for the handguns. That would be impossible to explain. John asked, "What happened inside?"

Jason looked down at the ground, his head hanging in shame. "I heard the sound of the back door splintering, it was one powerful blow. I opened my door a crack to see what the commotion was. I was unarmed and frightened. I saw Madame Xiulan pass by my door. She stopped like she knew I was there, and turned her face to the crack where I hid. Her eyes sparkled, her body was bent and there was blood on her clothes. What happened upstairs?"

"I shot her, and she fell out a window."

Jason's eyes widened in fear and disbelief. "What?"

"Jason, I need you to focus. What happened next?"

The man looked around like he expected her to come at them out of the dark. "She knew I was there. She smiled an evil smile, she had fangs, and she went up the stairs to the girl's dormitory. I heard the screams and cries but I did nothing to stop her," he sobbed the last part.

"If you went up she would have killed you," John said but didn't tell him how.

"Why did she do this?"

"She's evil. She promised to kill you all. You heard her when she called me earlier tonight." With his free left hand John took Jason by the elbow and walked toward the house. The right hand held the gun ready and his eyes scanned for movement. "Let's go help the girls." They walked through the broken glass and wood framing from the window, up the stairs to the porch, and entered the front door.

Inside Jason turned on the lights then hesitated at the bottom of the stairs. He looked up, the yellow light did little to calm his fears. He didn't want to think of what he would find up stairs. The girl's screams were still fresh in his ears.

John saw him hesitate. "You wait here. I'll go up," he said. Jason nodded a quick affirmative. "Watch to see if she returns. Use the gun if she does."

Fear lit in the man's eyes and he looked at the forgotten gun. John sighed at the reaction and started up the stairs. Jason was in a world he never imagined, a deadly world. His mind rebelled at the unreality of everything he'd seen and heard.

John ascended the stairs, purposefully making noise as he walked the treads. "Hello, I'm coming up," John called out. He wondered if any of the girls remembered the English he'd been teaching them. Hopefully in their panic and fear they remember his voice from the past week of visits. Faces peered out from behind other doors and cowered back, disappearing. It seems she'd only killed girls in only one room. He arrived before she could slaughter everyone. The other orphans were frightened but safe. The gun was still ready in his hand as he walked the corridors of the converted mansion. He didn't see her leave and he was merely guessing she left.

Xiulan could be in the building somewhere, waiting for the right moment to attack. John walked up another flight of stairs and passed the spot where they broke through the railing. "Hello." He tried to sound friendly. He needed his tone to be reassuring. The door was still open to the room where he confronted Xiulan mere minutes before. "I'm coming in. Don't be afraid." He could smell the blood.

He put the gun in a jacket pocket and turned on the light as he entered the room. He regretted the action. The bodies of the dead girls were exposed to the harsh yellow light. In the dark they could be denied. Now the scared girls could see their bloody, lifeless friends tossed like old dolls. "Damn," John whispered to himself. He needed to get the girls out of the room.

The girls were still huddled against the wall where he last saw them. They were frozen with fear. John slowly walked up and held out his hands. "Come with me downstairs." He ignored the four bodies of the dead girls but he could smell their blood, it stirred hunger in him. He motioned for them to follow him, a kind of universally understood gesture. The children looked at him then at each other.

One of the girls stood up and slowly came forward. Her big eyes took in the sight of her dead friends. She silently walked and took John's hand. He motioned for the others. One by one they overcame their fear and joined him. He led them out into the hallway and to the stairs. They were puzzled by the damaged stairs and spoke among themselves. He didn't understand.

They walked by the spindles from the railing on the stairs and looked at the broken window. When he neared the top of the last stairs he called down. "I have the girls with me." Jason stood at the bottom of the stairs, waiting, the gun now hidden.

"We need to get the rest of them down. They can sleep in the dining hall. It should be large enough to accommodate them all." John's pragmatism surprised Jason who merely nodded. John went up to each of the rooms and brought down the girls to the dining hall where Jason waited.

Jason pulled John aside. "What do we do now?"

"I don't know," John whispered "You have four bodies upstairs drained of blood."

"What?"

John realized Jason didn't know what was going on, what happened upstairs. "Madame Xiulan is a jiangshi."

"A hopping vampire?"

"Without the hopping. Or a hungry ghost if that makes more sense," said John, he remembered what the monk told him. "No matter what she is you have a problem upstairs. Call the police, call the army. The girls will tell them what happened." Would the police or army believe in jiangshi? Possibly considering the deaths in Beijing. "Give me the gun."

"Why?" Jason asked.

"I'm going to go kill Xiulan."

"With a gun?"

"It's a start," said John. "I'll cut off her head to be certain."

A light dawned in Jason's eyes. "The machetes."

John nodded. Jason slipped him the gun without the girls seeing. "I'll call the police. And lock the doors as best I can."

"I don't think she'll be back tonight," said John. "If I'm successful she'll never come back."

"She'll kill you," he whispered and guided him away from the children. "She's a monster."

"I've survived so far."

"How will you find her?"

"I think I know where she'll go." John turned to look at the kids. The older ones were consoling the youngest who had been in the room with Xiulan. She was definitely a monster. "I'll call you tomorrow night. If I don't, she killed me and may come back." John turned to leave then thought for a quick moment. "Please don't tell the police about me or about the banking we did. This was an attack by a mad woman. They'll never get the chance to question her even if she kills me. It's your word alone. And if I don't call tomorrow night," John sighed in dismay. "Wait three nights then have the army go to her house. Burn it down. And clear out the caverns below."

Jason blinked in disbelief. He never would have thought John would be so violent or cold. How could a priest be so heartless?

John left out the front door and disappeared into the night. Jason locked the heavy door then went to secure the back door as best he could. "Caverns?" Jason whispered to himself. His world was tilting wildly out of control. He needed to find some normalcy in the sad dark night.

Chapter 36
Xiulan's House

On foot John arrived at Xiulan's mansion before one in the morning. He listened to the sounds of the neighborhood for a minute. The night was mostly silent, some hushed conversations from a dwelling nearby, but no sound from the compound before him. He stood on the corner and looked at the two streets framing the south and west sides of the mansion. He could see a quarter mile in four different directions.

He turned up the street and walked to the north. He sprang up and landed on the wall then jumped down into the deserted compound. There were no lights on, the doors to the large house to the north were open and so were the doors to the caretaker's house. He noticed the flies buzzing around the gardener's shed and the smell of death wafting from it. It wasn't profound on the street, but in a day or two it would be noticeable outside the compound. He might need to do something like dispose of the bodies or take them below. It would depend on what happened tonight.

John moved to the smaller house first, gun in hand, ready to disturb the quiet of the neighborhood with the booming sound of gunfire. The two minutes of bullets and smoke in the cavern below had gone unnoticed. There was too much earth muffling the sounds. If it had been heard, someone would have come looking for the reason.

The caretaker and his wife were dead. The man had his throat torn out and the woman's head was at an unnatural angle to her torso. The smell of blood was thick in the room. They had died only a few hours ago. Xiulan found them as he'd left them and killed them where they lay. He searched the rest of the house. He found a dark shirt and jacket in a closet to replace the torn garments he wore. They were a bit small but intact. He transferred the contents of his pockets to the new jacket.

From the caretaker's house he entered the larger house to the north. Her house; the one he chased her through two days before. The house where he stole her financial information, the house which had the arsenal he raided, dozens of stolen military weapons were in an elegant cabinet.

He searched the house and finished in the office. The phone line was pulled from the wall and the phone ruthlessly destroyed. He found his note crumpled on the floor. She knew he'd been successful stealing her fortune. He looked at his watch. He went to the cabinet and pulled out two more AK's. He needed to stop her before she ever got in grasping range of his neck.

When she came to his hotel she was unarmed. She'd obviously been here to see the chaos he wrought. For her to leave unarmed was foolish. Maybe she'd been a vampire so long using modern weapons wasn't the way she thought about violence.

John exited the empty house leaving the doors as he found them. He didn't want her to know he was there when she came back. He opened the doors to the underground and walked down the stairs carefully, rifle sweeping side to side, ears and eyes straining for any indication of occupancy. She could be down in her crypt already. As he moved down the stairs the stench of death became stronger.

He moved down the corridor and reached the doorway to the cavern, it was the girls. Pale yellow light from bare bulbs burned endlessly illuminating the scene. The corpses of the girls lay where they fell, or more correctly where they were blown apart by bullets rending their flesh. He gazed at the carnage he caused and wept. Monsters can cry. He leaned against the doorjamb, sobs wracked his body. His actions were necessary but horrific. He killed children. John shook his head. "No," he hissed through gritted teeth. "They weren't children. They were vampires trying to kill me." It was cold comfort.

Blood congealed on the floor cold, thick and unappetizing. The bare earth was a poor tomb for the corrupted innocents. John figured he would carry the guilt for a long time despite the knowledge they would have killed him, again, if he'd done nothing to defend himself. He crossed, carefully avoiding blood and flesh to search her crypt on the far side of the cavern. Empty. It was as he left it, the harmony of the chamber disrupted by his previous search.

She wasn't in the compound above or the underground cavern below. John sat on the bed in the crypt and waited. He didn't move anything in the cavern by either walking or touching with his hands. He wanted it to look exactly as she found it the night before. He wanted her to feel safe when she returned.

If she returned. She might not come back. She spent the previous night somewhere else. There was no guarantee she'd return to her compound. She might have numerous places to hide. John had none. His safe refuge at the hotel was gone. The police would be searching his light proofed room. They would have his name and now be looking for him. All his clothes and what few possessions he had at the hotel were in the hands of the authorities, as well as a military pack full of money and magazines for the pistols. All he now possessed in Beijing were the clothes on his back. Luckily his passport, wallet, which he filled with stolen yuan from the backpack, and the banking information for the stolen money were on him when she broke down his door.

He looked at his watch. Dawn was hours away. He sat silently on the bed away from any direct line of sight to the main door to the cavern, staring at the crack of door of her crypt, listening for any sound marking her return. Time ticked away slowly. He waited, sitting as comfortably as he could. He didn't want to shift around much, silence was the goal.

No. Her death was the goal; silence was his ally in that quest. From where he sat he studied the room. It was small, not a roughly carved space like the cavern outside the door. It was rectangular with squared corners. There were dark wood panels, paintings and embroidered tapestries were on two of the walls. There were lamps with colored glass shades lighting the space. Two polished, gleaming, ivory elephant tusks, three feet long, gently curved up toward the ceiling from a wide writing table. A round stool, backless, was under the wood table, a leather bound book lay open, the writing was in Chinese. She had a journal? That would be a fascinating read, or horrific. From where he sat he could see the writing was not in English.

The back of the heavy banded door had sturdy locks. The room was a furnished bunker in case of a frontal assault. Something about the room seemed off, but John couldn't figure out what bothered him.

Time ticked on. He looked at his watch again. The earth was tumbling through the galaxy, rotating, and the sun was inexorably moving across the surface of the globe. It would render him dead to the world in minutes. She hadn't come back. He moved from the bed and shut the door. He secured all the locks and sat down on the edge of the bed. He pulled the pistols out of his jacket and slid them under the pillow. He lay down on the bed holding the rifle ready as…

Sleep

Chapter 37
Body Bags

Jason left the frightened girls in the dining room for the amount of time it took to rush up the stairs to the third floor and lock the door to the room with the girls bodies. He didn't look in, just shut the door, turned an old fashioned key sealing the door. He needed to think about his next move. Whatever he chose would have repercussions beyond this one night. The orphanage might close if he made the wrong choice.

It took an hour to get the girls all to sleep in the large dining room. They were uncomfortable on the hard wood floor covered with blankets, their pillows brought down from upstairs supported their heads. It wasn't a perfect solution but Jason wanted all of the children in one room. The six girls from the room where Xiulan killed her victims were huddled together for warmth and security. He asked the girls to keep what they saw secret until the morning. If they told the others no one would sleep.

Intent on staying up all night, Jason went to the kitchen phone to make a call. It was a number he rarely used, maybe once every few years, but one that provided a service necessary to keep the orphanage open. There was an electronic tone on the line as the phone at the other end rang. There was no answering machine so after twenty or so rings a sleepy voice was on the other end.

"Yes?"

"Yaoting, it's Lujiang." Jason could almost hear the man on the other end of the phone straighten up and look at a clock somewhere in the room.

"Yes?"

"I need your services."

"What is the problem?"

Jason was silent for a moment as he determined how much to say over the phone. "I need a pick up."

"When?"

"Now. Before dawn." There was silence on the other end. The man was thinking, weighing the time of morning. "I'll give you five times your fee."

"I'm on my way," said the voice.

"Bring your unmarked van."

"My van?"

"Sadly, yes." Jason hung up the phone and walked outside to the back gate. He unlocked it and left it slightly ajar. His visitor would see it in the headlights and let himself in. Back inside the dining room Jason pulled up a chair so he could watch the sleeping children and the back gate at the same time. One small lamp illuminated burned in the corner casting long shadows in the big room. Jason didn't want to sit in a dark room overnight. Darkness would have set is imagination aflame with monsters lurking unseen. He needed the light as he watched the children sleep. Their breathing was a susurrus in the atmosphere of the room. It was soothing.

About forty five minutes after his call a van slowed at the gate. The driver's door opened and a man got out. He pushed the gate open and drove through. Jason got out of the chair and locked the dining room doors behind him. He didn't want any of the children could see them doing what needed to be done for the next twenty minutes. He walked out the back door and met the two men as they walked up the steps.

"Was there an accident?" The man was tall and thin, he was old enough to have skin tight on his face making his cheek bones stand out. His clothes were dark and of finer quality than Jason's, he had some wealth. Or more money than Jason did to spend on clothes. The other man was younger, brought along for lifting what the old man could not.

"No. Please follow me, cousin." Jason headed up the stairs to the third floor. He pulled the key from his pocket and unlocked the door. He turned the knob and pushed it open so the two men could see in. There was a shocked gasp when they beheld the scene. Four children were tossed like garbage, bodies draped recklessly on beds or lying on the floor, crumpled.

"What happened?"

"Jiangshi," said Jason. He thought about lying but most people knew of jiangshi and believed in them, so it was simple to tell the truth. "She killed four of my children."

"How did you chase her away?" asked the younger man.

"Someone else chased her away before she could kill everyone."

They nodded and walked in the room. The older man bent to look at the wounds. It was what he expected for a jiangshi. He turned to the young man. "Mingyu, go get four body bags from the van," The man nodded and left the room. "Will she come back?" There was fear in his voice.

"I don't know. Probably not tonight," replied Jason.

Mingyu came back and handed two body bags to Yaoting. They quickly and efficiently unfolded them next to the bodies and with care and reverence for the dead, put the small bodies in the thick dark plastic bags and zippered them shut. Jason said good-bye to each girl, saying their names and apologizing for not keeping them safe. Tears welled up in his eyes.

"What will you do with them?"

"Considering the jiangshi, cremation is best." Yaoting replied solemnly.

"Of course, of course," Jason nodded.

The two men and Jason each picked up a bag, cradling the small body in their arms like they were taking a sleeping child to bed. They walked outside to the van. With one hand Mingyu opened the back door and they carefully put the bodies on the floor of the van. Silently the young man went upstairs to get the last girl.

"I will send the money in the morning after the banks are open. Do I need to buy coffins?" Jason asked.

"No. We will take care of it," Yaoting replied. "I'm sorry for your loss." It was a reflexive statement of condolence, but one he sincerely meant. The young man returned and put the last body in the van. The two men got in the van and started it up. Yaoting put the van in gear and drove toward the entrance. Jason followed the van and locked the gate after they cleared it.

He walked back upstairs to the room and pulled the bloody sheets and blankets off the beds, replacing them with clean linens. Four mattresses were soaked in blood, he flipped them over. It would dry dark brown. He cleaned the blood from surfaces, floor and furniture, in the limited time he had.

The bloody bedding went into a large basket. He would see if they could be saved or with the five million US dollars at his disposal he might buy new ones. Hell, maybe new beds for all the kids. Being able to improve the lives of the girls with Xiulan's money didn't make up for the loss of four girls. It was a start, though.

Jason thought for a moment at the door to the dining room. The key was in his hand waiting to unlock it. Did he miss anything? The back door was still broken. The stairway railing was broken and the gaping maw of shattered glass in the second story window chilled the entire manor house. He needed large piece of wood to cover the hole. He would deal with those problems in the quickly approaching morning, after the rest of the staff arrived.

He unlocked the door, the girls were still asleep. He locked the door behind him, then sat in the chair and waited for the dawn.

CHAPTER 38
PATIENCE

Awake

He gazed at the ceiling, momentarily confused. This wasn't the closet in his hotel. He suddenly remembered where he was and sat bolt upright scanning the room for danger. Everything was as he left it some eight or so hours before. The banded door was still locked from the inside, the rifle still in his hands. Everything was the same.

John listened at the door before unlocking it and peering out into the cavern. The sad corpses of the dead girls still littered the floor. He decided he would do something about them even if it was taking a match to them. Vampire bodies were oddly flammable, though he had no idea why or what chemical change made them be so. It meant he was also flammable. What a strange realization.

He opened the door and sat back down on the bed. He was hungry but resolute. He would stay there until Xiulan returned. She had somewhere else to stay during emergencies, like right now, but this was home. He figured she would come back tonight to start setting her world back in order. The crypt and her home above had a certain specificity. Everything had a place, and things out of place were not tolerated in her world. The only chaos came from the children, and they occupied their own space.

John gripped the gun and sat down on the bed. He had time to wait. He glanced at his watch, and settled in. The sun went down at around five p.m. and would rise around seven the next morning. That left fourteen hours of vigilant boredom. He wasn't sure if he wanted her to return. If she didn't come back to her home he wouldn't know where to look for her. This was his only option. If she didn't show up would he just leave? She would continue to kill and rob and turn children into vampires if he did nothing. Maybe not in Beijing, she could easily go to another big city.

Without her millions it might not be as easily as it would have been. She was cash poor, having only a few thousand yuan remaining in the accounts. He smiled at the thought of her rage. It put her invincibility into question. He needed her to be shaken and uncertain.

John looked at his watch again. Thirteen minutes had elapsed. "This is going to take forever," he groaned quietly. Patience was easier for him if he had something to occupy his mind. In foreign surroundings, he had nothing. Silence and fear and the stench of death from outside the crypt settled heavily on him.

An hour passed. He got up and paced the room to keep his blood flowing. Blood. His hunger was growing sharper as he waited. He would need to feed after he killed her. Even the cold oxidized blood staining the floor outside made his stomach quiver. He sat down on the bed again, adjusted the gun in his lap. He practiced bringing it up quickly and pointing it at the doorway a few times to make the unfamiliar action more fluid.

The air shifted unusually, like a vague exhalation in the cavern bringing in the smells from the chamber. There was a light scuffing sound. John whirled to his left and brought up the gun as the ivory tusk passed by his head, missing him by a hair and impacting on the gun. It blocked the blow. The rifle shattered, the hardware separated from the stock. The impact numbed his hand and arm and he dropped the gun. Xiulan was behind him, tusk in both hands, her face was a calm mask with anger and hatred boiling underneath. A space had opened up in the wall, a panel slid to the side exposing a dark passage.

John realized what bothered him about the room. It was a dead end. Anyone hunting her would not give up when presented with a thick door. They would blow up the cavern to kill her. A secret escape route made sense. Like the one she used to escape him when he attacked her house.

She swung the tusk again like a bludgeon, she was going to kill him, crush his head. Quick, efficient. John dodged and rolled off the bed, stumbling out the door holding his throbbing arm. He reached into the jacket pocket with his left hand, then remembered he took the two pistols out of the jacket and put them under the pillow. Hopefully the pillow wasn't disturbed revealing the weapons to her.

He saw the three rifles on the floor as he exited, and knew they were the ones he emptied killing her demon girls. Even if the guns were loaded he would have a hard time picking one up with his tingling limb. Scooping up a rifle with his left hand and using it was unrealistic. They were a two handed weapons and generally right handed.

John crashed out the door. He needed room to run and he needed a weapon. He was halfway across the blood soaked cavern when there was a reverberating

"Boom!" and a bullet hit the wall near the door. Xiulan had found his guns under the pillow. He redoubled his effort and vanished from the cavern, slamming the door behind him. There was the sound of an impact, a bullet splatted on the other side of the thick wood panel. That was two shots. Did she find both guns or just one? When he escaped the bed he must have shifted the pillow exposing the gun or guns.

He fled to his right and up the stairs. He climbed the thirty feet in seconds, when he reached the upper doors he came to a crashing stop. The doors were locked. John turned and looked down. He could hear the door to the cavern open. He stepped up three steps so he was crouched below the sealed doors, pressed his hands against the wood door and lifted with his legs and arms simultaneously. Pain coursed through is shoulder and arm, which meant sensation and functionality was returning.

The wood groaned and the lock broke. The doors crashed open. He was out of the cellar and sprinting to the north house. There were guns in the office cabinet. Xiulan flew out of the low doors and stopped for a millisecond to see which way the hated man went. She saw him entering the north house. Her home. She had more guns in the office cabinet. He disappeared around the corner of the entrance before she could shoot him.

She moved cautiously. A gun was not her weapon of choice. No weapon was her weapon of choice. She rarely chose to fight. Fleeing danger was her default reaction to any dangerous situation. Inside her mind there was a part telling her to jump over the wall,

abandon her thirst for revenge. He had her money.
She needed it back.

She ran across the courtyard to the caretaker's
house and hid next to the doorway. She had a clear
line of sight to the door of the other house. She would
wait for him to come out.

Chapter 39
Mayhem in the Night

John cleared the corner of the doorway expecting a trail of bullets to follow him. Any rounds from his pistol would easily pierce the thin walls of the building. She'd be firing randomly, hoping to hit him, but there was silence. The only sound was his shoes on the polished wood floors. He went straight to the office and pulled an AK from the cabinet. His hand still tingled a little like ginger-ale but otherwise her attack had no lasting effect. He checked the clip like he'd been taught and pulled the bolt to see there was a 7.62x 39 round ready to go. He slung the strap around his body, grabbed a pistol, and slipped it into his pocket.

He moved to a defensive spot in the office and listened for sounds of her footsteps. A minute passed, then another. Did she leave or was she waiting for him to make the first move? So far she always had an escape route; one from her crypt and the one in that dead end room where she escaped him several nights ago.

John moved carefully, crouching, peeked out the door. The hallway was empty. He turned to his right down the hall to the dead end room. The door was open. He slipped inside and shut the door. From the feel of it, it was heavy and reinforced. It was probably thick enough to suppress a bullet. He hoped the same could be said for the wall surrounding it. John looked at the small door he'd seen before. The one she escaped out of the other night. He pried the panel open again and went to the other door to release the lock. In the dust of the floor on the other side was the single set of footprints from the other night. She hadn't used this exit to leave, but he could.

She thought he was trapped in the house. If he followed her exit he could come back into the compound from another way, surprising her. He set down the rifle at the opening and crawled forward. The other door opened into a dark empty room. There were tracks in the dust before him leading out a door.

John crawled into the next building and pulled the rifle after, shutting the panel on his side. He carefully followed the path she made through the house. She knew best how to escape.

There were no occupants as far as he could tell and her footprints lead to an exterior door. He opened the locks and pushed at the door. A dark courtyard, smaller than hers, was in front of him. The space was unkempt and overrun with weeds and dried grasses. No one lived here.

John stepped out and got his bearings. Xiulan's house was directly behind him. He leapt up to the roof and moved stealthily on the slick grey tiles. Since she didn't come looking for him, he guessed she was waiting for him to exit her house so she could shoot him. Or she had fled again which would mean he'd have to find her.

He moved across the neighbor's house, on the roof directly next to the dead caretaker's house. The angle was steep but he was quite surefooted. The roof provided cover if she was in the courtyard watching for him. He crouched as he approached the top of the roof. His head barely crested the tiles. He scanned the courtyard with his eyes. There was no sign of her.

John moved further south to the second wall of the interior. It was four feet wide and similarly tiled, but the angle was not as severe. He crept forward looking at the front of the house to the east. From the high angle he could see the door was open but he couldn't see in. He moved forward again. In the dark he saw the bottom half of a leg. Xiulan was leaning against the wall next to the door waiting for him. He needed to move very soon.

She saw him enter the north house but not exit. If he waited much longer she might figure out he used the same secret exit she had. For the moment he still had the element of surprise on his side.

John stood up on the roof, picked a spot in the courtyard that would give him a clean shot at where Lady Xiulan stood hidden. He clicked off the safety and jumped up and out. The rifle in his hands was already moving to aim the moment he landed.

He alighted close to where he planned, his legs flexed dissipating the impact of his landing, and he brought the rifle up to his shoulder. He was still moving a bit when he targeted her and squeezed off three quick shots. The sound was deafening, but at such close range she had no time to react. One bullet missed her head by inches, buzzing past her face. The next one went wider as the rifle bucked, and the third smashed into her right shoulder from the side and moved into her torso. Xiulan cried out in pain and fell to the ground clutching her side. His pistol skittered out of her hand.

John moved cautiously to the entrance of the house. The clock was now ticking. Gunshots had broken the silence of the night. He had to finish her fast. Xiulan jumped forward and grabbed the gun with her left hand. She was on her feet and fleeing deeper into the house.

"Shit," hissed John, running quickly and cautiously after her. He couldn't let her turn to shoot at him. The gun was at his shoulder when he entered the house. The caretaker's house was small. He remembered the layout from the other night. He saw her back in front of him and fired another three round burst. Two bullets hit her back. She arched and fell to the ground, rolling, screaming at an ear piercing volume.

John moved to her, pulled the gun strap from around his shoulder, and plunged the hot barrel of the rifle through her head. The screaming stopped. He pulled it out and plunged it into her neck, shattering her spinal cord. John turned and ran to the kitchen, the rifle clutched in his left hand as he moved. He grabbed a large knife and returned to Xiulan's body. He cut off her head with one powerful slicing motion.

Less than a minute had elapsed since he landed in the courtyard. She was dead, but he heard the neighborhood roused by the sound of gunfire. People might think it's the PLA, but human curiosity would drive them out of their homes to take a look, to see what was happening.

John wiped the gun clean of possible fingerprints with his jacket and dropped the rifle next to her body. The police may have fingerprinted his hotel room. If they had his prints from the hotel and found them here it would make leaving China problematic.

Blood was pooling on the hardwood floor under her body. He grabbed his weapon she had gotten from the crypt. He wished he had time to burn her and all the girls downstairs. The authorities would find some very strange things when they arrived.

John stood in the courtyard and looked around. The doors to the underground chamber were open. Even if he closed and locked them someone was going to find the horrors below. The smell of decay and the swarming flies at the gardener's shed would lead someone to those bodies as well.

The thing he regretted the most was the loss of the crypt below. He had nowhere to sleep. The hotel was ruined and the crypt would be found. He considered the empty house immediately to the north where he passed through, but that could be found too.

John looked at his watch. It was still very early. He had time to find somewhere safe. He jumped to the roof and scrambled across the tiles. He dropped down the next street over when no one was watching.

Where to go now? He wondered.

CHAPTER 40
AN UNUSUAL SAFETY

John stood on the street seeking shadows, lights burned in the windows and people looked out from behind thin curtains. They heard the gunshots from the other street and were frightened. Could it be another protest? He didn't know where to go. He couldn't go to the hotel. He couldn't stay in Xiulan's crypt. The authorities would find the caverns below when they came to either investigate the gunshots he fired minutes ago or the unmistakable smell of death in a few days. The neighbors would point out where the sound of gunfire came from. There would be a house to house search.

A thought came to John as he stood. When it was clear on the street he jumped back up to the roof and traversed the angled highway back to Xiulan's compound. He stopped in the dark and looked. There was no one there, yet. He jumped down and moved to the doors to the underground. He stepped down the stairs closing the doors after him.

He turned and bounded down the stairs covering twenty five vertical feet with two jumps. He entered the large cavern and shut the door. At Xiulan's crypt he picked up the three empty AKs and tossed them into the hidden passage she emerged from less than an hour ago. He gathered the spent clips and threw them into the dark space as well.

John shut the door to her crypt but didn't lock it. He entered the dark tunnel through the hidden panel and turned to close that too. There was a secure sounding click when the panel slid in place. A locking mechanism worked, holding the door shut. In the total darkness John couldn't see much even with his new eyes. He felt on the floor for the guns and clips. Using his shirt he wiped his fingerprints off of any surface of the guns he might have touched. He couldn't have his prints on them either.

John left the guns behind and concentrated on the dark passage. Xiulan had come from somewhere safe to surprise him in the crypt. If it were safe for her, it might be a safe place for him to spend the next day.

He stretched out his arms and felt for the walls. They were about five feet apart; he could run his fingers along both walls as he moved. From the sounds of his footsteps he sensed the ceiling was low. Reaching with his right hand he touched the cold stone a few inches above his head. It had been carved for someone shorter than him.

He walked slowly, carefully feeling along in the dark like a blind man, reaching out occasionally to make sure he wasn't walking into a wall or dead end. His fingers detected no breaks in the walls, no alcoves or doorways. The tunnel was long and didn't curve or meander. It was dug with a destination in mind. It was meant for quick exits in case of danger. An escape route wouldn't have unnecessary twists and turns.

In ten minutes of vigilant walking there was a gentle slope upward. He slowed and reached out, there was still nothing. He spoke, "Hey." It was his normal voice. He listened for the sound to bounce back like a bat with echolocation.

John continued forward again. "Hey." Still nothing. The floor continued to gently rise up. He heard his footsteps come back to his ears in a different way.

Something had changed. "Hey." There was an echo. He reached forward and touched wood. It wasn't a door, it was the rung of a ladder. Reaching beyond the ladder he felt the cold stone of a solid wall. Stretching up his hand went beyond where he had had a ceiling for the whole of this journey in the dark.

He set his foot on the lowest rung and tested it to see if it would hold his weight. In the dark, he had no idea how old the wood ladder might be. It seemed sturdy enough so he started climbing. It creaked under his weight with each step upward. John traveled up ten feet or so. The ladder ended and he touched a wood panel. Keeping his left hand on the top rung of the ladder he felt around the door and surrounding wall for any kind of release or way to open the wood before him. He found an indentation in the side of the framing and pressed. There was a soft click.

John pushed and the door. It didn't move. He remembered the panel at the crypt slid into the wall. He worked the fingernails of his right hand into the seam of the wood panel and pushed. It pulled out slightly and slid to his left silently.

The pale light in the room before him seemed like bright daylight after the Stygian nothingness of the tunnel. He waited, listening. There was no sound in the building. The room before him had no furniture. A layer of dust was on the floor only disturbed by vague footprints leading to the secret door. There was the telltale signs of movement painted in the dust in front of the door. Motes from Xiulan's earlier passage hung in the still, stale air.

John climbed out of the tunnel and waited. There was no sound. He slid the panel back into place and stood up. The walls and floor were wood. There were no windows. He crossed to the door and opened it a crack. A hallway was before him. He opened the door more and slipped out. On the floor were Xiulan's small footprints. He followed them; at least she would know where she was going.

Her path led to a room with a sturdy door, the interior had a mattress on the floor, and the dust had been recently swept away. This was where she hid out after he attacked her compound. John continued to explore. He became bolder as each room he searched was empty and the floors covered in a layer of dust. It was the perfect place for him to hide for tonight. Maybe he could stay until he was able to leave China.

He looked at his watch. It was early and his hunger was growing. He needed to feed. He sighed to himself. He'd been a vampire for only a few days and the hunger drove him to do the unthinkable. Hunting was harder than he thought. And he didn't like having to knock his victims unconscious. If he hit them too hard with his new found strength he could kill someone.

John found the exit of the house and stood in the small weed choked courtyard. It was about ten feet by ten feet, drab grey concrete walls and flagstones where a riot of growing plants took advantage of the cracks. There was a door leading to the street on one side of the space. John stood listening. Did the police use sirens? Was anyone at Xiulan's house? Exactly where was he in relation to her house? How far had he traveled? He guessed he was several blocks away but he didn't know in which direction.

John opened the door and looked out on the narrow side street. There was no one around to see him slip out of the empty house. The neighbors would know that no one lived there. Seeing a white man come out of it would be a cause for investigation. Before the door closed he studied the building and the door carefully. His search of the house didn't turn up any key or anything to unlock the lock on the outside door. By jumping the wall he didn't need a key.

An inspection of the exterior showed the outside didn't have a house number and it was similarly unkempt like the interior courtyard walls. He looked around the street and memorized everything he could so he would be able to return after feeding. Reluctantly he let the door close, the lock clicked. He pulled at the handle to test it, the door was secure.

John chose a direction and started walking. His hands were thrust in his jacket pockets, the collar raised up around his neck to hold the cold night air at bay. As he walked he made a mental map, at the center was Xiulan's house. If he got lost he'd have to find someplace to shelter during the day.

The streets were quiet. There wasn't much foot traffic, and no one was walking by that he could accost easily. There weren't any convenient dark alleys where he could drag a limp body. He stopped and looked around at the buildings. Most were one story tall, small fortresses keeping the dangerous world safely outside.

He would have to go into a house. He would have to attack someone in their sleep. Down the street there was a small second story structure on top of a house. It looked like it was a newer addition, the shape of the roof was different than the house it sat upon. There were steps from the lower level courtyard leading to a landing and a single door.

John moved quietly, when he was close he looked around and jumped on the roof, landing lightly on the tiles. He pressed his body against the wall near the window. Inside the structure he heard the sound of a single person breathing, and one heartbeat. This was his victim. This was his sleeping prey.

This was the thing he hoped he never got used to. If he got used to feeding on people he would truly be a monster.

Chapter 41
Boxing

The phone rang. Lujiang picked up the receiver and said hello in Mandarin.

"Jason, It's John."

"You're alive!" Jason exclaimed. "It's been two days. I thought she killed you. Does that mean she's dead?" Jason lowered his voice, the children were still awake and some of them were on the first floor. "How did you survive?"

"Yes, she's dead. Can I come see you in person tonight?" John asked ignoring the last question. "I need help."

"Is she really dead? I don't want her coming back here ever again."

"Yes, she's really dead. I'll tell you what happened if you really want to know. Can I come by?" asked John.

Jason hesitated. He was afraid of John but didn't want to say so, it would be rude. He survived a fight with a jiangshi; that was something to be respected and feared. "Alright, come by after the children are asleep and the others have left." He was trepidatious; the last aid he gave John got four of the girls killed. If Xiulan were truly dead, helping the priest again should be safe. Jason was concerned, what he kind of help did he need?

John arrived at the repaired back door after eleven. The door jamb was replaced and a sturdy door in place of the shattered one. He was wearing new dark clothes, clean, not slashed or bloody like two days ago when John tumbled out a two story window with a jiangshi and didn't get injured. Jason was suspicious about him and slightly afraid to be near him.

"Come in. Sit down." Jason said gesturing to a chair at the small kitchen table they sat at before.

John nodded and took the offered chair. He watched as Jason busied himself in the kitchen heating water in a kettle over the gas stove and pulling out a teapot. John could smell his fear and sighed. He waited for Jason to cross to the table and sit in the chair opposite him before speaking.

"Xiulan is dead."

"You killed her." It was a question and a statement.

John nodded. "With her death there should be no more bodies discovered on the streets carved up by a serial killer."

"That was her?"

John nodded again but didn't elaborate. The color suddenly drained out of Jason's face.

"Where are the girls she adopted?" Jason asked quietly. He stared at the table afraid of the answer.

"You really want to know?"

"I do."

"She changed them into jiangshi and, I'm sorry, but they're all dead now."

Jason's hands came up to his mouth in horror as if the gesture could hold back the sound of grief which involuntarily came from deep within him. He bowed his head and mumbled something in Mandarin. The faces of the little girls she adopted flashed through his mind. Innocent smiles and inquisitive eyes, they all trusted him to keep them safe, and send them to a loving home.

The kettle started piping as the water boiled. Jason got up like a man crushed by life and pulled the boiling water off the stove with mechanical movements. His heart ached. He poured hot water into the teapot and brought it and two delicate cups over before sitting down again. He rested his elbows on the table and rested his head in his hands. John could smell the tea leaves steeping, jasmine something from the aroma.

"You didn't know. You couldn't have known. If you found out what she was and what she was doing, she would have killed you." John used his best priestly tone, the same tone he used when counseling the grieving and heartsick.

Jason nodded in his hands, he wasn't crying but his eyes were wet with imminent tears. He would weep alone, after John left. Jason sniffed, lifting his head up, he looked at John. "You said you needed help." Having a task would be good. It would help distract from the deaths two days ago and the revelation of everything else.

"I'm in a bit of a bind." John watched Jason pour steaming cups of tea and he set one in front of John. Steam whorled lazily in the still air. "I need to get back to the States."

"And you are be sought by the police."

"Maybe. I don't really know for sure. There was an incident at my hotel with Xiulan which would be difficult to explain. But the police are a lesser problem." John said. Jason nodded and waited for him to continue. John took a breath, a pause to decide how to continue. He felt the need to be honest and was prepared to escape out the kitchen door. Jason's reaction would dictate the next thirty seconds. "Xiulan killed me. I'm now like she was and I can't take a normal flight back home."

Jason leaned back, his eyes widening in fear. John was prepared if he reacted badly.

"That's how you survived the fall out the window."

"And down the stairs."

Jason was abnormally interested in his tea as he thought. "So a plane trip is impossible."

"At some point I'm going to cross the terminus from dark to light and if I'm in the cabin I will either sleep or if sunlight hits me from a window, burn." John wondered if being set alight in a sealed pressurized airplane cabin would bring the aircraft down. Yes, probably. Fire is fire, in an enclosed aluminum tube, it would be bad.

"Have you thought of a cruise?" Jason asked. "Or maybe going on a cargo ship? Shanghai is an international port. You could find something there."

John frowned. "How long is the trip?"

Jason shrugged. "At least two weeks. I don't know for sure. It would depend on where you go and what kind of ship."

John considered the option. He didn't like the idea of being trapped on a boat for over two weeks with no way to escape. There was a chance of being discovered. He would inevitably grow hungry. That was an invitation for disaster and exposure. The image of the Demeter in Dracula landing on English shores with a dead crew popped into his mind, a man lashed to the wheel, guiding a boat of corpses. "I find that risky." John finally said.

"You're very rich, you could charter a jet."

The thought of such an extravagance went against every instinct he had about money. It would cost thousands to charter a plane from China and there was no way to ensure his safety once he was in daylight. "No. I think I need a box." John said.

"A coffin."

John hesitated then nodded; slightly shocked he was getting a coffin. It was cliché, but now seemed prudent and necessary. "I guess I need a coffin. I can have it, me, shipped back by plane. The flight would be fifteen to twenty hours. I'd be safe from sunlight."

"I have a cousin in the funeral business." Jason smiled but the smirk fled his face. He used Yaoting two nights ago to take care of the dead girls. The police were never called.

"Of course you do."

"They took care of the girls the other night." Jason whispered.

"Oh, I'm sorry." The memory of her attack on the orphanage was still fresh for both of them.

Jason shrugged. John watched the tea cooling in front of them. "I guess you didn't need tea."

"No." John replied, pushing the cup gently away from him. He would have to try to ingest something other than blood at some point. What would his body do? "Can you trust them?"

"Yes." Jason replied. "For enough money they can give you the paperwork needed to get a body to the United States. It should help you clear customs." Jason went to the phone and dialed his 'cousin' at home again. This time the man was still awake. "Yaoting it's Lujiang again," he was speaking Chinese. John sat watching.

"Don't tell me she came back," Yao said.

"No, she's dead, and thank you for your help the other night. I greatly appreciate it," said Jason. "But I have a friend in need of a coffin and some travel documents."

"That can be arranged," Yaoting said. "Come by in the morning."

Jason paused and looked at John. "Can he come by tomorrow night, after you close." The man on the phone was silent.

"That's the only time?" Yaoting imagined it was some underworld criminal running from the police.

"Yes." Jason said. "He can pay for everything."

"What are you mixed up in?"

"Everything is fine." Jason said though his voice didn't convince even him.

"Come by tomorrow night after we close," Yaoting sighed. "We will get your friend squared away."

"Thank you, cousin." Jason finished and hung up the phone. "Come over tomorrow night. I will take you to a place and we will have you shipped to America."

"Great," said John, his voice tinged with sarcasm. "Now I'm luggage."

After seven p.m. Jason and John were sitting in the conference room of a funeral home. The walls were off white and clean, the doorway accents and doors were of a dark stained wood. The furniture was comfortable, but not too comfortable. It was a simple, elegant room, one which hosted countless grieving people over the years. Two Chinese men in dark suits were across the small conference table from them. The older man was introduced as Yaoting, the younger, beefier looking man was introduced as Mingyu. The older man was clearly in charge.

"They don't speak much English so I will translate for you," said Jason.

John listened as they talked in Chinese, there were a few words he recognized. *Los Angeles, LAX.* The men glanced at John and nodded in understanding of what his needs were going to be. John was surprised they hadn't stopped the conversation or acted shocked. What he required was unusual. Had they transported a live person to another country in a casket before? If so, who would need such a service? The ideas which came to mind were frightening or sad. It could be either criminals or political refugees. The latter would need to escape especially after Tiananmen Square. They'd be persecuted and jailed had they stayed.

Jason translated when the man stopped speaking. "What you desire can be done," Jason said. "This is a longer trip than… others who made a similar request."

John interrupted. "They've done this before?" Yaoting's eyes flicked from John to Jason then back. *He speaks more English than he's letting on.*

"It has happened once or twice." Jason's answer was appropriately vague. He didn't need to know specifically what they did before but it made them seem qualified to do so now. Yaoting started talking again, Jason continued. "There are documents required to transport human remains." On his fingers Yaoting ticked off five things. "Death Certificate, Passport, Embalming Certificate, Export Certificate, Declaration of Casket Contents. The transfer is from mortuary to mortuary. We close the casket here and it is received at the other end by a mortuary in Los Angeles. And you'll require a supplemental bottle of oxygen, water, and he suggests a diaper like the astronauts use."

John listened carefully. He didn't want to say he had no need for oxygen or water, and certainly not a diaper. How was he going to get all those documents when he's not dead? And how does he get out if the casket is sealed in China? That requires trust and people on the other end to follow explicit instructions. If the coffin was opened in the daylight, he'd be dead for real. "I have a passport, but I don't want to use it and be declared deceased in some computer somewhere. Who knows how that might bite me in the ass later."

Brain and Yaoting spoke for a few minutes; John sat wishing he spoke Mandarin.

"Yaoting will take care of the last three documents as a funeral director, and he has a cousin which can help with the first two."

John sighed. *Of course, another cousin. My life is at the mercy of cousins who aren't cousins.* "All right. How long will it take and how much will it cost?" He wasn't concerned about the cost but he wanted to haggle. He watched the haggling that took place for the smallest of goods. It was part of the culture. Jason understood he wanted there to be haggling so no one would think it was too easy.

Jason and the old man started talking, it was fast, with both making points and looking aggrieved at times. After a couple minutes Jason told him the price and how long it would take. John made a face, all part of the act, then reluctantly nodded.

Yaoting said something to the young man, he got up and left the room. He returned in a minute with a 35mm camera. Yaoting spoke to Jason who then relayed the information.

"They are going to take a passport picture of you now, against the white wall. It will speed up the process." Jason hesitated a moment. "Then we will go down the hall for another photo."

"What photo do they need?"

"You, on a medical table for proof of death."

John raised his eyebrows. "Oh?"

"It will be included in the sheaf of papers."

"I won't have the Y incision of an autopsy." He'd seen many deceased in his job and knew what happened in an autopsy room with a corpse.

"The death certificate will say you died at a hospital of a heart attack while under emergency care. No autopsy necessary." Jason said.

"If that works, then okay." John walked to stand in front of a blank white wall. He remembered what his passport photo looked like. Look straight ahead, no glasses, no smile. Mingyu framed the shot and took several photos, a couple with flash and a couple without. He wouldn't know which they'd use until the roll of film was developed.

He spoke and gestured for them to follow. John looked at Jason. "You're coming with me?" He tried not to sound suspicious but couldn't help it. Suspicion and mistrust would keep him alive in the years to come. John didn't think the three men would be able to overpower him if they planned anything untoward. He could disable or kill them all easily.

"Of course," said Jason.

"Great. Let's do this and get out of here," John said confidently. "Lead the way."

They went out the conference room door and down a couple hallways. They passed through a door to the part of the mortuary not shown to the grieving family. This was where bodies were processed. The air became more antiseptic as they walked. Yaoting led them through a set of swinging white doors to a sterile, white tiled embalming room. The carpet of the hallway transitioned to tile. There were several drains in the floor for easy cleanup of fluids. On a table nearby was a body under a sheet. They were still prepping it.

"Please take off your shirt and lie down on the table," Yao said, Jason translated.

John stripped off his jacket and shirt and set them across the back of a nearby rolling chair. He sat on the table as Mingyu readied the camera with a flash attachment. "Ready?" John asked.

"Yes." Mingyu raised the camera. John swung his legs up on the table, lay back on the cold steel, and let his arms fall naturally on the metal. Yao framed up the picture then said, "Close your eyes."

John knew where everyone in the room was before he shut his eyes. There was a flash as the picture was taken. The unit hummed as it recharged for a few seconds. Another flash. It took five seconds.

"Done, thank you," said Jason.

John got off the table and dressed.

"Lujiang will call you when everything is ready for your travel." Yao said, speaking English for the first time.

John smiled at the man. "Thank you," John said. He and Jason said good bye and walked out of the funeral home to Jason's beat up old car.

Once behind the wheel Jason started the car and there was a grinding sound of gears as the manual shifted from neutral to first gear. He drove silently for a minute, the transmission crunching with each gear change. "The police came by looking for you this afternoon." His tone was conversational and unconcerned.

"You're telling me now?"

"I didn't want you to worry," said Jason. "John, my friend, it will all work out."

"I certainly hope so," John said. He'd done the calculations to make his time in the box easy. "I want an early night flight on a plane that goes as direct to LA as I can get. Something around seven p.m. would be great. If I'm sealed into the box right after sunset I will be awake at the start of the trip, and at the end when I arrive in LA. The rest of the time I will be asleep in the coffin. On the other end I'm going to have specific instructions. If the flight gets in early and they pull the lid off the coffin in daylight thinking they are saving my life, well, all this hassle will be for nothing. Maybe the funeral home picking up can be instructed to get the casket towards five o'clock. That should keep me safe."

"That can probably be arranged."

"You need to get a new car. And now you can afford to do it."

"Not too new. People would be suspicious," Jason said. "No one has a new car, certainly not me. The PRC might look closely at the orphanage." He shrugged. "If I can feed the children I'll be happy."

John looked at Jason and wondered how many shady dealings he'd done to be aware of optics. "True, very true." China seemed to thrive on under the table deals.

"How are you able to forge these documents?" asked John after a long pause.

"This is China. We don't create or innovate. We take something that someone else made, pull it apart to figure out how it works, then we make the exact same thing cheaper, faster and flood the market. It's done with toys, electronics, and the same skill can make documents. The passport doesn't need to be perfect. You're a corpse in a box." Jason said. "There's not a lot of scrutiny on a body. No one travels like that."

"It seems like someone has, otherwise they wouldn't have experience doing it," replied John.

Jason shrugged. "I guess." He concentrated on the narrow roads.

John was dropped at a corner near Xiulan's safe house. He trusted Jason but didn't want his new friend to know where he was hiding. John could tell Jason was uncomfortable with his condition. He fell into the primordial predator/prey relationship. Even if a lion were tame, it's still a lion.

John would wait until everything was ready for his departure. Jason would help, but John would contact him daily to check in. It was the safest thing for him to do. He would stay at Xiulan's deserted house. The authorities hadn't found it yet, so he would use it as his base while he lay low.

Xiulan was dead, her house searched by the police, then the army. Weapons and bodies were discovered. Being a dictatorship the government didn't have any obligation to tell the populace the truth about anything. The neighbors saw official vehicles at her house, but they were told lies if they asked questions. There was no news about thirty bodies or a cache of stolen government weapons; stolen from troops who were slaughtered at night.

The government released a story of a man found by the patrolling troops as he killed someone. He was shot and killed. A gruesome picture accompanied the story.

The nightly killings stopped so the people didn't care. They gladly went on with their lives thinking the government had done its job.

At the funeral home, in the white antiseptic preparation room, John was nervous. He had nine days to think about all of the things which could go wrong. If something went wrong he would die. And there were a host of possible ways it could go wrong. Someone on either side of the transfer could open the special coffin. He was going to be sealed in the way any corpse would be sealed in the box for transport. Unless he broke the coffin completely he wouldn't be able to free himself.

He was relying upon help from others and he hated giving up control of his own safety. But, honestly, once he was loaded in the box and unconscious, the plane could crash over the Pacific and he would never know. He would wink out of existence in an ironic way, prepared for a watery burial. Or he might sink to the bottom to be trapped forever, waking and sleeping and starving the whole time. At some point would he die?

John shook his head to clear the wild flights of doomed imagination and took a deep breath. The timing was critical to keep up the appearance to Yaoting that he was human. Jason was there to help with the masquerade. They discussed the steps several times and again on the trip over in his car.

The coffin for shipping bodies internationally was sitting on the ground. It was like other coffins in size and shape but this was lined in lead and would be sealed with screws. A large oxygen bottle was inside it, as was a small container of water with a tube so he could drink.

"Are you ready?" Jason asked.

John looked at his watch. It was just after 6 p.m. "Yes, I'm ready." He stepped into the coffin and sat down, arranging the air tank and the water bottle so they were comfortably situated. He put a small satchel at his feet. It held US dollars, his real passport, and what few possessions he had in China.

"Thanks for everything, Lujiang." John put the oxygen mask over his mouth and rested his head on the small pillow."

"You're welcome." Lujiang said. He appreciated John using his real name. Westerners had a difficult time with the language, John was no exception. He glanced at the clock.

"Wait." Jason pulled a jade pendant from around his neck, a milky green and white Foo lion. He put it in John's hand. The American had brought a lot of trouble to his life and his work, but he killed an evil woman. He avenged the killing of his orphans by Xiulan, now his girls were safe because of John. The children could find real homes. "Have a safe trip, Father." Lujiang looked at the waiting men. "Okay, go ahead."

"Thanks for everything," said John. He put the jade necklace in his pants pocket. He closed his eyes for the next part. It would freak him out to watch his own entombing.

The lid was put on the coffin, bumped into place with a hammer then Mingyu used a cordless drill to screw in long screws every few inches. John listened concerned about his plan. It was all a procedure dictated for health reasons. When the lid was securely in place the coffin was loaded into the van and taken to the cargo terminal at the Beijing airport.

John lay in the dark trying to remain calm. He would have an hour or two being awake in the coffin, when the plane hit the sunlight, if his calculations were right, he would be asleep. Until that happened he had a front row seat at how luggage was treated.

Finally he felt the plane leap into the sky. At some point...

Oblivion

****

Awake

So far so good. He was still in the casket. It was as pitch black as death would be, but he was alive. The plan to ship him by plane worked so far. He explored the tight surroundings by shifting his limbs slightly. There was a large bottle of oxygen between his legs; a thin clear tube snaked up his body to a mask which was held in place around his mouth and nose. He turned the knob and heard the hiss of oxygen in the box. In his left hand was a small flashlight. He found the button and turned it. Bright white light pushed back the darkness and he shone it around the claustrophobic space. It was small, much smaller than he expected.

The walls of the travel coffin were lined with fabric which hid the lead lining. The lead kept leaks from exiting the box. Directly in front of him the lid was slate grey, there was no attempt disguising the dense metal. The lid seam was tight against the rubber gasket on the sides. It was another precaution to keep possibly dangerous fluids in the box. The embalming process used a toxic brew of formaldehyde, glutaraldehyde, methanol, and other solvents to keep the body from temporarily decomposing.

Luckily John wasn't embalmed or dead. Well, the latter point could be argued for and against. He noticed there was a swaying to the coffin. He was in a vehicle. From the muffled sounds it wasn't in the air. He'd been off loaded from the plane after five p.m. Los Angeles time. If the instructions were being followed, he was headed to the mortuary, cousins of the mortician in Beijing. John put the flashlight to the side and pressed against the lid with both hands. It didn't budge. Yaoting had said there would be dozens of screws securing the tightly fitted lid in place. There was nothing he could do but wait for someone to open the box.

He thought of pounding against the lid of the box to be let out immediately, but if the people driving weren't in the know, they would have one hell of a shock. No reason to cause an accident. He remained quiet and waited. He'd become very proficient at waiting recently.

After a timeless hour in Los Angeles traffic, the vehicle finally came to a stop. He heard the sound of car doors opening and closing. Then there was the sound of doors at the back of the vehicle opening. The box was released and slid out of the back on rollers onto a rolling stand. The wheels bumped and shimmied as the travel coffin was taken into a building. He could hear talking in Chinese and English as they rolled the box.

When he came to a stop her heard a man say something in Chinese. Another man replied, there was a faint sound of doors closing and the click of a deadbolt.

Boom, boom, boom. Someone knocked lightly on the lid. The sound was like a drum in the interior of the coffin. John waited a second and knocked three times. Boom, boom, boom.

"I will have you out in a few minutes," said an accented male voice. There was a hint of awe and concern in his tone. By John's calculation he'd been in the coffin something between 20-27 hours. If the men in China tried to repeat this with a living human the coffin would be put to its rightful purpose.

A drill whined and the sound of long screws being removed from the lid filled his ears for the next three minutes. A lot of screws. When the noise of the drill traveled all the way around the circumference of the coffin, a small metal pry bar was thrust between the lid and the side. Leverage cracked the tight fit and light plunged in the dark space.

John lay with his head on the pillow. His eyes immediately found those of the Chinese man. He was middle aged and had soft facial features. His eyes betrayed his wonderment and showed a little fear. To the men on either side of this shipment, John was human, they didn't know his true nature. For a human to survive such a feat of endurance, sealed in an air tight coffin, it showed superhuman calm and patience.

The man set the lid to the side and John sat up. He pulled the oxygen mask off his face and set it aside so the tube didn't get tangled as he got out. He didn't want to raise any suspicions. When they looked at the tank later they could wonder how he could survive with so little oxygen. He would be far away by the time they discovered it.

John climbed out of the coffin and stepped onto the tile floor. He looked around, noticing the clock on the wall and set his watch to local time. This body prep room was white as well, similar to the one he was in when he went into the box. "Thanks," he said.

The man looked him up and down. A body never gets out of the coffin on its own. The sight was incongruous to all of his experience. "You're welcome," he replied. "I'm Zhang." The man held forth his hand. John shook it. "How was the trip?"

"I don't recommend it." John shook his hand. "Nice to meet you," he said without giving his name. Zhang noticed and understood. It was best for him to remain anonymous. "Is everything prepared?"

"Yes. There's a rented van outside with a casket in the back. It's rented for the week. There's a US map on the passenger seat. You can return the van at any of the Hertz lots in the nation, airports are probably easiest. Keys are in the ignition, the gate will open automatically when you approach." The man eyed him. Why did he need a casket? He didn't mind selling a new casket, but usually it had one destination. The ground.

"Great. Thank you," John gestured at the coffin. "For everything. Are you able to call Beijing and let them know I made it safely to LA?"

"Yes."

"Tell Yaoting and Lujiang it all went off without a hitch. Can I have all the documents that went with this shipment?" John reached into the coffin and scooped up the satchel with his money, information on Swiss accounts, and his real passport. He slung it over his shoulder and looked at the man expectantly.

"Of course," he handed over a large brown envelope; it was a quarter inch thick. There was Chinese and English writing on the outside with his fake name and a list of all the documents inside. It had numerous official stamps on the exterior. John took it and slid it into the satchel.

"Which way gets me to the van?" he asked.

"Follow me," he said. Zhang walked with the unknown man and wondered what circumstances drove him to travel in such a dangerous manner. Was he on the run from the Chinese mafia? Could he be a political dissident? Some rabble rousing American fleeing the communist government? Zhang decided it was best the answer remain a mystery.

"How do I get to the freeway to Vegas?"

Zhang told him they were in Exposition Park, near USC and gave him simple directions to the 110 freeway, and from there simple directions to the Interstate 15 going north.

"Great. Thanks again." John stepped out the doors of the mortuary. He looked at the night sky. His last view of the night was six thousand miles away and a long trip in a coffin ago. He was amazed he made it to the United States alive. It made him wonder how vampires traveled. He'd need to find someone to mentor him, tell him the vampiric secrets he was obviously missing.

The waiting cargo van was white, the Hertz logo emblazoned on both sides. There were double doors in the back and a sliding door on the passenger side. It had no windows on the body except for the front windshield and the driver's and passenger's doors. The light came on when he opened the driver's door. There was a chiming sound telling him the keys were in the ignition. He waved at Zhang, got in and started it up. He adjusted the side mirrors and carefully backed up.

The gate in the wall surrounding the mortuary slid to the side with a herky jerky motion then it became more fluid. When it was clear John pulled out and turned right. He went down the block, pulled into a parking lot, and shut off the engine. There was a Rand McNally road map for the entire nation on the passenger seat. He opened it up and flipped to the back where the mileage tables for destinations listed cities. He looked at Los Angeles to Denver. 1076 miles. That was too far to travel with his time limitations. He flipped to the map of Southern California and followed his path to Denver with a finger. He knew the road to Denver meant going up I-15 through Las Vegas. He flipped to the mileage table and looked up Las Vegas. It was 270 miles. Four hours travel time.

He looked at his watch and started the engine.

CHAPTER 44
OLD FRIENDS AND NEW

John arrived in Las Vegas the night he was unboxed. He found a place to sleep in the daytime, a cheap motel comprised of separated bungalows far from the Vegas strip. It was built in the fifties off of State Route 95 and meant for the burgeoning car travel of the time. John paid for a bungalow in the back of the complex and told them not to disturb him. He paid cash in advance for two weeks. The owner nodded and agreed enthusiastically. Few people now stayed so far from the action and with cash up front, he'd do whatever John might need. John hoped the owner would keep his word. He needed seclusion.

The next night after an uneventful daytime sleep, John returned the Hertz van to McCarran Airport. He took a taxi to a used car dealership before they closed and bought a cargo van with cash. He had thirty days to get it registered in Nevada. It would get him to Colorado and from there he didn't know what his next move would be.

On his third night in Las Vegas he decided to call upon an old friend. He thought about calling first but figured he'd surprise her. He drove to the neighborhood from memory, and pulled to a stop in front of her house. When he was pursued by Malcolm and his vampires almost three years ago he asked for Maggie's help and she let him hide out at her house before they went vampire hunting. At the time she thought his story was crazy, but came around when confronted with the reality of vampires asleep in their coffins. Three years was not a long time but his world was vastly different.

John approached the door, fear and apprehension threatened to overwhelm him. She saved him when the police station was attacked. Malcolm's vampires raged through the building killing everyone. They barely escaped alive. They'd gone through life and death together. They survived the kind of experience which forged close bonds in a short amount of time. He hoped she still cared for him. He hadn't called in months despite thinking of her often. He was afraid. He felt too much for her and talking to her frequently was a dagger twisting in his heart.

He rang the bell. With his heightened hearing he could hear her footsteps, her muffled voice said something. Was she alone? Was she talking to herself? He would flee if she had company. He didn't know how to deal with her. He needed help. He needed understanding and there was no one he could turn to.

Being a newly turned vampire he discovered the disadvantages being a lone nocturnal creature in a world where most business happened between 9 to 5. He had no way to do anything in the daytime. No wonder all the vampires he'd met had humans to help them. Night was limiting, subject to the seasons and his position on the globe. He wondered what happened to Norwegian vampires in the summertime.

Her footsteps stopped just inside the door, the porch light flicked to life. He blinked rapidly. The eyepiece of the viewer darkened for a moment. He thought he heard her take a deep breath before unbolting the locks and turning the knob. Was she anxious? John certainly was. He had no one to turn to; no one would understand his predicament. Maggie might. She was there, she survived, she saved him from dying.

He stood expectantly as the door swung open. She stood looking at him, a half smile gracing her lips. She looked like he remembered. He hadn't seen her for a year and a half, or was it two years?

"Hi Maggie." John said. He waited, wanted to gauge her reaction to seeing him. They talked on the phone occasionally, though less frequently as time passed. He told her about Rome after he got back. She was the only one he told about the vampires in that ancient city. She admonished him for his stupidity and tried to get him to promise to never get involved in the affairs of vampires ever again. He promised but ultimately failed.

"John." She pursed her lips and looked him over with a police officer's scrutiny. "Come in."

He smiled. Vampire myths said they couldn't enter without being invited and he knew that was wrong, but he was also pleased she was still friendly. "Thanks," he said. He entered and she shut the door behind him. He waited, unsure what to do. Maggie stood in front of him studying his face. He was surprised when she hugged him fiercely. He encircled her with his arms and melted into her, thankful she still cared. Though how much would depend on her reaction to his news.

She smelled of soap, and lilac shampoo, and warm skin, and underneath it all, blood. There was another smell. Something unusual. It was a smell vaguely remembered. One he recalled from performing christenings.

Maggie led him into the living room. It was mostly the way he remembered, the surprising addition was toys strewn about the floor, and a toddler sitting watching a Disney video he recognized. "Sit down." She sat down near the boy and gestured for him to sit on the couch next to her.

"You're, you're a mother?" John asked in disbelief. His face registered complete shock, so did the tone of his voice. "You never said anything when we talked on the phone."

"No, I didn't. His name is Thomas. Tommy, after my dad." She moved forward slightly and said, "Tommy, this is my friend John." The boy looked over at him. The child had a mop of dark hair and bright, intelligent eyes. He turned his attention back to the TV. "It's a terrible babysitter, but it focuses his attention and gives me a bit of a break."

"Wow," John said, his voice quiet, he was genuinely astonished. He stood gazing at the child. "That's great. I'm happy for you. Why didn't you tell me?"

"You're job doesn't like unwed mothers."

"Well, my *former* job has a bigger problem with abortion," John said. He didn't know how to tell her he was no longer a priest. He'd figure out the vampire admission as best he could. He didn't want to freak her out.

"Former?" she stammered. Her face flushed with unexpected emotion. "What do you mean former?"

"I'm being forced to leave the priesthood." A dark, serious expression crossed his face. "As soon as I talk to the Bishop, that is. I'm sure there's going to be ramifications. And paperwork."

"You leaving the church?" she asked. There was something in her voice, was it anger? Possibly hurt?

"Yes. There were circumstances beyond my control," he replied. "I have to leave."

"What happened?"

"The Church sent me to China to find out how one of our nuns died," said John. "And I had some trouble in Beijing."

"What kind of trouble? Did you get involved with vampires again?"

"How old is Tommy?" he asked, partially deflecting her question, but also curious she could have a boy so big. He wasn't an infant, his limbs were plump with baby fat but he wasn't a baby. He had to be walking at least.

"Nineteen months." There was an expectant note in her tone. "He was born in August. What kind of trouble did you have in China?"

John studied the boy more closely, he did a quick mental calculation and gasped in realization and recognition. "He's..."

"Yours," She nodded, conceding the earthshaking truth in a simple fashion. "Yes."

Suddenly speechless he stood up and paced the room, staying away from them. Maggie was hurt by this. She wanted a different reaction from John. Happiness, joy, some positive emotion at learning he was a father. What he exhibited was troubled pensiveness.

"I didn't want to hurt your career," she said simply. "Being a father, a real one, would be bad for you."

He stopped, his back was to her as she spoke. He nodded his understanding. "Yeah. It would be tough to explain. Or maybe not so tough after all he'd seen and done in the past two years. Those actions and revelations would be harder to explain.

"What happened in China, John?" she asked again.

He turned to face her and shrugged, defeated. "I died."

The statement crashed into her. Maggie immediately understood what he meant and turned her body, placing herself between him and her son.

"I'd never harm you or Tommy." His voice betrayed his hurt feelings. "I'm still the man I was."

"But now you drink blood," Maggie said. "And live forever."

Forever. The word hit him hard. He hadn't considered the possibility that he would watch Maggie and others would grow old and die while he remained unchanged. He looked at his son. His son. A reality he never imagined or dreamed of. A future he never entertained or thought about. He sired a child. His boy would grow, possibly marry and have kids of his own. They could meet their unchanging, unnatural, vampire grandfather. What would it be like to watch all his friends and acquaintances grow old and die? Devastating. Death served a purpose. No individual had to deal with generations of dead loved ones. No wonder the vampires he'd met tended to stay among their own kind. Humans were ephemeral, temporary. Brief flames extinguished by time. Being solitary might be one way to safeguard his heart from constant, devastating loss.

"I don't know about forever. I'm having a hard enough time with right here and right now," John said quietly, moving away from them to sit on the floor against the wall. He wanted to show he was no threat to them. He needed to show her he was safe to be around. He hugged his knees into his chest and wallowed in deep despair. If she rejected him he didn't know what he would do.

Tommy watched with curious eyes, it was past his bedtime and he was tired, but he didn't want to sleep and new people were interesting.

"How did it happen?"

"I was foolish like I'd been in the past with them. A Chinese vampire named Xiulan was evil in a way none of the others ever were. Those vampires had some shred of humanity left, empathy for their victims. She didn't and I died. But because she was evil she couldn't just kill me, she turned me. I came back chained to a roof. She left me to burn when the sun rose."

"But you escaped."

"Yes," John said wearily. "And I killed her and her spawn." He didn't want to tell Maggie that he'd killed dozens of little vampire demon girls. Children, really, feral, deadly, but physically and mentally children, and he killed them all. The optics of his actions were difficult, horrifying. Saying the words didn't tell the true nature of the danger he was in at the time nor the danger they posed to Beijing. Killing the demon girls was a good thing. He was sure he saved people's lives by doing so. But the price he paid was his death and his new unnatural life. Killing their master kept her from continuing her reign of terror.

Maggie stared at John. She'd wanted to see him again for ages, wanted to tell him he was a father. Now he was in front of her transformed. He wouldn't grow old. He might live a very long time, but to do so he needed blood. She knew he'd never harm her or their son. She wondered how such a gentle man could drink blood from a victim.

"I'm glad you kept Tommy," John said, his voice a choked whisper. "He's the last remnant of my humanity."

"Oh, John," she said. Maggie looked at him with sad eyes. She loved him in her own way. They'd been through life and death together. He was a good man and she could tell he was lost and broken. She coaxed Tommy off the floor and guided him over to John. He let go of his knees and reached out gathered the boy in his arms and sat the toddler on his lap. The boy reached out and touched John's face. He smiled and bounced the boy on his lap. John smiled genuinely.

"Hello, aren't you a big boy?" He said with and made the required baby talk, overly exaggerated words and silly faces. Mixed in with his voice was awe and joy. The child, his child, smiled and giggled. Tears welled up in John's eyes. Maggie lifted the boy from John's lap and perched him on her hip.

"I'm going to put Tommy to bed. Stay here. I'll be back in a few minutes unless he puts up a fight. Sometimes he's tough to get to sleep. It's like he doesn't want to miss anything." She hefted the child up. "Who's a tired boy?" She asked in a sing song voice, one every mother developed. "You are! Yes you are. I can tell. Are you going to go to sleep easily tonight?" Tommy nestled into her shoulder as she carried him into the guest room he'd seen on his first visit to her house years earlier. She didn't offer him the comfortable bed when he came looking for refuge from the forces hunting him.

After ten minutes she returned and sat cross legged on the floor in front of him. He could smell her shampoo, and the blood coursing thru her veins.

"You're fucked and not in the fun way." She smirked. Then seriously she asked, "What are you going to do?"

"Night clerk at 7-Eleven," he joked. "I'll get a studio apartment with a light tight closet for the daytime. Buy a house with a basement. Put my coffin down there and sturdy locks on the door to keep noisy fools and deluded priests out." He shifted his position and sighed. "Actually I have some money, I think it will be okay for the money stuff." He was more than okay, he was wealthy.

"You have a coffin?"

"Yeah. Actually it's my second. The first one was a box for shipping human remains. That's how I got back from China. I Fed-exed myself." He made an embarrassed face like he couldn't believe his own predicament and the measures he'd taken to survive.

She glanced at the carpet and looked sad. "I'd help if I could." She reached out and gingerly took his hand in hers; she turned it over in her own. She remembered his hands. It appeared unchanged from the ones she recalled caressing her body and holding her in the night. It seemed like a normal hand, normal skin, but a bit cool to the touch. She weighed it, felt the skin, traced the smoothness with her fingertips, pressed the veins on the back of his hand. They popped up like normal. Curious, she flipped his hand over and felt for a pulse. "You have a pulse, very slow but it's there."

"The rumors of my death are true, but my nature is inexplicably changed." John said. Again with a shrug, "I'm still figuring it out."

"I want to help but I don't know how."

"Thanks, I know you'd help if you could." John smiled. "It's very strange. I never thought much about my death. I always had it figured out, at least the after-life part. I'd die after years in service to the Lord, and I'd go to heaven. Then I go and die in China fighting evil vampires, and this is my after-life. Walking around," he paused, his face clouding over. "Drinking blood."

"I'm sorry."

John shrugged. "I guess I really do have an immortal soul now," he said sardonically, bitter about the future before him. "I took it on faith that such a thing existed. And if I don't die, well, there you go. Immortal soul."

She could tell he was getting despondent. He was starting to spiral down into a dark place. Maggie looked for the right words to help him, provide some solace, a remedy to his tumultuous situation. She wanted some simple combination of consonants and vowels which, in the proper order, would calm his troubled soul. Provide him a balm for the crisis he faced. She couldn't think of any. Keats or Byron would be woefully inadequate to help John right now.

She looked at him seriously. "We could drive to the desert. Bullets will harm you." Her tone was calm but not cold. "You saw what a few rounds from a rifle did to that Simone woman."

John considered the option for a moment not bothered by the fact she offered to assassinate him. Bullets killed all the vampire children. In his mind's eye he could still see the horrific carnage he caused. He shuddered at the thought. "Malcolm said she lived through the shooting." He didn't want to tell her she was right and he had first-hand knowledge.

She nodded. "I forgot." Maggie repressed much about that night. It was the only way to stave off nightmares. Monsters were real, and she had a child to protect. "We could watch the sun rise," she suggested.

"I . . . I think that would hurt," John conceded. He didn't want to die a painful death. He didn't want to die, but the possibility of a vampiric life stretching for years shook him deeply.

"I think most deaths hurt unless you die in your sleep. You're aware and in pain. That's got to be frightening." He suddenly looked hopeful so she quickly added, "I'm not pounding a stake through your heart." She remembered what it looked like seeing the point piercing the sternum and puncturing the heart of the vampires at the church. The way they woke and screamed, it had to be painful. As any stake pounded through a heart would be.

"But you're willing to shoot me."

"There's a difference between moving a trigger a quarter inch, a five pound expenditure of pressure, and pounding a stake through your heart."

"Excellent point," John conceded. He winked at her. "Though you held the flashlight, I did the dirty work with the whole hammering thing."

"Okay, I held the flashlight," she said, her natural competitiveness coming forth. "But when you were being questioned by the police and the vampires attacked, who picked up an assault rifle and killed heavily armed, well trained men? Who blew the brains out of Simone when she was about to have you as a snack? Me."

"Potato, tomato." John grinned.

"Seriously, what are you going to do?"

He sat silently for a long moment, thinking.

"I deserve to exist." In that instant he decided to live, whatever he had to do, well, within reason. The steps he needed to do to survive would be a changing target. John was adamant, there was steel in his voice. "I don't know if I can continue as I am, but I'm not going to purposely quit my life. "

"Seriously, how will you survive? Finding any type of job will be tough."

He didn't answer for a long moment. "I took Xiulan's money to draw her out after she escaped," John said. "I killed her, now I have her money. She was wealthy, very wealthy. Over a hundred years of accumulated wealth. And she was having her demon girls steal more off their victims."

"Demon girls?"

"She was taking orphaned girls and turning them into vampires. There are many abandoned girls in China due to the one child policy. People want boys. Girls have little value. She turned the eight year old girls into vampires." His voice broke in grief. "She trained them to kill and steal."

"That's horribly evil."

John nodded.

"What did you do to them?" Maggie shifted on the sofa, curling her legs under her. It was a defensive position, a closing off to him. She anticipated unpleasant information.

"I killed them all." John declared flatly. "Xiulan and all her demon girls."

"And then you stole her money." Maggie's ethics, police and other senses of right and wrong, were somewhat offended the priest she knew and loved was a thief and mass murderer. His circumstances were unique, but it didn't make it right.

"I stole it before I killed her. Can you steal from a two hundred year old dead woman?" John retorted calmly.

"Technically, yes," she replied. "It would be considered stealing from an estate.

"Of a walking dead woman. In China."

"In China they'd probably kill you for stealing."

"Too late."

Maggie stared at him. John had changed from the man she knew, there was an anger and bitterness roiling under the surface. She figured death would do that. "So you've killed."

"Nothing new there."

"Children."

"Vampires, feral child vampires, heartless killers," he corrected. "There's really a huge difference."

"And you've stolen." Maggie continued.

"Father Hadrien would have something to say about that." John mused aloud.

"Who's he?"

"He's a priest who helped me in Rome with some ethical dilemmas. I think I mentioned him to you."

"Okay, what would Father Hadrien say?"

John didn't answer. Hadrien would have been shocked at the deeds John did to survive.

"What would God say?" Her voice was quiet. She didn't like the changes she was seeing in him or approve of the deep changes in the way he looked at life.

"Well, if we're having a conversation, me and God, I'd ask what's the big deal turning me into a vampire?"

Maggie said nothing.

"That's the question. If God has a plan for everyone, what was his intention for me?" There was a bitter edge to his voice. He knew the ramifications to his new life better than her. "Seems to me there is no plan." His voice changed from anger to loss. "And there is no God. It's just random numbers and you have to find a way through the chaos."

"I'm sincerely sorry."

The phrase was simple but it helped. It helped calm his rage. "I know," he answered quietly.

"What are you going to do with your sudden windfall?" She almost used the words 'stolen lucre' but changed her mind. Money is neither good nor bad. Judgment depends on how it's spent.

"First I need to find a place I can… live, for lack of a better word. A city big enough to…" John's voice trailed off. He didn't want to say certain words. *Hunt. Feed.* "I don't want to get mixed up with other vampire's territories. I don't know for certain, but I bet there are vampires in most big cities. Sean said as much."

"It makes sense." Maggie conceded. "After you are set, what then? You have money. You could start a church like Malcolm. Vegas was a brilliant place, and Malcolm had a sweet set up."

"He did."

"You could do that too," Maggie said. "Money and food walked in the door. His church is still sitting empty, no one wants a church where people died."

"I'm sure. But I could never do that. Religion isn't a con job for me. He was as opportunistic as any mega church pastor on TV." John thought for a long moment and sat down next to her. He took her hand, she didn't shy away from his touch. "I'd like to be able to see you and Tommy from time to time if you'll let me. I'll support him. Right now I'm nineteen months behind on child support. I can help support his grandkids."

"Not funny." Maggie pulled her hand away.

"Maybe a little bit funny," John smiled weakly. "No? Okay," he sighed. "I'm sorry, Maggie, if I can't joke about this, it's going to be a long eternity."

"You're going to have eternity." Maggie was suddenly angry. "I'm going to have, what? Seventy or eighty years if I don't get killed in the line? I'm a single mother and the father of my son will live forever." She fell silent for a long moment. "I kind of love you, you asshole."

It was a difficult thing for her to admit. No man, or woman, is an island, but Maggie spent a lot of effort trying to be one. Now the island had two occupants, her and Tommy. She would fiercely defend and protect him. She always wanted to be a mother but dating was difficult. Circumstances gave her her heart's desire. It was difficult being a single mother, but worth all she had to do to make it work.

John's face fell. Maggie loved him. Her admission stabbed at the very heart of him. If he were human and heard her say that, what would his reaction have been? Would he have left the priesthood and married her? He did love her in some way. That kind of love, a deep romantic love, was a rusty and unused emotion. Other priests left the church to get married. Humans fall in love. Would he have left the only life he knew for her? He couldn't answer that question.

He looked at his watch. It was late. She had work in the morning. For him the night was early, he would go see the Strip with his new eyes. The lights would be wondrous. And he needed to feed before going to the bungalow off of I-95 to sleep.

"I should go," he said as he stood up. "It's late and you have work tomorrow."

"Where are you staying?"

"Someplace safe," John stated. Even with her he felt the need to be cautious regarding his temporary sanctuary. "I'm going to be in town for a few days. Can I come by tomorrow night? See you and play with Tommy? I've got some catching up to do, if you'll let me."

Maggie thought for a long moment and nodded. "Sure." She knew they'd be safe from his new blood thirsty nature. He was a compassionate man, transformed, but still the same person she loved. Well, mostly. A dangerous animal was birthed in the soul of this gentle man. She would watch him around Tommy, but trust he wouldn't harm their child.

"That's great. Thanks," John smiled and stood not knowing if he should hug her or turn and leave. Maggie set his mind at ease when she jumped into his arms and hugged him fiercely. She nuzzled into his chest then raised her head to kiss him. Surprised, he kissed her back. They stood together kissing until he broke the embrace. "I really should go," he said breathlessly.

Reluctantly she released him and nodded. "Come by at six tomorrow. You'll be up then?"

John shrugged and smiled, "Yeah, as soon as the sun goes down."

Maggie furrowed her brow. "How does it work? The sunset, sunrise thing?"

"No idea." John turned and walked to the hallway. "See you tomorrow." He paused in front of the hallway mirror. He still recognized himself. This would be his visage for unknown years. He remembered who he was from before, but he was changing, an interior evolution was inevitable. In the future years and decades would he recognize his human face or would he see the monster circumstance might force him to become?

There are two people in every mirror. The one you see, would the other be a reflection of an inhuman creature?

John unlocked the door and stepped out into the embrace of the night.

ABOUT THE AUTHOR

Bradley Upton is an actor who has been writing as long as he can remember. He exhibited exquisite canines in the web series **Dark Commandos** as Dreyfuss. He's been seen in **Days of Our Lives**, **The Guardian**, and **Criminal Minds** among others. Regionally he was in the casts of **The Winter's Tale** and **All's Well That Ends Well** at the Old Globe Theatre in San Diego.

An avid traveler he's been to 16 countries and has plans to take a bite out of the rest of the world when he has time and resources.

Instagram @bruwrites

Katherine Kirkpatrick, Fresh Look Photos